Leftover Soldiers

Book 2

Aftermath and Opportunity

by

Bert Entwistle

Books by Bert Entwistle

The Drift,
Jack Bannister Mystery #1

Uranium Drive-In,
Jack Bannister Mystery #2

The Taylor Legacy,
An American Family Saga

The Black Rose Banker

Murder in the Dell

New Mexico,
A Novel of the Old West

Leftover Soldiers,
Book 1, Life on the Western Frontier

Leftover Soldiers,
Book 2, Aftermath and Opportunity

Looking Back,
Stories of Real American Pioneers

Leftover Soldiers, Aftermath & Opportunity
Book #2 in Leftover Soldiers series

Published in the United States of America by Black Mule Press
Colorado Springs, Colorado

Available at amazon.com. book stores and from the publisher,

westernimages@msn.com

(719) 287-8063

Copyright © 2020 Bert Entwistle

First Edition, August 2020. Revised 2022

Library of Congress Control Number: 2020920181

ISBN: 978-0-9896761-6-8

Price: $16.00

For Kyra and Eli

The Newest Members of my Colorado Family

Author's Note:

Leftover Soldier's, Aftermath and Opportunity, picks up where the multi-award-winning *Leftover Soldiers, Life on the Western Frontier,* left off.

After the last battle of the Civil War in Brownsville Texas, the four main characters, Union soldiers Delbert Beale, Tom Lee Daggart and Sylvie Parker, and one Confederate soldier, Boyd Stamps, found themselves working as buffalo hunters in the Texas Panhandle, and Sylvie disappears in the middle of the night. When the hunting trip ended, Del, Boyd, and Tom Lee take jobs driving a herd of Texas Longhorns from San Antonio to Cheyenne.

Del and Boyd decide the new town, with the proposed transcontinental railroad running through the territory, might hold their futures. Tom Lee has a girl back in San Antonio and can't wait to get back home.

The end of the Civil War began an unstoppable rush of Americans and immigrants from all over the world looking for an opportunity for a new life in the West. As the men settle into their new jobs, the West shows the newcomers just what it will take to tame this wild, wide open country.

The railroad brings ranches, towns, and jobs to the new territory, and along with them, every kind of outlaw and con man in the country looking for quick money. Boyd Stamps takes a job as cow boss on a ranch outside of Cheyenne, and Delbert Beale hires on as the Deputy U.S. Marshal, working out of Laramie, another new railroad town fifty miles to the west. When Tom Lee Daggert returns to San Antonio, he is hired to run the Thomas & Case livery stable.

The men look for their place in the dangerous country that would come to be called "*The Wild West*" by journalists and authors.

The Indians are relentless in their war with the whites, the army, and the new railroad. As efforts to forge a treaty at Fort Laramie go on with many of the Indian tribes in the summer of 1868, others are still attacking wagon trains and killing immigrants.

The Wyoming Territory becomes the first place in the world to grant women suffrage rights. Boyd's partner, an incredible woman reporter named Anny, and her "*Wyoming Women's Betterment Society*" work non-stop to make it happen.

The men find love and their futures in the prairies and mountains of the West. Overcoming everything that this wildly beautiful and dangerous country can throw at them, they carve out a place for themselves and make their lives in the newly opened American West.

Chapter 1

Laramie, Dakota Territory

Deputy Marshal Delbert Beale leaned back in the chair with his boots on the desk. Exhaling a long cloud of cigar smoke, he watched as the prisoner paced back and forth in the small cell.

"Please Marshal, you gotta help me . . . Please sir . . . I ain't never done nothing like this before. Do you know what's gonna happen to me when they take me to Cheyenne?"

Beale shrugged. "Ain't my problem son. I expect you knew better than to take someone else's cattle when you did it."

"It was only a couple of steers Marshal; I swear I'll pay it back, I can work it off . . ."

"How old are you Bob?"

"Almost eighteen sir."

"Where's your family at?"

"All I had was my uncle and the one cousin — those are the ones you shot."

"Well, I could see a judge maybe giving you a little sympathy, 'cause of your age and all," said Del. "That is if the steers were the only things you and your clan stole from that man. Was that all you stole Bob?"

1

The boy lowered his head and began to cry. Shaking his head, the tears turned to heaving sobs. "No sir, there were horses too."

"Everyone knows you can't steal a man's horse in this country. It'll get you a rope for sure."

"Sir, are you saying they're gonna hang me?"

"That's what usually happens to horse thieves," said Del.

Before they could say anything else, the front door swung open, and two rough-looking men in long dusters and muddy boots walked in. "I'm Jake Barnes," said the biggest man. "This is Billy Jefferson. We're here for the prisoner."

"You got the warrant?" asked Del, crushing out the stub of his cigar.

"Right here Marshal, it's for one Robert Lee Baker, age seventeen, for cattle rustling and horse theft."

Del looked at the warrant and the wanted poster, then back at the prisoner. "He's all yours, you got shackles?"

"I do. The poster says there were three of them in on it. What happened to the other two?"

"Dead and buried."

"Good enough for 'em," said Barnes." Del opened the cell, and the two bounty hunters shackled the still sobbing boy's hands and led him out the door. "Did he have a coat? It's gettin' nasty out there."

Del grabbed an old blanket and tossed it to him. "Best I can do, but it might keep him from freezing before you get to Cheyenne."

"Yeah," said Jefferson. "We wouldn't want him to freeze up before they had a chance to hang him, now would we?"

Del sent a telegraph to his boss, Territorial Marshal Wesley Tompkins, in Cheyenne, telling him that the prisoner was on his way. Walking into the River Cafe, he ordered a big breakfast and coffee. The waitress sat the cup down and filled it.

"Marshal, I expect you're gonna want some sugar for that, right?"

Del nodded, "That would be good if you have some."

Dolly Truett, a slightly plump middle-aged woman with dark, pulled-back hair smiled at him. He could see her blue eyes light up when he looked at her. "I've been saving some just for you, I'll get it."

"Remember now, the last time I was here, you said that you'd call me Del, and I'd call you Dolly. We've known each other for a while now."

"You're right Del, I forgot. Let me get that sugar."

Finishing up he left a tip on the counter and said goodbye. "Thank you Dolly, I'll see you at supper."

"That will be nice, I'll see you then."

Del wondered if there was something more going on with her than just a casual friendship. *Maybe one day I'll ask her,* he thought to himself.

The next morning had turned even colder, and the wind was worse than usual; spring had been slow in coming this year. Stoking the stove, he settled in for what he hoped would be a quiet day. He studied the new wanted posters for a minute, then hung them on the wall between the one with his old nemesis Sylvie Parkers' face on it and a row of others wanted for various crimes. There hadn't been any news about Sylvie for a few months, but he was not ready to take down the poster yet; there was no doubt he was still doing business around here somewhere.

He shuffled through a pile of mail that had been on his desk since yesterday. The local school teacher had been helping him with his reading and writing over the winter, and he was now able to do his day to day paperwork without problems.

One of the envelopes was addressed to him in a woman's hand. It was an invitation to the wedding of Anny Werner and Dean Timms in Cheyenne. Timms was an old friend and rancher outside Cheyenne, and Anny Werner was the town's telegrapher when he hired on as Deputy Marshal in Laramie. He would be looking forward to the wedding in June and seeing his old friends. Pinning the invitation on the wall, he lit up a fresh cigar and put his feet back up on the desk.

Chapter 2

Colorado Territory

The four men waited nervously, tucked into a narrow side canyon that fed into the Poudre River. The leader, a large black man with very dark skin and a full beard, watched as a swirl of dust moved toward them on the river road. When the stagecoach got close enough, the leader spurred his horse, and all four men rode out, firing their pistols in the air and surrounded it. The driver reigned to a stop, set the brake, and raised his hands. The guard quickly threw down his shotgun and did the same thing.

"You got no fight here," said the driver. "We don't want nobody hurt. Take what you want, and leave us be."

Three members of the gang wore white hoods, the black man with the full beard was not covered. "How many passengers you carrying," asked the leader.

"Just three, a woman with her young daughter and one older fella, looks like some kind of businessman."

Riding up to the door, he pulled it open and looked inside. "Everybody out — now!" The woman stepped down from the coach and held her young daughter's hand as she climbed down. The man never moved from the seat.

One of the gang opened the door on the opposite side. A paunchy, middle-aged man sat perfectly still, clutching a leather bag on his lap.

"Old man, are you deaf? You were told to get out . . ." Pointing his pistol at him, he cocked the hammer. "Now, you can get out like my friend told you to do, or I can shoot you where you sit, it's up to you."

The man got up and moved to the door without speaking. After lining up with the other passengers, the black man checked the woman's bag, tipped his hat, and told her and the little girl to get back into the coach. "Just wanted to be sure you didn't have a pistol hidin' in that pretty little bag of yours, Ma'am." Standing face to face with the man, he reached for his bag.

The man tightened his grip and pulled back. "Old man, if you don't let go of that bag, I'm gonna put a bullet right through your head . . ."

The man shook his head, refusing to give it up. The blast of the pistol startled everyone, and the man dropped to the ground in a bloody pile. Pulling the bag from his hands, he motioned for the rest of the gang to move out. Mounting up, he spoke to the driver before he rode off. "That ain't much of a guard you got there. He threw down his scattergun before we even got to the coach."

"He just didn't want to see anyone get hurt is all," said the driver.

"Well, I guess I messed that up, didn't I?" Laughing out loud, he spurred his horse and disappeared down the road. Several miles up a side canyon, the four robbers rode into their camp through a long stand of aspen trees. Dumping the bag onto the ground, they found a leather wallet and a cloth bag. Inside they found eight-hundred dollars in paper money and two-hundred dollars in gold coin.

"Boss, how did you know he'd have all this cash with him," said one of the men.

"Three days ago, I was in a bar in Denver and overheard him telling someone he was gonna buy a couple of new bulls at a ranch to the west of here. He even told the bartender what stage he was gonna be on."

"Now wasn't that nice of him . . ."

Sylvie Parker nodded and grinned, "It sure was, now, let's pack up and head out. I got a chubby little whore and a big bottle of whisky waiting for me."

Del picked up the telegram and read it out loud;

To: All Law Enforcement.

Stage robbery in Colorado Territory on Poudre River road.
Four men on horseback. One passenger robbed and murdered.
Three robbers with masks, and one large, black man with heavy beard and no mask — the apparent leader. Del, this looks like Sylvie's work, be on the lookout, they are believed to be headed back north. Good job on the Baker Ranch rustlers.

Wesley Tompkins, Territorial Marshal.

Del wrote out a new message on the pad and handed it to the telegrapher.

"Sir, that will be two dollars and twenty-five cents for Cheyenne and four dollars and fifty cents for San Antonio."

"Charge it to the Marshal's Office."

The agent nodded and began to transmit the messages. One was to inform Dean Timms and Boyd Stamps on the Timms Ranch outside of Cheyenne of the situation with Sylvie, and one was to inform old friend Tom Lee Daggart in San Antonio. Sylvie was unpredictable, and he wanted to be sure his friends knew he was still around, and he was now wanted for murder. Del also told them that he would see them at the wedding.

Chapter 3

Cheyenne, Dakota Territory

Anny Werner wrote out the telegrams from Del. One was for Boyd Stamps, and one was for Dean. After finishing with the telegrams, she walked to the livery and had them hitch up the buggy. On the ride home, she stopped for a minute and watched a band of pronghorns' race across the prairie and cross in front of her. Close behind were three Indians on horseback chasing them. As they disappeared across the dry hills, she made a note in her journal:

May 13, 1868: *"Today I watched nine pronghorns pursued by three Indians at full gallop, racing against a brilliant blue sky. I believe them to be Arapahos from their dress. Many new Indians are in the territory since the start of the big treaty gathering at Fort Laramie. Two hawks were also wonderful to watch, such graceful fliers and hunters."*

*

Driving under the **Timms Land & Cattle** sign, she pulled into the barn. One of the ranch hands tied up the horse and helped her from the buggy.

"Good afternoon Miss Anny, how was your ride home today?"

"It was wonderful James. I saw pronghorns and Indians running across the prairie and two hawks chasing their supper in the grass."

"Did the Indians say anything to you Ma'am?"

"No, I think they had their own supper in mind, but I love to see those things," said Anny. "I get more notes for my journal every time I go out."

"You 'bout ready to make that book Ma'am?"

"It's getting closer now. I'm looking for someone that might publish it for me."

"I sure hope you'll have an extra copy for me, I like readin'."

"James, you will have your very own copy, I promise."

*

Dean was building a fresh fire when Anny walked in. She walked straight to him, wrapped her arms around him, and kissed him.

"Hello, my wonderful cowboy . . ."

"Hello, my favorite lady telegrapher. Did you have a good day?"

"You know more than one lady telegrapher do you?"

"No, just the one is all."

"Then I better be your favorite," she said, kissing him again.

"There will always be just one," said Dean, still holding her tight. "How was your work today?"

"It was slow, though you and Boyd did get this telegram. You should let him know right away."

Dean read it and put it in his pocket. "I'll get it to him as soon as he comes in."

"There is something I want to talk to you about. I think maybe now is a good time."

Adding another log to the stove, he sat down and pulled her onto his lap. "So tell me, what's on that beautiful mind of yours?"

"Well, it's the telegraph office. I have been training a new telegrapher for more than a month. Dean, I want to quit the job."

He tickled her ribs playfully. "It's not a woman, is it? You might have some competition for the favorite woman telegrapher job if it is . . ."

"No, it's not a woman," she said, pushing his hands away, "now just stop it and listen. I want to quit the job and stay on the ranch.

10

There's plenty for me to do here, and I would be able to spend more time on my writing."

"So go ahead and do it. I'd rather have you here anyway."

"Aren't you worried about losing the extra money?"

Dean kissed her again. "No, the matter is settled, you stay at the ranch. Let's forget about it for now and go to bed."

"That's what you always say."

"You don't like that idea?"

Taking his hand, she pulled him from the chair, "No, I love that idea — come on."

"You know," said Dean, "there are people around here who would say that the two of us living together without being married is living in sin."

"I never cared what any of those people thought before, so I see no reason to start now. All those old church women are just jealous they don't have a handsome cowboy of their own. Besides, come June, we'll be properly married, and then what will they have to talk about?"

"I'm sure they'll find something," said Dean, following her into the bedroom.

*

Riding alone to the line shack, Timms cleared the last of the aspen trees and saw Boyd feeding a couple of horses in the small pen. He tied up next to the gate and waved to him. "Come on inside when you're done. I need to show you something."

Finishing up the feeding, he turned out Dean's horse and headed for the shack. Hanging up his hat and coat, he put on some water for coffee. "What's so important that you'd ride all the way out here on such a miserable day?"

"I wanted to give you this telegraph that came yesterday."

Boyd read the message and dropped it on the table. "You want coffee?"

"Yeah, that would be good. You heard anything about Sylvie recently?"

"Nope, I figured he was long gone from this country by now."

"Well, you can add him to your watch list along with the Indians."

Boyd poured them both a steaming cup of coffee and set a pan of biscuits on the table. "I gotta say, there have been a lot of Indians around here lately, some from tribes that I never saw before."

"It's that big pow-wow up at Fort Laramie. Tribes from all over the West are meeting there to talk with the government about another treaty."

"If the government wants their land, they'll take it anyway," said Boyd. "Ain't no treaty ever stopped them before."

"That's true enough. They just want to protect their precious railroad all the way to Sacramento," said Dean.

"Yeah, I heard it'll be in Laramie any day now. The government is giving the railroads plenty of land to build anything they want. The Indians don't stand much of a chance living the old way on their own land."

"Damn . . .!" said Timms, spitting his first taste of coffee across the cabin. "That's the strongest coffee I ever drank; did those hands drink this while you were trailing them longhorns up here?"

"That's a long story. I'll have to tell you about it someday," said Boyd. "It's already raining and blowing hard; it might be best to stay here tonight."

"I hate to leave Anny alone, but I guess it's a good idea. You got anything to eat besides biscuits?"

"We got plenty of beans and jerky. We won't starve for a while."

"Sounds good to me. I'm gonna lay down for a bit. Wake me when it's ready." Timms woke up to a warm cabin filled with the sweet aroma of beans cooking. "Smells damn good in here Boyd, in fact, I don't think I ever smelled any beans that good before."

"Better get used to them. It looks like we're gonna be here a while, take a look outside."

Cracking the door open, Timms could see a foot of snow on the ground, and it was still coming down hard. "Good thing we got all them beans, though things could get a mite odorous around here with two of us eating them."

Before they could eat their first bite, the door slammed open, and two snow-covered cowboys came rushing in with the wind. Forcing the door closed, they looked at Dean and Boyd. "Well shit

Bob, looks like we're just in time for chuck," said a big cowboy named Ezra.

"Get warmed up boys. I'll throw some extra beans in the pot for you. I figured you boys had been got by the Indians by now," said Boyd.

"Hell no, ain't no self-respectin' Indian gonna get caught out in this mess," said Ezra. "They all got 'em a squaw keepin' them warm in their lodge."

All four cowboys spent the next two days in the line shack, keeping warm, finishing off a jug of whisky, telling stories, and eating Boyd's special beans. When the sun came out, the four men left to ride through the deep snow and check on the cattle. All four cowboys couldn't be happier to have the fresh, bitter-cold air biting at their face.

Chapter 4

Walking into the manager's cabin, Boyd knocked the snow off his hat and coat and hung it up. After feeding the stove, he laid back on the bunk, pulled the blanket over his head, and fell asleep.

Waking up to the blanket being pulled off him, he rolled over to see Flora Dere standing next to the bed. "Move over I'm cold."

He slid over to make room, and she crawled in next to him and pulled the cover over both of them. "I need your heat; my teeth are clattering. Where have you been? I was worried you were lost in the storm."

"You were worried about me? said Boyd. "That's the first time I ever heard you say anything like that to me."

"Boyd Stamps — that's just plain horse pucky!" said Flora. "I do worry about you when you're gone. You just don't seem to notice it."

"Flora, it's just that sometimes I think that you don't really like me. It seems you like to give me a hard time more than anything else."

"Damn, you southern boys can be so slow at times! Do you think I would spend all this time with you if I wasn't interested? We've been keeping company almost since the day we met, and you haven't even tried to kiss me yet!"

"Uh . . . I'm sorry Flora, I'm not so good at these things. Can I kiss you now?"

"You damn well better kiss me right now, or I may have to find another cowboy to keep me warm."

Boyd leaned toward her, and Flora kissed him; gently at first, caressing his lips. He felt his face flush, and his hands shook.

"Are you okay, Boyd?"

"I am. I liked it very much. Can we do it again please?"

Flora broke into a big smile and put her arms around him and kissed him again and again. Do you want me to stop?

"No, no, please don't stop . . ."

The ranch started by Monroe Timms and his son Dean had been steadily growing since just after the war. Now that the railroad had reached Cheyenne, he was sure it would only get better. He wished that his father had lived to see it. Before long, he would have his first chance to sell his cattle to someone that would load them on a railcar headed to the eastern slaughter plants.

His brother David, outside of San Antonio, would be sending up another herd to add to his, this time, a better balance of cows, heifers, and some good bulls. He had decided the range had more than enough grass and water for more cattle.

As the snow from the spring storm melted away, the cowboys working the herd found a few dead cows in the washes and low spots, and several that had been butchered by Indians. The loss totaled about ninety head.

Boyd sat at the table with the members of the Southeast Four Cattlemen's Association. The group included Dean Timms, Clifford Platt, Wilf Rikard, and Flora Dere, the daughter of Basquiat Dere, who ran the family business when her father was absent.

"Everyone around here says this was a bad winter, worse than they can remember," said Dean. "If that's right, then I believe we'll be fine, actually better than fine. I think we're all gonna be very rich in a few years. I've hired Case to trail up another herd that my brother put together; they should be leaving Texas any time now. The prairies and foothills around here will be covered with our S/4 brand as far as the eye can see."

"How many are we gettin' this year, boss," asked Boyd.

"Around 2,500 maybe 3,000, it depends what David puts together this time."

"That'll be a lot of work boss. We'll for sure need more hands and at least a couple of new line shacks and branding wagons," said Boyd. "Maybe we should start with a smaller herd this year and get the shacks and corrals built first."

"Boyd, you are a great ranch manager," said Dean, "but you worry too much. All that open country will hold more cattle than we could ever put on it. Find a good spot for the new line shacks and pens, and plan on hiring some more hands."

"I'll start on it right away."

"And one more thing, they'll be bringing up more horses this time. I want the corrals and the barn enlarged to make more room," said Timms. "We're gonna start raising and breaking horses to sell to the locals around here."

"I'll start looking for a couple of new wranglers."

Clifford Platt interrupted the conversation, "Dean, I don't want anything to do with the new horse business. I have enough to do just keeping up with the cattle I got."

"Nor do I," said Rickard. "I'll stick with the cattle business, and I think I'm going to start growing some feed at my place."

"Flora, what about you and your father?" asked Dean.

"We're with Wilf. We're already talking about growing some feed ourselves."

"Well, I'm sorry all of you feel that way, I think this is a good opportunity to make more money."

"Dean, I think maybe we're all a little concerned about keeping track of so many head on all that open range," said Platt. "So don't make any more of those decisions on cattle numbers without talking it over with us first."

*

Boyd walked into the cabin and sat down on the bed. His head was filled with the extra work he'd been given. The door swung open, and Flora walked in. "What's wrong with you? I can't believe you just sat there and let him give you all that extra work like it was nothing!"

"He's the boss Flora, what did you expect me to do, get mad and quit?"

"Just tell him the truth! Tell him this operation isn't ready to grow that fast." Throwing her hat and jacket on the bed, she sat down beside him. "You're the ranch manager. You're on the range every day. Do you think we can handle that many more animals?"

"Well, it'll be a whole lot more work for sure."

"Between the weather, other rancher's cattle, the rustlers, and the Indians, how are you going to manage our herd across hundreds of miles of open range?"

Boyd just shrugged. "I guess we'll figure something out."

Anny Werner finished her last day as Cheyenne's telegrapher; she had mastered a job generally reserved for men and did it well. The new operator was a young local man named Franklin. A bit of a slow learner, but after more than a month of training, he appeared to have a good grasp on it. As she handed him the keys to the office, she walked out the door, sad for leaving but excited for what might be coming next.

The wedding, having babies, and writing, now consumed her thoughts. On the ride back to the ranch, she stopped for a moment to watch a pair of coyotes running across a grassy meadow. Opening her journal, she started to write about them when out of the aspens rode a dozen or more Indian men, women, and children. They rode within a hundred yards of the buggy without acknowledging her presence, and she added it to her journal.

May 20, 1868: *Twice in as many weeks, I have been fortunate to see Indians on my way back to the ranch. While watching two coyotes play, what appeared to be a family group of Indians, four strong-looking men, five women, and several children. They were dressed like none I have ever seen before. The men were very tall and straight. They were decorated in paint of several colors on their bodies and their horse's bodies, as well as feathers and headpieces. They paid me no mind as they rode by so regal looking.*

*

Boyd hired four more hands and took them to the site of the first new line shack. Nestled into a grove of giant fir trees, it was good protection from the weather on three sides, and the front provided a good view of a long grassy meadow with a small stream winding through it. When the supply of tools and materials were unloaded, the men muscled off the new cast iron stove and two water tanks.

"You're gonna want to build a pen for the horses first," said Boyd. "There's plenty enough trees here for the posts and the cabin. I'll have the metal roof sheets out here in a few days."

One of the new men, a young, muscular Mexican named Ernesto, spoke up. "Señor, as long as we can make tortillas and beans, we can build the cabin and pens, no problema . . ."

"If you need meat, there are plenty of deer, elk, and pronghorns around," said Boyd. "If you find any crippled-up cattle or old dry mamas, you can take one of them if you need it."

"Sí Señor, we will work hard for you, do not worry."

"I'm sure you will Ernesto. What I'm worried about are all the extra Indians in this part of the country, stay clear of them whenever you can. If they kill one of our cattle for their own food, let it go. If they start stealing them, that's different."

"Señor Boyd, what will I do if they are stealing many cattle from you?"

"Run 'em off if you can, but don't shoot them unless you have to. You have guns, right?"

Ernesto nodded. "Sí, we all have rifles and pistols."

"One more thing . . ."

"Señor?"

"Here is a copy of a wanted poster. It is for a murderer and thief named Sylvie Parker. The Marshal thinks he may be around here somewhere. He's a large, bald-headed black man with a heavy beard and the darkest black skin you have ever seen. He likely has a couple of other very bad men with him. If you see him, send someone back for the Marshal right away."

"Sí, we will be watching for him and the indios."

"I'll be back in a few days with the rest of the supplies and the new wagon on the next trip. It will have everything you're going to need out in the field."

Chapter 5

Territorial Marshal, Wesley Tompkins, sat across the desk from Del, looking through several new wanted posters. "Del, Cheyenne and Laramie are just growin' too fast. The railroad can be a great thing, but too damn many outlaws, con-men, gamblers, and other bad characters come with the tracks. There were three killings in Cheyenne just in the last week. When you put whisky, gambling, guns, and whores together with cowboys and railroad men every night, then throw in a few Chinamen, you can count on bullets flying and blood flowing. I've requested six more deputies. I figure four more for Cheyenne and two more for you."

"Yeah, it's the same here," said Del. "Since the tracks reached town, it's filled up with the roughest bunch of men this side of the mountains. There's just the two of us right now for the whole county, more deputies will help out a lot."

"They should be ready to start in about two weeks. The town of Laramie will eventually be setting up a formal city government, and they'll be taking over policing inside the city. That'll free up you and your men to work the county. Did you get the telegram from Tom Lee about Sylvie breaking into his house and terrifying his wife a while back?"

"I did. San Antonio is a long trip; he must have gone down there until things cool down from his last murder in Colorado. I see they raised the reward for him, maybe that'll help."

Tompkins pushed back from the desk and stood up. "Yeah, it's high enough now that the committee is interested. A couple of them are talking about hunting him down."

"It's a real shame it'll have to end like this," said Del, "he was a good soldier."

"He ain't the first ex-soldier to go bad, and he won't be the last," said Wesley. "How's the problem with the outlaw brothers coming?"

"Not good. They've threatened people, stolen their stock, burned some out, and forced them to sign over their property deeds. So far, nobody has caught them in the act, and we have nothing to arrest them for. They hole up in the saloon during the day and do most of their business after dark. They recently started killing landowners by ambushing them in the dark. I'm sure Laramie's committee is working on a plan right now."

Tompkins nodded. "Good, the railroad is bringing in a lot of good folks too. It's time to clean out the trash to make room for them. Let me know how it comes out. One more thing, are you good with staying in Laramie? I can get you back to Cheyenne if you'd rather."

"I think I'm good for now. I'm just getting to know everybody around here. Maybe somewhere down the road though?"

"That's fine. Just let me know if you decide you want to make the change. I'm not gettin' any younger, if you get my meaning."

"Thanks Wes, I understand, I won't forget it."

"Is there somewhere I can get a meal? I'm starving . . ."

"Sure, follow me. I'm kinda hungry myself. It's the River Cafe, just on the other side of the road."

*

Abe Deal, his brother Joe, and father Verlan had been in the Laramie area since the first tents lined up to form a main street. All three had been Confederate soldiers and raiders and rode with Quantrill on the Lawrence, Kansas massacre. After the war, they turned to rustling and horse theft and were suspected in several murders. After too many run-ins with the Texas law, the family headed north. They understood what would happen to the area when the railroad reached Laramie, and set up shop selling whisky and other stolen goods.

Within a year, they had swindled two men out of one of the first large, log buildings on Main Street and ran their business out of the saloon they now call the Whisky & Blood. Abe Deal had appointed himself and his brother the first lawman of the county, running roughshod over the local ranchers and early citizens.

When Delbert Beale was appointed the official Deputy Marshal of the county, a local vigilance committee had already been operating in secret. After the recent murders of a farmer and his wife, they all agreed that it was time to put the Deal clan out of business.

Early one morning, they gathered in the street just as it began to get light. On the leader's signal, six committee members rushed the saloon, instantly overwhelming the brothers and their father Verlan, taking them prisoner without firing a shot. Within minutes, the committee had marched them to a nearby unfinished cabin, threw their ropes over a rafter, and prepared to hang them.

The three men had been quiet on the walk to the cabin. Abe asked only that he be allowed to remove his boots, so his mother would know that he died 'with his boots off'. The committee granted him his last wish then promptly hung all three.

The Laramie and Cheyenne "committees" continued to clean up most of the roughest elements of the new towns until official law and order finally reached them. When Del was asked about the lynchings, he explained that he had been out of town searching for a horse thief when it happened.

*

Waking up to gunshots in the street, Del pulled on his pants and boots, grabbed a Winchester, and headed out the door. A crowd of townspeople had gathered around a body in the street. Del could see the tall black boots and the blue uniform of a soldier lying in the dirt.

"What the hell happened here?"

"There were two soldiers having a meal in the cafe," said one of the men standing near the body. "They got into a screaming argument about something. I don't know what it was about. Then the one soldier pulled out his pistol and shot this one right across the table."

"You were in the cafe," asked Del.

"Yessir, just a couple of tables away from them. The shooter ran for his horse, and the other guy stumbled outside and fell over right here."

"Okay, someone get the doctor, and I'll find the post commander."

"That won't be necessary, Marshal," said a voice behind him. "I'm Colonel Theodore L. Hayes. I'm in charge of Fort Sanders. I was just down the street when I heard the shot. We'll take care of finding the shooter, and he'll get a military trial, that is, if he isn't killed first."

"Thanks Colonel. I can have him taken to the undertaker until your men come for him."

"That will be fine. One of my men is already headed to the fort for help. They should be here within the hour."

"I gotta say Colonel, this is a first for me," said Del. "I never heard of one soldier killing another one in town, especially right across the breakfast table."

"The soldier in question has been disciplined recently. He is something of a rogue. However, I never thought him capable of a cold-blooded murder like this."

"Good luck finding him, Colonel. Looks like we're gonna end up with another outlaw on the loose. If I can do anything to help, let me know."

*

Dolly smiled when Del walked into the cafe. "Good morning Del, how are you doing today?"

"I'm always good when I see your smile, you know that."

"Here's your coffee, I'll be right back with a little sugar for you."

"Hold on a minute please," said Del, "I want to ask you something first."

"What is it?"

"Are you free to go on a buggy ride tomorrow? The weather is so good that I thought we might take a trip down by the river?"

"I would like that very much Del, should I make a lunch for us?"

"That would be nice. I'll come by in the morning and pick you up."

*

Del pulled under two large cottonwood trees and tied off the horse. After an hour of pleasant conversation and lunch, Dolly couldn't hold back any longer. "Del, I feel like you have something you want to say to me, but you're holding back."

"You're right. We've been seeing each other for a while now, and I know I want to be with you, but I've been afraid to ask."

"Del, I would like to be with you too. What's bothering you so much that you can't tell me about it?"

"Dolly, you need to know, I'm not such a good man. I've done bad things in my life that most people would not approve of. I am worried that you wouldn't want to be with me if you knew about them."

"What I know for sure, is the Delbert Beale I have been spending my time with is a good man, and he is the one I want to be with. We both have a past, and that can't be helped. I'm only interested in the future, hopefully, our future together."

Del pulled her toward him and kissed her. "Dolly, I want to marry you . . ."

"I thought that's what you wanted to say, so please don't take this wrong, but I don't really want to get married to you."

"I'm so sorry, I knew I shouldn't have asked," said Del, pushing away.

She took his arm and pulled him even closer. "Del, listen to me, I want to be with you too, just not married. I would like us to live together as if we were man and wife if you will have me."

"Why don't you want to marry me?"

27

"Like I said, we both have a past, and this is the way it has to be. If you need time to think about it, I understand."

"I don't need any time; I want to be with you."

Chapter 6

As the first light reached the hills, Boyd rode into an open meadow with a long string of beaver ponds. Stopping to let his horse drink, he watched a bunch of S/4 cattle with fresh calves feeding alongside the creek. On the far side of the meadow, two does and a new pair of spotted fawns fed along the edges of a cluster of aspens; the spring grass was nearly high enough to conceal the fawns.

"I guess I can see why Anny Timms writes everything in her journal," he said to himself. *"It would be nice to keep memories like this close by."*

After an hour of checking cattle on the lower range, he rode into the first of the S/4 line shacks. Everything looked good; several horses fed in the corral, the water tanks were full, and the woodpile was well stocked. Inside, the shack was in good order, and the extra tack piled neatly in the corner.

Boyd knew he'd made a good choice hiring Ernesto as his new cow boss. Things were always in order whenever he made the trip.

Mounting up again, he rode through the scattered herd and toward the next shack.

After a few miles, he saw several sets of unshod hoof prints crossing the trail heading east. A flock of ravens circled the trees in the same direction. Following them into the aspens, he came on the remains of a butchered cow. All the meat on the carcass had been taken, including the tongue, as well as the hide.

It was the work of Indians; white men were never that thorough. There was no doubt they were on the move, most likely headed for the treaty business at Fort Laramie. He knew they wouldn't be back through this area any time soon.

When he got back to the ranch, he found Dean sitting in his cabin. "Boss, I just got back from riding a long circle. The spring rain we've been getting has everything good and green. The calves are healthy and getting fat. I saw two places where wolves or coyotes got a calf, but other than that we're looking good."

"You see any Indians?"

"No sir, none this trip," said Boyd, not mentioning the butchered carcass.

"If you see any of those red bastards, you know you gotta kill 'em . . ." said Dean.

"Yes sir, we'll take care of them."

"I hate them sons a bitches. They're all thieves and murderers. Here, have a whisky with me," said Dean, sliding him a glass.

Boyd had half a glass in front of him before he could say no. Downing the whisky, he sat the glass upside down on the table before Dean could refill it.

"What the hell Boyd, one more ain't gonna kill a good old southern boy like you . . ."

"It's been a long day boss. I just need to get a little sleep."

Dean shrugged. "I guess I'll have to drink alone then."

"Where's Anny today," said Boyd, changing the subject.

"I think she's in town for some writing supplies or something. I never really know what she's up to."

"You got you a good woman there boss. Everyone in the area talks real highly about her."

Dean nodded. "She is that for sure. She helps everyone with anything they might need. She and some other ladies formed a group to talk about things like why women can't vote in our elections. They want to vote and sit on juries and all kinds of other silly things."

"Yeah, I think Flora has been to a couple of those meetings too. Do you think that could ever happen?"

"I don't see any way in hell that women would ever get the vote. What would be the point? They don't know nothing about politics. But if the idea of meeting with her friends and talking about such things make her happy, then I'm happy. She can talk about whatever she wants."

"Well, goodnight, I'll see you in the morning; we need to talk about the next herd that's coming up."

"More cows mean more money for us Boyd."

"I hope you're right boss."

"You'll see. The new slaughterhouse is expanding to serve people in the area, and we now have a real school and even a church or two. You just watch, it won't be long before the railroad will have to put on extra cars for all the cattle we're gonna ship back east."

*

Anny was busy at the table writing in her journal when Dean walked in. "How's my favorite ex-telegrapher today?"

"I'm doing good. I'm working on a drawing of something I saw yesterday. Maybe one day, I will be good enough to include one in my book."

"What did you see that was so interesting, if I may ask?"

She turned the journal toward him. "As I came through the gate, a jackrabbit raced across the road in front of me."

"And you thought that was interesting enough to make a drawing?"

"No, I wasn't finished with my story. A few yards behind the rabbit was a weasel in hot pursuit! I didn't know that either one of them could run that fast. What do you think of my drawing?"

Dean studied the picture and handed it back to her. "I think it's good, and it would look good in your book. Have you done others?"

"I'm working on a few more. I'll show them to you later."

"Did he catch her?

31

"Catch her . . .?"

"Yeah, the weasel, did he catch her?"

"Oh, I don't know, they disappeared into the grass."

"He likely made a couple of good meals out of her."

"Why do you assume that the rabbit was a female and the weasel was a male?" said Anny. "You know it could be the other way around."

"It's just the way of the world my love. The men are the ones in charge."

Deciding to change the subject, she closed her journal. "Dean, the wedding is getting close now. I talked to Reverend O'Malley today. He said that he would be happy to do the service. I'm starting to get excited; I hope you feel the same way."

He leaned over and kissed her. "You know I love you, and I can't wait for you to be Missus Dean Timms."

"Dean, I want kids, a whole bunch of kids if we can. It's the one thing I've wanted the most for my whole life, right after a husband, of course."

"My love, we can fill the whole house with kids if you like. I can always use some new cowboys to run the ranch when I get old and feeble."

"Then it's settled," said Anny, hugging him. "We'll have a house full of kids and grow old and feeble together."

*

Dean heard Anny calling for him as she came in the door. "Dean, look, I've been published! The Leader printed my story! I'm a published writer — look!"

He read the short article about the treaty meeting taking place at Fort Laramie and the increase of Indians in the area. "That's wonderful, I'm so proud of you."

"Dean, the publisher wants to know if I would consider going to the fort for my next story."

Dean shook his head. "Anny, I don't know about that, I don't trust the Indians, and I think it's just too dangerous for you. Maybe you could write one on the railroad or on how the town is growing instead."

"Oh Dean, everyone can see what's going on around here, but they can't see what's happening at the fort. Besides, I've seen Indians many times before, and it was always very exciting, but I never felt in danger at all."

Knowing how much this meant to her, he agreed to it with one condition. "If you really want to go to Fort Laramie, fine, but I'll send a bodyguard with you."

Anny hugged him and kissed him over and over, "Thank you, my wonderful husband to be! I can go tomorrow!"

"Wait a minute, slow down. Let me find you someone I trust, and then we'll get the wagon ready. Everything will be ready the day after tomorrow. Just don't stay too long. We got important things to do."

"We have important things to do? What would they be," said Anny.

Dean looked at her with a huge grin. "You've already forgotten what we have to do on the twenty-eighth of June?"

Anny thought about it a second, then her face flushed. "Of course not, we have to go to a wedding that day!"

*

The wagon was packed with extra food, bedding, and her small oak writing desk, a gift from Dean on their first Christmas. Two horses were already hitched up, with an extra saddle horse tied behind. Morgan Reese, a longtime family friend, and employee of the Timms family, sat with the reins in his hand and his foot on the brake. He was a quiet giant of a man, standing six-foot-five and two-hundred and sixty pounds. He had grown up on the prairie, living among the Indians of Montana, and was completely fearless in any situation. He could also speak many Indian languages and would be very helpful to her on the trip.

"Anny, I trust Morgan with my life under any circumstance," said Dean. "He will stay with you at all times, and whatever he says is the way it has to be. Are you good with that?"

"Certainly, we've become good friends since I moved out here. He knows everything about the mountains and the prairies, and I love his stories about the Indians. I think he is a wonderful choice."

Dean pulled her tight and kissed her. "Please be safe, and don't trust anyone out there, not Indians or white men, nobody but Morgan, you understand?"

Anny kissed him once more and climbed onto the wagon. "Don't worry, I will be fine. I'll be back in a few days."

Chapter 7

Del headed east into the mountains, with Raylan Davis, his main deputy alongside him. Spotting the landmarks given to him by a local rancher, they rode up to the base of a stack of rocks left as a marker. Several steps into a stand of aspens, they found the body, just as the rancher had described it.

A young white man's body lay face down with three bullet holes in his back. Wearing only blue trousers, they rolled him over and found four more bullet holes in his chest and belly. "They must've wanted him dead pretty bad," said Davis, looking the body over. "One round that size woulda done it just fine."

Del nodded. "Looks like maybe someone used a Spencer on him, big as the holes are."

"I imagine there's quite a few of those around since the war ended," said Davis.

"Yeah, there is. I know a few that still carry them," said Del. "Pull off his trousers. I need to take them back to town."

"You want his trousers?"

Del nodded. "I may know who this is, but I need to confirm it. The trousers should be enough to do it. Let's get him in the ground before it gets dark on us."

*

Del rode into Fort Sanders and tied up in front of Colonel Hayes' office. He greeted him at the door. "Hello Marshal, this is my wife, Susan Mackey Hayes. We were just having some lunch. You're more than welcome to join us."

Del took off his hat and nodded, "Good afternoon Ma'am, thank you for the invitation Colonel, but this is just business."

"Gentlemen, I will take my leave while you attend to your business," said Missus Hayes, "very nice to meet you Marshal."

"Thank you sweetheart. Marshal, what brings you here today? You taking a day off from chasing rustlers?"

"Not exactly. I found a young white man about ten miles to the east of here. He was shot seven times. These were all that were on the body," said Del, showing him the trousers. "Colonel, are these Army issue?"

Hayes looked at the bloody trousers. "They are, and the most recent issue at that."

"Are you missing any men Colonel?"

"Just the one that shot the trooper in the cafe a few days back. It has to be him. You buried him I assume?"

"We did, but he's very shallow. We stacked up some rocks so you could find him easy enough."

"I'll need you to take a detail to the grave. We'll need to dig him up and rebury him here. Any thoughts on who killed him?"

"All I know is that he was shot seven times by large caliber bullets. I think someone may have emptied a Spencer into him."

"Was there anything else left at the scene," asked Hayes. "No horse or gear?"

"No, he'd been picked clean," said Del, "the trousers were the only thing left."

"Any chance it was Indians?"

"All the tracks were from shod horses. I think this was done by outlaws or rustlers."

Hayes handed the trousers to his aide. "Put these in the storeroom and mount a detail to pick up a dead soldier. Seven rounds from a Spencer is really unusual. Any thoughts on why so much overkill?

"My guess is that someone has an old grudge against the Army," said Del. "I'd say that whoever did this left the trousers to make a point."

"You got any guess as to who that might be," asked Hayes. "If so, I need to know. He may have been a murderer, but he was still a soldier. He needs to be buried here, and his killer needs to be brought to trial."

"Colonel, I have an idea, but I don't have any evidence right now. As soon as I find anything, I'll let you know, and you can help me track them down. Deputy Davis will take you to the body. Thanks for your help."

Raylan Davis took over the duties of sleeping at the jail when there were prisoners. Del and Dolly rented a small set of rooms at a local boarding house. "This is nice Del. I just wish we could just stay here together forever. I get very nervous when you aren't here, and I worry about you when you're off chasing outlaws."

"If I had my choice, I'd stay here with you all the time. But I have three deputies now and that'll keep me home a little more," said Del.

"Doesn't it bother you living on the prairie for days at a time? I would think all that time on a horse and sleeping on the ground every day would be painful."

"It's not my favorite thing to do, but when I was in the Army, we chased Indians all over the desert for weeks at a time. I guess I just got used to it."

"Well, at least I can keep you comfortable when you're home."

"I like having that to look forward to. It keeps me going when I'm gone. Dolly, did you ever think about moving to a larger town, like maybe Cheyenne?"

"No, I like Laramie just fine. Why do you ask?"

"I was offered a job as a deputy there, but I turned it down."

"I like it here, it's much smaller and that suits me," said Dolly.

"I agree, but it's gonna grow faster now that the rails are here. Before long, they'll be setting up some local government stuff, like a local sheriff position. I've been asked if I would take it instead of the Marshal job. That way, I wouldn't have to be gone on so many long trips. If Laramie is good with you, when the time comes I may consider it."

*

After sending a telegram to Marshal Tompkins about the dead soldier and who he suspected the killer might be, he had breakfast with Dolly and walked to the office. Raylan had been on duty for several days while waiting for the trial of a local man caught stealing two horses from his neighbor. The man in the cell laid on the bunk, snoring loudly.

Del looked at his watch, then snapped it closed. "It's time. Raylan, hook him up and get him over to the courthouse, the judge is waiting."

The prisoner, a bald-headed, contrary old Irishman with a matted red beard everyone called Mad Mick, walked without incident to the log building that had been recently constructed as a county office. After the jury was seated, the judge pounded his gavel until the room quieted down. "Mick Maguire, you have been accused of stealing two horses from your neighbor, one Clyde J. Harper, how do you plead?"

"I ain't pleadin' to shit, cause it don't mean nothin' anyway. Yer gonna hang me no matter what I say, so you can just go screw a goat for all I care!"

The judge pounded his gavel until the laughter died down. "Mister Maguire, what makes you think I would hang you anyway? I haven't even heard your story."

39

The old man ran his fingers through his beard, then sent a long stream of tobacco juice across the floor. "Ever since you been here, I seen how you work. You done hung all kinds of black men, white men, Chinamen, Mexican men, even an Indian or two, but hardly any Irishmen, so I figure I gotta be the next one on yer gallows."

After the gallery and jury stopped laughing, the judge banged his gavel again. "I will have quiet in this court right now! Mister Harper, tell us about your missing horses. Do you have proof that the defendant took them?"

"Yessir, my son saw him tear down the fence and lead the horses out. We caught him just outside of the pen tryin' to get away."

"Mister Maguire, do you have anything else you would like to say to this court?"

"Well, yes sir, I do . . ."

"Let's hear it then."

"Can I watch you screw that goat before you hang me?"

The courtroom erupted in laughter again, and the judge, now red in the face, pounded his gavel over and over until things quieted down. "Mister Jury Foreman, you heard the testimony, what say you and your fellow citizens in the business of Clyde J. Harper versus Mick Maguire?"

Doing his best to hold back his laughter, the foreman stood up. "Your honor, he's obviously quite guilty."

"Mick Maguire, a jury of your peers has found you guilty of horse theft. I sentence you to be hung by the neck until you are obviously quite dead. Execution will be a week from today at twelve noon. Court is adjourned. Marshal, take him away."

*

Del slid the tray of food under the bars and pulled up a chair alongside the cell. "So, why'd you do that, Mick? You knew it would just make things worse."

"Marshal, I was livin' down along the river before there was even a town or railroad here, long before Mister Clyde J. Harper and his two thievin' sons were anywhere around. I had staked out my 160 acres and was workin' it. I just proved up on it last fall. Then the Harpers and the rest of the outlaw gangs moved in. They shot my animals, tore down my fences at night, and tried to burn me out. I was told by those sons a bitches that Irish trash like me wasn't allowed around here."

"What'd you do then?"

"I grabbed my 10-gauge and ran him off . . ."

"You shot him?"

"No, I just shot in the air over his head. I told him if he came back, I'd take his head off. Seems he was old man Harper's number two son."

"What about stealing the horses, what was that all about?"

Maguire finished the food and laid back on the bunk. "I was the one that turned 'em out, but it weren't gonna be for my personal use though. My plan all along was to let them loose. I was gonna make it look like they broke down the fence and took off. Then, when the Harper boys came looking for 'em, I was gonna shoot every goddamn one of 'em. I still got my old .50/.70 Springfield from my buffalo days; it wouldn't be all that hard to do."

"So, how'd you get caught?"

Maguire shrugged. "Just stupid damn luck is all. I had just pulled the fence rails down and started to shoo out the horses when the shithouse door opened and who walks out but the same asshole I shot at!"

"Now that's for sure some bad luck," said Del. "Then what happened?"

"I took off running for my horse, but he spooked. As old and fat as I am, I couldn't outrun a porkypine if my ass was on fire, so they caught me easy enough."

"Were you really gonna kill all of them?"

"That was my intention, there was no way I was goin' to let them push me off my land, and there was nobody around to stop them, so I decided to do it myself. Kinda like what the committee did to the Deal brothers a while back."

"Mick, I wish you woulda come to me before it got this far. I understand the problems you were having, but it's too late for me to do anything about it now."

"No matter, Marshal, I'm sixty-one-years-old. I'm tired, broke down, and I got no money, no animals, and probably no cabin by now; I'm ready to go."

42

"You got any family I can contact? You need to choose someone to leave the homestead to."

"No, I ain't got no family. I was an orphan when I was ten years old. I was passed around to a couple of families for a few years until I set out on my own. When the war started up, I tried to join the Union Army, but I guess they musta had plenty of men, 'cause they said they weren't needin' any stinkin' Irishmen. So, I joined up with the South. I guess the smell didn't offend them near as much, and I ended up in Texas. Were you in the war, Marshal?"

"Yeah, I was with the Union, in the Western Army, mostly I just chased Indians out on the desert. You said you were a buffalo hunter?"

"Yeah, I did that for a couple of years, then moved around for a while and finally settled here. I was hoping to start a new life and maybe even a family."

"I spent some time hunting buffalo myself. It's a pretty tough job," said Del. "I'm sorry it didn't work out for you Mick, but I promise you that I'm gonna look into the Harper problem."

Maguire stuck his hand through the bars toward him. "Thank you Marshal, I appreciate that."

Del shook his hand, "What about your place? What do you want to do about it?"

"I heard you and the lady from the cafe are together, that right?"

"It is, why?"

"Get you a lawyer down here, and we'll draw up the legal papers, and you two can have the place."

"I don't really know what to say Mick. You must have someone to leave it to?"

"I do Marshal — you. If you don't do this, Harper and his bunch are going to end up with the place. Now get that lawyer over here before they decide to hang me early."

Chapter 8

Dean could see a swirl of dust coming toward the barn. As it got closer, he could see Anny waving to him. Morgan Reese pulled the wagon up to the barn, and Dean grabbed the reins, tying them off to the fence. Anny jumped down from the wagon and into his arms, smothering him with kisses. "Oh, Dean, it was incredible! I have so many things to tell you about. There were Indians everywhere, they're magnificent Dean!"

He took her arm and started to walk her to the house. "Anny, you've been gone more than a week. I was worried about you being around all those rough people."

She kissed him again and pulled off her shoes and hat. "I'm sorry if I made you worry, but I never felt threatened or scared in any way. Morgan is the perfect bodyguard; he never left my side the whole time. It was clear that no soldier or Indian would care to challenge him. Oh, Dean, I know now that this is what I want to do. I want to document everything I see in this beautiful country."

"What about us?" asked Dean. "What about our wedding and our family?"

"Nothing has changed, I will be ready for the wedding, we will be married and have many babies, just like we planned. I will go on my trips, make my notes, and come back home and do my writing here."

"As long as the family is the most important thing, and your trips aren't too long," said Dean. "I guess it's okay, but I'll never be able to stop worrying about you when you're gone on a trip."

"Dean, nothing in my life has ever been more important than my dream of a big family. I am about to get the first part of my dream, a wonderful husband, then lots of babies will make the rest of my dream come true, and nothing will ever change that."

*

Anny read the new telegraph to Dean at supper. "This is from Tom Lee down in San Antonio. It says that he and Sancha are sorry that they will not be at the wedding because Sancha is heavy with child and unable to travel so far. He wishes the best for us."

"Have we heard anything from my brother David?

"Nothing yet," said Anny. "They still don't have a railroad connection, and it would be a long, tiring ride on a stagecoach or wagon."

"I suppose so, but it would be nice to see him again. They've got two little ones I've never seen."

"Del and Dolly will be here, and Boyd, and of course, Flora."

Dean interrupted, "You still don't like her after all this time?"

"No, I can't stand her. You just wait, she's gonna hurt Boyd real bad one of these days."

"I hope you're wrong about that. Who else is on your list?"

"All the association members and their wives, and most of the other ranchers and wives around here."

"Everything else is ready? The preacher and all that kind of stuff?"

"Yes husband to be, all that kind of 'stuff,' as you call it, is ready. Next Saturday, I will be Missus Anny Werner Timms! Are you as excited as I am, my husband to be?"

"I'm excited, sweetheart, but I just don't show those things like you do. I am very excited to have Anny Werner as my bride." Dean poured himself a tall whisky to note the moment. "Are you sure you won't have a drink with me? Just one?"

"You know I can't stand the taste of that stuff, so no," said Anny, "water is good enough for me, and tea with fresh milk when we have it."

"Exactly where are we going to hold this wedding? Have you chosen the spot yet?"

"I think I would like to have it on the top of the long, grassy bench just below your father's grave. It's a pretty spot. We can see all of the ranch, and it will be like he's watching over things and giving us his blessing. Is that okay with you?"

46

"That's wonderful. I think he would like that. It looks like you've thought of everything."

*

"Morgan, tell me about the trip," said Dean. "Do you think Anny could be in danger if she continues to do this?"

"It is a pretty rough bunch of people up there. Each of the Indian tribes camp in their own area and come and go as they please. The army has meetings with them in their groups and meetings with the different chiefs. At night, the tribes dance and raise hell and challenge each other to fight. During the day, they gamble and race their ponies while the chiefs meet with the army."

"What about the army? Can they keep the peace while the Indians are there?"

"There's a lot of soldiers at the fort, and they're all well-armed and are instructed to be extra cautious. I don't think they would let anything get out of hand."

"Can you keep her safe if she keeps doing this?"

"As long as she stays with me, she will be fine. I think that some of the Indians are taking a liking to her. They have not seen many white women before, particularly one with such fair skin and red hair, The idea of her trying to ask them questions seems to interest them. I told her if she brought out a bunch of small gifts, they would really like it."

"Gifts? What kind of gifts are you talking about?"

"It doesn't have to be much, just buttons, ribbons, beads, tokens and things like that. Bring enough so that they all get a little taste."

"Anything else she should know when she's on these trips?"

Morgan nodded. "I didn't say anything to her, but I think maybe she needs different clothes. The long full dresses, fancy bonnets, and coats are not well suited for the trail."

"What would you suggest?"

"I think she would do better in men's trousers and shirts and a bandanna and wide brim hat. It would be much better in the weather too."

The idea of his wife dressing like a cowboy on the range never occurred to him before, but Dean had to agree it would be much more practical for travel on the prairie.

*

Anny sat at the table with her notebooks and writing tablets spread out in front of her. At the top of a fresh page, she wrote the date and the location.

Fort Laramie, June 21, 1868

The fort is everything I hoped it would be; wide open, wild, and spectacular! Tucked into a deep bend of the North Platte River under a cloudless sky, rows of whitewashed barracks, workshops, barns, and tents of every shape and size fill the scene. Blue clad soldiers are everywhere, fulfilling army tasks of every description. More horses than a person could count are scattered all around the property, and cannons and wagons line up against the cottonwoods, awaiting their call of duty.

Adding to my excitement is the sight of the Indians . . .!
Riding their ponies at full gallop, whooping and hollering as
they go, they are truly magnificent to watch! They play some
form of gambling games and race each other during the day,
then sing and dance in the light of their campfires late into the
night. They can be somewhat scary upon first encounter, but my
companion, Morgan Reese, a quiet giant of a man, is always at
my side and commands respect where ever we go.

An oversized American Flag flies above the parade ground,
snapping sharply in the breeze. It is a new one, with the thirty-
seventh star already added. We set up camp under the branches
close to the river for a source of water. Morgan secured the
wagon, staked out the horses, and made us an evening meal. He
spent the night sleeping on the ground near the fire, and I spent
the night in the reasonable comfort of the wagon. However, I
cannot say that I slept very much the first night, with my
excitement level so high. When I finally drifted off, it was to the
distant sounds of Indians singing and dancing.

*

Closing up her journal and writing tablet, she put them into the
desk drawer. Looking out the window, she saw Dean and Boyd
standing near the corral, talking very animatedly. Boyd appeared
to give up the conversation in frustration and walk away, and Dean
turned toward the house. Stepping inside, he went straight for the
cabinet, poured himself a whisky, downed it quickly, then poured
another. "Goddamn it anyway . . .!"

"Dean, what's the matter? Are you okay?"

"Yeah yeah, I'm fine. I just don't understand Boyd sometimes. He's still fighting me on running more cattle. Hell, the new herd is on the trail already. It's too late now anyway."

"You don't think Boyd knows what he's talking about?"

"No, it's not that. He's a good man and a good manager, but I've been in this business a long time, and I think he's just too conservative. We've got plenty of range, plenty of water, and plenty of grass, and it's all free! He wants to cut down on the headcount and start growing feed close to the ranch. We ain't a bunch a goddamn farmers! If there's enough grass and water for the buffalo, then there's plenty for the cattle." Throwing back the whisky, he picked up the bottle, walked into the bedroom, and shut the door.

*

The monthly meeting of the S/4 cattleman's association was held in Dean's bunkhouse. Everyone except Basquiat Dere attended. Like usual, Flora Dere took his place. "How's your father these days," asked Dean.

"About the same. Since the horse accident, his back still bothers him. Bouncing around in a buggy or on a horse is too much for him."

"We all hope he gets healed up soon," said Dean. "I have two issues I'd like to talk about today. First is the fact that our manager thinks we should consider cutting down the herd size. He's concerned that the range won't hold any more cattle. I think he's wrong, but we all need to talk about this today. Boyd, would you tell everyone your concerns please."

"Well, we all know that the prairie has plenty of grass and water and that we're all doing very well right now. A range-fed steer cost about a dollar and forty-five cents to raise; we've been able to sell that steer for as high as twenty-three dollars or more. The railroad is going to be a giant boost for all of the ranchers in the area, and soon we'll be shipping cattle east; that will increase our profits even more."

"That's the reason I'm having trouble understanding why you feel we shouldn't get more cattle," said Dean. "Things are going even better than we expected when we formed this pool; now you say we should cut back? I'm sorry, but that doesn't seem right to me."

Boyd shrugged. "I guess it don't matter much anyway; the next herd is on its way. I've got the new line shacks built and the pens ready, and the cowboys are hired. They're getting set-up with the new branding wagons right now."

"Dean," said Clifford Platt, "I want to say this one more time for the record. I want no part of the new horse business and no part of any additional cattle beyond this new herd. I hope we're clear on this?"

"Flora, Wilf, do both of you still feel the same?" asked Dean.

"I do," said Flora.

"Same here," said Rickard.

"Well, I can't say as I agree with you," said Dean, "but that's the way it will be."

"I have a question about range loss, how bad is it right now?" asked Clifford Platt.

"As far as an average year goes, it's running slightly high," said Boyd. "We are noticing more loss this year; I suspect it's from so many Indians passing through."

"Do we try and stop them?" asked Rickard.

"No, that would bring more trouble than it would be worth," said Boyd. "A cow here and there is a cheap price to pay for peaceful Indians."

"Boyd, you know how I feel about it," said Dean, "I think you ought to shoot every one of those thieving red bastards. We need to teach them to stay away from our property."

"I know that's how you feel Dean, but when this treaty deal at the fort is over, things will get better. It's best not to stir them up right now."

"I agree, just leave them be for now," said Platt. "There's already more cows out there than we can count."

"Wilf, Flora, you feel that way too?"

They both nodded. "When the new herd gets here, we'll have a hell of a lot more to worry about than a few Indian-killed cows," said Flora.

"Dean, what else do you want to talk about?" asked Flora. "You said you have two issues on your mind."

"Yes. I think it's time for the association to grow. I want to make it available to other, smaller outfits and any new ranchers that want in."

"Why? asked Flora, "we're all making good money with the four members we have now. How will new members help us?"

"I have the same question," said Rickard. "What would the benefits be?"

"We are doing good right now," said Dean, "but as this town grows, there will be more homesteaders looking for their own hundred and sixty acres, the railroad all but guarantees that'll happen. I want a bigger association of ranchers that can represent our issues. Basically, it's all about safety in numbers. In a few weeks, we will officially become a territory, and Cheyenne will be the capital. We need to make a strong association to keep our place in the business."

"Dean, I don't always agree with some of your ideas," said Clifford Platt, "but I understand what you're saying about keeping our place in the business. I think we should have a special meeting to discuss it. How does everyone else feel about it?"

Wilf Rickard nodded his head, "I agree, at least to talking about it."

"Flora? You good with it," asked Dean.

"I can't say I'm in favor of it either, but I do think it's worth discussing. Let's plan on having a meeting here next Saturday."

Chapter 9

"Dolly, I have to be there, it's all part of the job," said Del. "When it's over, we can take a ride down to the property and see what needs to be done to make it livable, unless you want to come with me now."

"No thanks, the last thing I want to see is a man hang. I've seen more than enough of that sort of thing; I don't need any more, and when you get back, I'd rather not hear about it."

The gallows had been finished just in time for the execution. Mick Maguire was shackled with his hands behind his back and led up the steps of the platform. Standing on the trap door, they shackled his legs together and put the noose behind his left ear.

The executioner, a tall, thin man wearing a black bowler hat, stepped alongside him. Holding a bible in one hand and a black hood in the other, he looked at the prisoner. "Mick Maguire, you have been found guilty by a duly appointed court of law and sentenced to die by hanging on order of the judge of said court. Do you have any last words?"

The prisoner shook his head and stared straight ahead. Placing the hood over his head, the executioner pressed the bible against his heart and put his other hand on the lever. "May God have mercy on your soul."

It was over quickly. The body was put in a cheap pine coffin, laid out in a wagon, hauled to the cemetery, and put in the ground; everything was done in less than an hour. Del pushed a crude wooden cross into the ground and walked away.

*

Tying up the buggy at the homestead that had been given to them, it was obvious that Maguire had chosen well when he staked out this site. It was just far enough outside of town to avoid the railroad land and had the Laramie River as one boundary. Del saw mostly good flat grass-ground. He could see where the fencing had been torn down and the remains of two burned down outbuildings. Close to the river, on higher ground, were the damaged remains of the cabin.

"Dolly, you've been quiet all the way out here, something wrong?"

"Not really. I guess I'm just sad about Mister Maguire. What happened to him just wasn't right."

"I agree, but there wasn't any way to change things."

"What would have happened to the place if he hadn't signed it over to you?"

"If they found no heirs, it would be put up for auction," said Del. "I'm sure old man Harper was set to buy it; his property runs along the north side of this one."

"I suppose that won't make him a real friendly neighbor?" said Dolly, as they walked around the remains of the cabin.

"I'm sure he's not too happy about it, but I doubt him or his boys are gonna bother the Marshal's place. What do you think about living here? We can fix it up into a good ranch. I always wanted to raise a few horses; this would be a perfect place."

Dolly looked over the property for several minutes then slid her arm through his. "Del, this is the closest I've ever come to having a real home. I think we can make it into a wonderful ranch. There's just one thing though . . ."

"What would that be?"

"I would like to name it the Maguire Ranch."

Dean nodded. "I like that idea. From now on, this will be the Maguire Ranch. I already have a stone ordered for his grave; it didn't seem right to leave it unmarked."

*

As the engine slowed, Dolly saw the Cheyenne station come into view. "How about this deal," said Del. "It's fifty miles through the mountains from Laramie to Cheyenne, and now it's nothing but a short train ride. Sure beats the hell out of fifty miles on the back of a horse or in a stagecoach."

"It's a great improvement, but the smoke from the engine can be bad. Del, I see Wesley on the platform, and Anny's standing next to him."

Stepping off the train car, Anny greeted both of them with a hug, and Marshal Tompkins shook Del's hand. "Good to see you Del, you keeping a lid on Laramie?"

"Doing our best, but it seems like just about the time you got one bunch under control, another one starts raising hell."

Tompkins nodded and lit a fresh cigar. "Just the nature of the job. By the time the tracks get to Rawlins, things should start calming down around there."

"I expect so," said Del. "When all the Indian business at the fort finishes up, it should get even better."

"Speaking of Indians, they been giving you much trouble recently?" said Wes.

"Not really, a few ranchers claim they're rustling from them, but I haven't seen any real crimes to speak of. How about you?"

"Mostly a lot of whining from people like Dean," said Tompkins, "sorry Anny, no offense meant."

"None taken," said Anny. "The Indians may have taken a few this summer, but nothing serious; he just hates Indians and pretty much anything he perceives as taking money out of his pocket."

"Sounds like every rancher I ever knew," said Del. "There's so many cattle out there now that I don't see how they think it's possible to keep track of all of them."

"I doubt they can," said Tompkins. "Del, how did the hanging go? Any problems with the executioner? It's the first time we have used someone outside the department, most guys don't like to do it."

"Everything went fine. He was very professional."

"Good. Are you and Dolly staying at the Dakota House?"

"We are," said Del. "We're heading back the day after the wedding."

"You hungry? The Chophouse is right next door, and it has a fine steak dinner, and best of all, it's on the government. I eat all my meals there. It's the best food in Cheyenne."

"I like that idea. Let us get to the room and rest up a little. We'll see you there in an hour if that works?"

"Del, Miss Dolly, I will see you there," said Tompkins, tipping his hat.

*

The morning was cloudless, with a slight breeze coming over the hills. The Timms Ranch hands were setting up chairs in front of an arch built for the occasion. It looked out over the Timms property, with the ranch house set against a stand of tall aspens and the creek wandering through the meadow in between. Local ladies had decorated it with white linen and fresh wildflowers. Several water barrels with long planks laid between them formed tables and were covered with more linen sheets.

An endless stream of local women had filled the table with more food than most had ever seen in one place before. Buffalo, pronghorn, turkey, and enormous platters of beef as well as breads, biscuits, and beans covered most of the main table. At one end was a large punch bowl full of sweetened lemonade and another of sweetened tea. At the opposite end were pies and cakes and sweet treats of all kinds.

By 11 am, the chairs were filled, and the pastor from the local Methodist church was in place under the arch. When the pastor decided it was time, he called for everyone to be quiet; the wedding was ready to begin. Looking to the back of the crowd, he motioned for the bride to begin. Slowly, Anny Werner, dressed in a beautiful white dress with light blue trim, walked down the aisle, accompanied arm and arm by her old friend and bodyguard, Morgan Reese.

Waiting at the altar was Dolly on one side of the pastor and Boyd on the opposite side. Dean stood next to him. The pastor signaled for everyone to be seated, then he motioned to Morgan to be seated and began the service. After the pastor read the special words Anny had chosen, he chose a passage from the bible, read it to the couple, then closed the book and pronounced them husband and wife. He told them they could kiss each other if they would like.

Dean grabbed her and pulled her to him, kissing her for a long time. When they separated, the crowd began to clap, and Anny embraced him and kissed him again and again; the crowd continued to clap until they turned to face them. "Thank you everyone," said Anny, "thank you all so much for being with us today!"

The celebration went on for several more hours, and the food and punch were going fast. While Anny visited with the guests, Dean gathered at the punchbowl with a few friends. Reaching under the table, he took out a box and opened it. Pulling out a new bottle of whisky, he uncorked it and held it up. "Gentlemen, dump that woman's drink and have a whisky with me to celebrate!"

The men wasted no time pouring out the punch and holding up their cups. When they were all filled, they toasted Dean and his new bride. Quickly throwing back the first whisky, they held out their cups for more. After several more toasts to everything from the wedding, the ranch, the cattle, and how much they all hated Indians, the bottle was empty. Grabbing a second bottle, Dean uncorked it and the toasts began again. By the time the guests were gone, there were half-a-dozen drunken men left, and Dean was the drunkest one of the bunch.

Boyd and Morgan shooed the rest of the drunks away and laid Dean flat on the ground. "I'm sorry, Anny, I think he's gonna be out for a while," said Boyd. "The wedding was wonderful; I hate that he messed it up like this."

"Thank you Boyd, can you two get him to our room at the Dakota? I would really appreciate it."

Morgan picked him up and tossed him over his shoulder, and carried him to the buggy. "He'll be fine. We'll put him on the bed. If you need us for anything, let us know."

*

Stepping off the train in Laramie, Dolly and Del met Raylan coming out of the station door. "How's my town doing," asked Del, "still quiet?"

"Well, not exactly quiet . . ."

"Raylan, what the hell's going on?"

"Clyde Harper, and both his boys were murdered two nights ago."

"Murdered? All of them?"

"Yessir, all three are dead."

"Do you have any suspects?"

"No sir, nothing yet."

"Who found them?"

"Isaac Bell, from the feed store. He was makin' a delivery in the morning and found them strung-up from a beam in the barn."

"Well damn Raylan, I thought all that stuff was finally over in Laramie; it looks like I was wrong. We'll talk about it when I get to the office in the morning."

"I'll see you there. How was the wedding?"

"It was good, though the groom got a little drunk, but overall, it was good."

Dolly listened to their conversation about the hangings as she and Del walked to their rooms.

"Del . . ."

"What is it?"

She thought for a moment then shook her head, " . . . never mind."

"Dolly, if there's something you want to ask me about, go ahead."

"No, it's nothing. I'm just glad to be home is all."

"Me too sweetheart, me too. Let's take a ride down to the property tomorrow. I'd like to get an idea of what we'll need to get started on fixing up that cabin."

"Are you going to go to the Harper place while we're there?"

"I have to Dolly, it's part of my job to investigate what happened."

"Then I'll stay here; besides, I need to get back to the cafe; tomorrow is baking day, and I'll be making the pies for the rest of the week."

"Okay, bring home one for us, please."

"I will. I'm going to bed, I love you Del."

Del nodded, "I love you too." He walked through the cool night air to the jail. Inside, he sat down and put his boots on his desk. Pouring himself a whisky from the bottle in his desk, he lit a fresh cigar and exhaled a long cloud of smoke toward the empty cell.

*

Anny was writing when Dean came in and put his arms around her from behind. "Sweetheart, I am so sorry about embarrassing you and our friends at the wedding. I'm ashamed of the way I acted. Will you be able to forgive me?"

"We've all done embarrassing things in our life," said Anny, "it's over, and we can get back to business as usual."

Dean hugged her and kissed her several more times. "Thank you for being so understanding to this old fool."

"I do have some exciting news to share," said Anny, changing the subject.

"Well, let's hear it," said Dean, still holding on to her.

She pushed him away and picked up a copy of the current Cheyenne Leader. "The paper wants to publish my story from the fort. They said it's long enough for two pieces and want me to keep reporting on it until everything is finished. I will have my own by-line too; '*Anny Werner Timms Reporting*,' isn't that exciting?"

"I'm happy for you, Sweetheart, but that means you will be gone on more trips?"

"It does, but I'll try and keep them short and be here for you as much as I can. Besides, they will eventually have all that treaty business finished, and it will be back to life as usual."

"I suppose so, but I'll still miss you. When do you want to go again?"

"I think the day after tomorrow if it's okay with you and Morgan."

"Morgan will do whatever I tell him. I'll have him get everything together tomorrow."

"Thank you. I will get my things ready right now."

"Anny, there is one thing I forgot about . . ."

"What would that be?"

"The clothes for your trip. We talked about you wearing men's trousers and such?"

"I took care of that already. I showed them to you, don't you remember? I have a new split skirt, long sleeve shirt, oversized hat, big bandanna and boots, the whole western outfit. Although I have to admit, it may be a while before I'm completely comfortable in the new boots."

Dean looked surprised, "You showed them to me? When?"

"Just before the wedding."

"Well, I guess I must be getting old, 'cause I sure don't remember that."

"Maybe you just had a lot on your mind. It's not important, it's all taken care of anyway."

Chapter 10

Twenty four-hundred cattle and nearly a hundred horses covered the gentle hillsides and meadows several miles below the South Platte River. A narrow creek wandered its way through the grassy flats that had been fattening up the herd for three days.

Case looked at Roly and motioned him to move out. Passing the signal down the line, the lead cowboy gave his signal, and the herd riders started to move them out. "Roly, find us a good place to cross," said Case. "After the wagons get across, keep 'em moving until you find a place to bed them down for tonight."

"You got it boss." Rounding up the wagons and two extra hands, they headed for the river. Finding a well-used buffalo trail, they crossed without a problem. The herd began to string out, following the leaders and moving steadily, feeding as they went.

The cowboys expertly moved them along, following Roly's lead toward the river.

It was obvious that the herd smelled the water as the pace picked up for the last mile. With the cowboys whooping and hollering and pushing them hard, the lead cow plunged directly into the river without slowing down. The water was not over a foot deep, and the herd moved steadily across, and the drag men pushed the last of the herd onto dry land.

Roly and the rest of the wagons kept moving north for a few more miles until they found a spot with good water and grass for the night. "How close to Cheyenne you figure we are boss," asked Roly.

"This isn't where we crossed last year," said Case, "but I'd say about two days or a bit more."

"Looks like the good lord got us through another one boss."

"Well, the good lord had some help from a damn good bunch of cowboys too."

"We didn't lose any men this trip," said Roly, pulling the harness off the mules. "I believe that God protected all of us."

"I'm sure God helped with that too, but I like to think our rifles and pistols had something to do with it. We also had extra men watching for Indians this year."

"Sure, but it was God who guided you to make all of those decisions, he watches out for everyone, even if you don't believe it."

"Roly, I'm tired and hungry and don't want to debate you anymore, I just want to have some chuck and rest."

"God Bless you Case," said Roly.

"I'm going to Cheyenne tomorrow and get with Dean Timms. I need you to hold down the place until I get back."

"No problem boss, me and God will watch over things 'till you get back."

"That makes me feel a whole lot better . . ."

*

Case and two of his trail hands rode under the "Timms Land & Cattle" sign and tied up at the ranch house. Greeting them at the front door, Dean shook everyone's hand. "Case, it's damn good to see you again. All of you, come on inside and tell me all about the trip."

Sitting around the table, Dean set up four glasses and poured them a drink. "It was longer and drier than last year. Finding enough water was the hardest part," said Case, finishing the glass of whisky.

Dean opened the bottle again, and Case put his hand over the glass. "No thanks, no more for us until we get this herd to the ranch. Can we get a few extra hands to guide us the last few miles? You probably want to send your wranglers along to help cut out the horses and move them where you want them."

"I'll get them started right away. You sure you don't want one more drink first?"

"We're sure," said Case. "It's a long ride back, and we need to keep a clear head. We've seen a lot of Indians the last couple of weeks."

"Did they give you much trouble on the trail?"

"The Comanche's were worse than usual; we had a couple of serious fights with them all the way up to the Arkansas River. We didn't lose any men, but we lost maybe a hundred-fifty head to the Indians and the rivers, but they really wanted the horses. They ended up with twenty or thirty, but they paid dearly for everything they got."

"Did you kill a bunch?"

"We did, including one old chief down by the Colorado River; I got a good bunch of feathers from that one."

"You coulda killed every last one of those stinkin' red bastards as far as I'm concerned," said Dean, pouring another whisky.

"I don't think there's enough bullets this side of the Mississippi to get them all, but we made a good dent in the local population," said Case. "Dean, we need to get moving; we don't want to be traveling through Indian country in the dark."

*

The herd pushed steadily toward the ranch, crossing the rails and covering the last few miles without a problem. Dean leaned against the fence rail next to Anny, watching the waves of cattle and horses move into the valley and scatter out along the creek. Case rode up to the fence and stopped. Pulling out the makings, he rolled a cigarette and watched as the cattle filled the landscape. "Well, what do you think boss?"

Dean watched the herd for another minute, amazed at how many animals there were. "I think of dollars Case, lots and lots of dollars filling up the association member's pockets. What about you, what do you think?"

"Dollars for sure, but good luck managing so many cattle out there, you're gonna need a lot of hands on horseback all day every day. The branding alone will be a serious bit of business."

"We'll get it done, no problem. You and Boyd both worry too much. This is going to be the biggest, most successful ranch in the West. You just wait and see."

"Well, good luck with that, I hope you're right. We'll see you in the morning and get everything squared up."

Dean Timms just nodded as he watched the new herd scatter.

*

"Boyd Stamps, exactly how are you going to keep track of all these cattle," asked Flora. "There aren't enough cowboys in Laramie County to watch over all of them."

"Flora, you knew Dean already had plans for more cattle and horses. There's nothing you or me or anyone else could do about it. I'm gonna do my job the best I can, keep him informed, and hope he figures it out."

"You're the one who should be running this outfit, not him. Everyone in the association says so too."

"I'm just a hired hand, I don't give orders, I take them," said Boyd. "Why don't the association members tell him what they think should be done?"

"The members really are a little nervous about the new herd, and you know they won't have anything to do with Dean's proposed horse business."

"If that's so, then why won't they speak up?"

"It's money Boyd, it's all about the money. Right now, they're making a lot of money, and they don't want that to stop."

"What about your father? Does he feel the same way as the others?"

"Of course he does. Like I said, it's all about the money."

"I'm tired of talking about cow business. Let's go to bed and talk about something else."

"Why Mister Stamps, you old reb, whatever do you have in mind?"

"Miss Dere, I have told you many times before to never call me a reb."

"Really? Well sir, what is it you intend to do about it?"

"Just get under these blankets, and you'll find out quick enough."

*

Dean watched as Anny and Morgan pulled out of the ranch on their next trip to Fort Laramie. When they reached the fort, Anny was excited to get started with her interviews. "Missus Anny, how are your new boots feeling," asked Morgan.

"They are about the same, very stiff. I suppose they will get better though. But my new skirt is wonderful, far better than the old dresses. And, I really love my new hat. Does that make me a cowboy now?"

"No Ma'am, it makes you a cowgirl."

"Oh, of course, a cowgirl! I'll be the cowgirl reporter. I like that."

They spent the day walking through the fort, making notes on everything she saw. She interviewed soldiers and travelers and every Indian that would stand still for her while Morgan translated. Sometimes, she made small drawings at the bottom of her tablet to help her remember the scene later.

Morgan introduced her to Nathaniel Taylor, Commissioner of Indian Affairs, an old friend of his. After nearly an hour long interview, he told her that he would take her around to the different camps the next day. Too excited to fall asleep, she stayed up and wrote in her journal by the light of the campfire.

Taylor had a buggy ready in the morning, and they rode the short distance to the Arapaho camp. For the next hour, Anny walked between the lodges taking notes and making quick drawings in her tablet. "Missus Timms, the older man sitting by the fire smoking with the younger men is Black Bear, one of the Arapaho chiefs," said Taylor. "You may want to sketch him; he is important to the tribe signing the treaty."

She studied the chief for a moment then made a quick drawing. "Mister Taylor, may I speak with him?"

"Missus Timms, I should warn you, not all Indians are friendly or even want to be here. I doubt he will speak enough English to be understood. Morgan, do you think you can translate well enough for her to speak to him?"

Morgan walked to the fire, squatted down next to Black Bear, and talked for a minute. The old man nodded and told the younger Indian men to leave. When Anny walked to the fire, Black Bear motioned for her to sit beside him. Her hands shook noticeably while she tried to compose herself enough to speak. "Morgan, what do I do now?"

"Did you bring him a gift?"

"Oh, yes, I forgot. I have them in my bag."

"Then find something and offer it to him, it is a gift of friendship."

Anny took out a silver-colored medallion with an eagle embossed on one side and a flag on the back, hung from a red, white, and blue ribbon. The old chief's face lit up with a huge smile, and he nodded his appreciation. She nervously asked every question she could think of and wrote down everything as quickly as Morgan translated it. She also sketched Black Bear wearing the medallion. When they got ready to leave, he leaned toward Morgan and said something to him.

Walking back to the wagon, Anny looked at Morgan. "What did he say to you as we were leaving?"

"He said that you and him are now friends, and you can come and speak with him whenever you wish."

"I have to say, that's pretty impressive, Missus Timms," said Taylor. "It usually takes the Army longer than that just to get a chief to sit with them, let alone talk to them. Maybe they should hire you to make friends with all the chiefs before the negotiations begin."

"That was very exciting for me. Any time Morgan and I can talk with them or help in any way, just ask. How long do you think that it will take to finish up negotiations with all the different tribes?"

"It's hard to say. I think they would like to get it done by fall, but not all the chiefs have shown up yet. Keep in mind, they're not all as obliging as Black Bear. We're not sure if some of them, like the Oglala chiefs, will show up at all."

"Thank you so much for your help Mister Taylor, and to you, Morgan, for translating for me. I have so much to report about already. I may never finish it all."

"You're very welcome Missus Timms. The government could use some accurate reporting on the proceedings going on here. We're so remote that most of the country has no idea what the real West is like, or what is happening with the different Indian tribes."

"Mister Taylor, I promise I'll do my best to paint an accurate picture, so the people will know what's happening out here."

Chapter 11

"Ernesto, it looks like four horses, and one is missing a shoe, and the others look to be worn out," said Boyd as they followed the tracks along the bank to where they crossed the creek. "It looks like they got away with at least ten or fifteen head. Let's see where they're going. Have you got your pistol?"

"Si, right here in my belt."

Following the trail through a winding gap in the trees, they stopped short of a long narrow sage flat with a lone calf lying in the middle, bawling for its mama. "What do you think Ernesto?"

"Señor Boyd, I think we should be careful, the rustlers could be waiting for us to check on the calf."

"I agree. Let's tie up here and see if you're right. You take the east side of the meadow, and I'll take the west side. Stay back in the trees and work yourself along the edge and see what you can find. If someone is waiting for us with a gun, you know what to do."

"Si Señor, I will take care of business, no problema."

Both men started to work their way slowly through the trees, stepping quietly as they went. Boyd could see where the rustler's trail had left the sage and disappeared around a low ridge. Before he could go any farther, he heard a single gunshot from across the flat. Watching the opposite tree line, he saw Ernesto step out and wave his hat. Boyd gathered the horses and walked to where he'd seen him.

A tall, skinny man lay on his back with a rifle still in his hands and a bullet hole just above his left eye. "Señor Boyd, when I told him to put his hands out so I could see them, he turned toward me and raised his rifle."

"You did good Ernesto, looks like he was waiting behind to kill us. It's one less rustler we'll have to deal with." Looking closely at the dead outlaw, he recognized him. "They call him Chicken Jack. I've seen a wanted poster on him. He was a Confederate soldier from Florida who deserted early in the war. He's wanted for horse theft and robbery in several states. I guess he thought rustling was more profitable."

"Chicken Jack is a very strange name for a man," said Ernesto.

"I suppose they call him that because he's got the longest, skinniest legs I ever saw. There is a reward for him, I think a hundred dollars or so. We'll bring him in, and you can collect it. You can also keep his gear and his horse if it isn't stolen; it must be tied up nearby somewhere."

"Sí, muchos gracias. Perhaps you can help me send the money to my family?"

"I can do that. Let's get him over his horse and head to the shack for tonight. We'll take him into town in the morning. Did you check on the calf?"

"Sí, they broke her legs so she couldn't walk. I had to kill her. What about the rest of the rustlers?"

"Nothing we can do tonight. When we see the Marshal, he can decide what to do about them."

*

Flora Dere was at the cabin when Boyd walked in. "How's my handsome cowboy today? Things good out on the range?"

He hugged her and gave her a kiss. "A little more excitement than usual, we had some rustlers working the upper valley. Ernesto and I followed them for a couple of miles, and he ended up killing one of them."

"What about the others?"

"They got away with a few head. Marshal Tompkins is sending out a posse to hunt for them. It looked like they were headed west, so we sent Del a telegram to be on the lookout for them in his part of the world. They all carry the S/4 brand, so they should be easy to spot if they're in the area."

"How do things look with all the new cattle? Are the cowboys able to manage things okay?"

"They're working their asses off; they're branding them wherever they can find them. We need to give them some kind of a bonus when they get it all done, maybe giving them one of the new horses or something."

"Sit down and relax a while. I have some pronghorn and potatoes ready to cook up."

"That sounds wonderful," said Boyd, as he sat down in front of the fireplace. Closing his eyes, he slid off to sleep before Flora finished talking.

*

After her third trip to Fort Laramie, Anny had filled several more tablets full of notes and drawings. She had begun to be known and accepted by everyone at the fort, including many of the Indians. On the last trip she met and interviewed General Sherman and Senator Henderson, chairman of the Committee on Indian affairs.

With the help of Nathaniel Green and Morgan Reese, she had met and spoken to many Indian tribal leaders. Black Bear, the Arapaho chief, had invited her back and told her about his life on the prairie. The publisher of the Cheyenne Leader loved her work and increased her space in the paper, allowing her to write articles as long as five-hundred words about her time at the fort.

Dean walked in and sat next to her, kissing her on the cheek. "Welcome back."

Anny closed up her journal and kissed him back. "Thank you, sweetheart. Did you see the paper? It says that congress is going to vote on making us a territory any time now. Are you excited about the idea of Wyoming becoming an official U.S. territory?"

"No. I think it's gonna be more laws and regulations that most cattlemen won't like. If Cheyenne is the capital of the new territory, the politics will just complicate everything. That's why we need a strong cattleman's association to keep our business from changing."

"Well, I think becoming a territory is wonderful. On the twenty-fifth of July, we'll be an official territory and now have a path to statehood. It won't be long, and we'll be able to take a train all the way to California, I think that's pretty exciting."

"I suppose, but it also means more people will be migrating into this country, and it won't be all that long before we'll have more damn farmers than we know what to do with."

"I think you're worried about nothing; it would take a hundred years to fill up this country, even with the railroad."

Dean shook his head. "I've just seen politics get in the way too many times before."

"Well, there isn't any way to change it, so we just as well enjoy it," said Anny. "I forgot to tell you; I am now a paid writer!"

"You got paid? What did you write?"

She held up the Cheyenne Leader. "Right here on the front page, my story on the Fort Laramie treaty business. Mister Becker paid me a dollar for the first two pieces I gave him. He said he would pay me a dollar apiece for my next stories."

"Anny, that's wonderful. Maybe you could start writing about other things too."

"What kind of other things are you thinking of?"

"Like the cattle business for example. Now that most of the railroad workers will be moving on, it's the biggest industry in this part of the country. The other day I heard someone call it the "Holy City of the Cow.""

"I hadn't really thought of it like that," said Anny. "There are plenty of things I could write about. I'll talk with Mister Becker and see what he thinks."

Dean poured himself a whisky and raised his glass, "To Mister Becker then," and downed the drink.

Anny watched him pour a second whisky and drink it. "Dean, I want to talk about something else."

"And what would you like to talk about my love?" said Dean, refilling his glass.

Anny put her hand over the glass and stopped him from pouring. "Dean, please don't drink anymore, I want to talk about something important here . . ."

"Fine, I'll wait until we're done, go ahead."

"Dean, you know how badly I want a child."

"Of course I do, sweetheart, but I don't know what to do about it. I guess it'll happen when the time is right."

"That's the problem Dean, we've been together quite a while, and I'm afraid I may never get pregnant. I've been thinking, maybe we could adopt a child?"

"I guess that would be okay. Do you know of any children that have been put up for adoption?"

"Yes, there are several young children at the fort that need a good home."

"Why are they at the fort?"

"They're Indian children Dean, found by the troopers."

"Indians? No! Absolutely not! There won't be any goddamn filthy Indians in this house ever!" Picking up the bottle, he filled the glass again, "The subject is closed."

Anny picked up the paper and read her first paid story to herself.

*

Cheyenne Leader

Each trip to Fort Laramie is more interesting and exciting than the last. At another visit with my new friend, Arapahoe Chief Black Bear, he regaled me with stories of life on the prairie before he'd ever seen a white man. He often touches my hair and gently curls it around his finger. I realize that he has likely never seen a fair-skinned red-haired woman before. On my second visit with him, he took my hand and put it on his head, showing me his hair. It was somewhat sticky and gritty, and in long tight braids tied with strips of hide and decorated with a single eagle feather.

I find the Arapahos to be a very handsome and well-dressed tribe, at least as far as the plains tribes that I see represented here. To my uneducated eye, they appear to be a stoic lot, calmer, and more apt to observe before they act. This view could, however, be somewhat tainted by my newfound friendship with the old chief.

I met U. S. Army General William Tecumseh Sherman on my second day. He is the highest ranking member of the army in charge of the military side of the business. He's very lean, and I dare say somewhat rough-looking with a thin face and a scruffy beard. He was, however, polite and straightforward, answering my questions without hesitation. He explained how difficult it was to get all of the various tribes to sit and talk when other tribes are camped nearby. Some tribes that are expected to be there, like the Oglala, with their chiefs Sitting Bull and Red Cloud, have yet to make an appearance.

A party of fourteen wagons, each pulled by a team of horses, came into the fort while I was there. They camped in a tight circle just outside the compound. The travelers looked very tired and road-weary from many months on the trail. The leader was a short, roundish, middle-aged man dressed from boots to hat in heavy, black wool clothes, including a long black frock coat that brushed across the dirt. He introduced himself as Pastor Jonathon James Jeffers, leader of his own congregation called the First Church of the Blessed Lord, all were believers from Ohio. He said they were on their way to the Oregon goldfields. When asked why such a devout group would want to undergo such a difficult and dangerous trip, he explained that: "... even the poorest, most wretched of men need the word of God, and we intend to teach them the gospel and save their souls." It appears unlikely that this group, however noble their intentions may be, had any idea of what was ahead of them. The mountains between them and their destination are a formidable barrier at the best of times.

My friend Morgan, an experienced mountain man for thirty years, tried to explain to them it was very late in the season to start for the mountains and that it might be best to stay at the fort for the winter and start out again next spring. Pastor Jeffers instantly puffed up with some indignity and loudly explained that he and God would get his flock there without incident and that we should not concern ourselves with such things that are not our business. When Morgan offered to find an experienced guide to help them, Pastor Jeffers simply turned his back and walked off. Although not a strong believer myself, all I can say about that is good luck, and I hope God's divine intervention will indeed take care of this misguided flock of believers.

Chapter 12

"Basquiat, I'm glad to see that you're up and around again," said Dean. "It's been a while since we've seen you at the table."

"Thank you. It's good to see all of you too. I assume that daughter Flora has been doing a respectable job representing the Dere Cattle Company interests?"

"She has indeed. She's very involved in everything that goes on with the association."

"Wilf, Clifford, you're both looking well," said Dere, leaning his cane against the table. "Boyd, are you keeping all those rustlers and Indians away from our herd?"

He took off his hat and nodded. "Me and a bunch of good cowboys are doing the best we can."

"Good to hear it son. Dean, I understand you have something you want to talk about, something besides regular business?"

"I do. I want to talk about the expansion of the association and building a new home for us to do our business in."

"And why do you think we need to enlarge our association," asked Basquiat. "I think we would all agree that financially at least, we are pleased with the return we are currently receiving on our investment. How can more members improve it?"

"I'm concerned that with the new territory coming, and Cheyenne as the capital, we as cattlemen won't have any representation with the politicians," said Dean. "If we form one larger association to include all of the area ranchers, we will become a strong voice for keeping our business the way we want it."

"What makes you think that our way of doing business is in jeopardy," asked Basquiat.

"The completion of the railroad is the main reason. There'll be more people, more towns, and more roads, and all of that will take more land, and where do you think that land will come from? From us, that's where. All those miles and miles of raw land out there are taking care of thousands of head of our cattle. That's our land and our livelihood, and we need to protect it."

They all sat quietly for a minute, thinking about what Dean had laid out. Wilf Rickard was the first to speak up. "Dean, everyone here knows that we're running our cattle on government land. Every acre of it is open range. None of us have any more claim to it than anyone else."

"You're absolutely right Wilf, and that's why we have to protect the way we do business. That's why a large cattleman's association can help all the ranchers fight the politics that will most certainly change our way of life."

"I think that it's inevitable that the range will eventually be opened up for other uses," said Flora. "Maybe we should be thinking about other ways to run our business?"

Clifford Platt had been quietly listening to the conversation and finally spoke up. "Dean, like I've said in these meetings before, I think we need to talk about growing feed and stockpiling it for emergencies. Flora's right, the politicians could end the idea of open range at the drop of a hat."

"I think that's reason enough to create a strong group of cattlemen to represent our interests," said Dean. "I can tell you right now that I plan on fighting to keep the open range system exactly as it is."

Basquiat tapped his cane on the floor, causing everyone to quiet down. "I believe we're all thinking more or less along the same line here. I agree that we want to protect our interests the best we can, but history is against us if we think we can keep operating like this forever. I suggest that we call a public meeting of all the ranchers we can reach and talk about our future and the possibility of an association of some kind. Clifford, Wilf, what do you think?" Both men nodded their agreement.

"Boyd, you haven't said anything yet. What do you think?"

"I'm just a hired hand here, but I do think we should be looking at how we're gonna handle all these cattle in the future."

*

Anny and Morgan sat on the ground in front of the army tent, fascinated by the negotiations going on inside. Two gray-bearded men dressed in mountain buckskins and fur hats translated back and forth between the white officials sitting in chairs and several Indian chiefs sitting on the ground in front of them. Smoke from the pipes of the Indians and the mountain men, mixed with the cigars of the whites, swirled around inside the tent, floating out the open flaps. Anny noted it and did her best to capture it in a drawing.

General Sherman listened intently, his gaze darting from Indian to translator to civilian and back. When some point had been made, he raised his hand and pointed to a civilian, transcribing the information to write it down. The Indians often became very animated, shaking their heads and raising their voices, only to have the mountain men try and calm them down.

From blankets just outside the tent, Anny and Morgan sat with a small group of Indians, watching the negotiations and the reactions of the crowd. The Indian men watched and smoked, sometimes nodding their heads and pointing at those in the tent. They talked loudly between themselves and often laughed at what was being said.

The Indian women all sat quietly, wrapped in blankets up to their necks, a few holding their babies against their breast. When the negotiation ended, Anny and Morgan walked through the encampment of lodges, watching the daily activities of the women. She watched as they did the work in camp and cared for the children while the men were across the valley racing their ponies.

"Morgan, is this the way it is with all the tribes?"

"Not sure what you're askin' Ma'am."

"I mean, do the women always do all the work in camp?"

"Pretty much all the Indians I ever been around are just like these. The men do the hunting, the fighting, and take care of the horses. The women take care of everything else in camp and raise the children."

Anny watched the women work for a while longer then told Morgan she was ready to pack up and go back to the ranch.

"Everything okay, Missus Anny?"

"Everything is fine Morgan. In fact, everything is better than fine. I'd like to get started as soon as we can."

"It is too late right now; we would be traveling in the dark all night. But we can leave as soon as the sun comes up tomorrow."

"Then that's the plan. I have a bunch of notes to transcribe. I can do that tonight after we eat. I have a new project I want to get started on as soon as I can."

*

"Anny, you've been buried in those tablets all day," said Dean. "Morgan told me you came home two days early. Is everything all right?"

"Dean, do you know that Indian women do all of the work in the village and raise the children?"

"Uh, yes, I think that's the way it is. Why?"

"I've decided I want to write about women," said Anny.

"You don't want to write about the business at the fort anymore?"

"No, I still want to write about everything I've been seeing, but I realize that everything I've been writing has a very male point of view. I want to put more women in my writing, not just the Indian women, but all women."

"Do you think that the readers will be as interested in your stories if there are a lot of women in them?"

"I don't see why not; half the population of the world is women."

"I just don't think women would be very interesting to read about. It's men who do all the really important things," said Dean. "The fact of it is, women do take care of the home and the children while men are off doing other, more interesting things, things that women just couldn't do. That's just the way it is."

"Well, my wonderful rancher husband, I believe you are full of beans, and I'm going to prove to you that there are just as many interesting women in the world as there are men."

"What does Mister Becker down at the Leader have to say about your idea?"

"I haven't told him yet."

"Let me know what he says."

*

In the back of the Florquist Dry-Goods store on Cheyenne's main street, a group of local women had gathered for the first formal meeting of *The Cheyenne Women's Betterment Society*. Bruce Florquist, a former fur trapper from down in the Green River country, opened up his store after hours for their meetings. Anny Timms had invited all the local women she knew. Sixteen showed up at the first meeting, mostly out of curiosity, including Flora Dere.

"Thank you all for coming tonight," said Anny, handing a sheet of paper to everyone. "I have been considering doing this for a long time. On the paper is a list of some of the things I hope to address in the group. Wyoming is now an official U.S. Territory and on its way to eventual statehood. I couldn't think of a better time to make ourselves heard."

"The new government is gonna be a bunch of stupid old white men, just like always," said Flora, from the back of the room. "What makes you think we can do anything about it?"

"Like it says on the paper, I think women need to be part of the new territory's political system," said Anny. "We deserve the right to vote and make decisions on things that will affect our future."

"The right to vote? We all know that'll never happen. You're just wasting our time with all this," said Flora, standing up. "I don't know about the rest of you, but I've got more important things to do than waste my time on this, goodbye."

"What about the rest of you?" asked Anny. "Does anyone here feel the same as Flora?" Three more women left the room, and she waited until things quieted down. "Well, that leaves a dozen of us who are still interested. Thank you for staying. I'm excited to see that so many believe it's time to talk about women's progress."

"Missus Timms, I'm in favor of the things you've put down on this paper, but I wouldn't have the first idea how to go about getting them done."

"Marie, I apologize. I should have started the meeting differently. I know some of you, and I should start over again with introductions. I'm Anny Timms, my husband is Dean Timms, and he runs the Timms Land and Cattle Company. Some of you may know me from my time as the town telegrapher before I was married. Perhaps we could go around the group and introduce ourselves?"

The women were the wives of ranchers, shopkeepers, a barber, a bartender, and two who were unmarried. They bonded quickly, and within two hours, they had formed the heart of the new association. By the time they left, they had made out a formal agenda, schedule, and renamed their new group: *The Wyoming Women's Betterment Society,* changing it from Cheyenne to Wyoming to give the sense of covering more of the territory.

"What a wonderful meeting. I'm so glad to get to know you and see that we all share so many of the same concerns," said Anny, as they all got up to leave. "I will see you at the next meeting, and please feel free to bring along any of your friends who may be interested."

Chapter 13

With the cabin on the Maguire Ranch nearly finished, Del fenced off two pens for his horses. He had a local carpenter build a barn with six stalls and a tall hayloft. "Dolly, I think we're about ready to move in, what do you think?"

"When will the stoves and windows be in? It might get kind of cold without them."

"They'll be here any day now, but I can keep you plenty warm 'till then."

"I'm sure you can, but I think I'd like to have the stoves and windows in place just the same."

Del saw Raylan coming down the lane and walked out to meet him. "Marshal, we just got this wire from Cheyenne, rustlers got off with some of the Timms cattle. They think they are headed west and asked us to be on the lookout for any animals with the S/4 brand."

"Put the word out. I'll be in the office in a while," said Del. "Anything else going on I should know about?"

"Ike King got drunk and shot out the front window of the laundry."

"Really? What'd old man Yang have to say about that?"

"When I got there, he was red in the face, babbling in Chinese and looking for Ike with a shotgun. I got Ike's pistol and Yang's shotgun in the office, and Ike in the cell."

"He's a good hand but was never much good at holdin' his whisky. It ain't the first time he's done something like this. I'll be back to town in a while."

"What did Raylan want?" asked Dolly.

"I guess Ike King got drunk and did a little shootin' at the laundry. I gotta go sort things out. It's gettin' late anyway; we should head back."

*

Sitting at his desk, Del worked his way through an assortment of paperwork. The prisoner had been passed out since he got back. When he woke up, he looked around and realized where he was. "Marshal, goddamn it to hell! What am I doing in here? I didn't do nothing but have a couple of drinks," said King.

Del looked at the sad, disheveled figure staring at him through the bars. "Ike, will you just shut the hell up! This is at least three times you've been in that cell, and I'm gettin' tired of looking at your sorry ass."

"Marshal, just let me out. I didn't hurt anyone. I need to get back to the ranch."

"Listen dumbass, you shot out that big front window of Mister Yang's laundry last night, and you're gonna have to pay for it or go see Judge Chapman."

"That lying little Chinaman said I did that? That's crap. I ain't shot that pistol in weeks."

"If it hadn't been for Raylan, that lying little Chinaman would have taken your head off with his ten-gauge, and now I got both of your guns. So, here's the deal. I talked to Yang, and if you pay for a new window, he won't press charges. If you don't do that, you'll have to see the judge."

"A new window? What would that cost?"

"Yang says it will cost forty-five dollars."

"Forty-five dollars! Where the hell is it coming from, New York City?"

"No, just Cheyenne."

"Screw Yang, I ain't paying him nothing."

"It's up to you, you pay him, or you go see the judge. How'd it work out for you the last time you went to see the judge?"

King shook his head, remembering the last time he went before him. "Not so good. I ain't got any money. I spent what little I had at the bar last night. Can you tell my foreman out on the YK where I'm at?"

"Yang's gonna want the cash up-front before he agrees to anything."

"Aw, screw that old man, Marshal, that's two month's pay. I'll get it to him when I get some saved up."

"Or, I could give him back his ten-gauge, and we can see what happens," said Del.

"Okay, okay, can you ask my foreman to come and see me. Maybe I can get him to advance me enough to get squared up."

"Ike, I got another idea if you're willing to listen."

King shrugged. "Sure, why not. I ain't really got nowhere to go, now do I?"

"I'll make you a deal," said Del, lighting a fresh cigar. "I'll pay off Mister Yang out of my own pocket, and you can work it off by doing a few things for me."

"What kind of things?"

"How long you been working out at the YK?"

"Two years, why do you want to know that?"

"All the ranches between Laramie and Cheyenne have been hit hard by rustlers. Every cattleman on the range has lost animals over the last year or so. What I want to know is who are the worst of them. I already know you and some of the YK boys are involved. You let me know who's doing the serious rustling, and I pay off your debt to Yang."

"Marshal, I swear, we ain't never done more than grab whatever unbranded calves we find. I ain't turning in any of my friends for that."

"Ike, as far as I am concerned, you can have all the unbranded calves you want. I know everyone out there does it. I'm looking for the gangs that are stealing large bunches of cattle. You know the ones I'm talking about. I want the murderers, rustlers, and horse thieves, and I want to put them out of business permanently."

"And if I don't?"

"If you don't, I can guarantee you a good stay in jail."

King laid back on the bunk, "Well shit Marshal, I guess I work for you now."

"Ike, you're at the saloon nearly every Saturday. Just keep me up to date on what you know, and what you've heard. You know the ones I'm looking for. You do that, and I'll pay your bill and stay outta your way, am I clear?"

"Yeah, yeah, clear, now can I get out of this cage?"

Del opened the cell door and handed him his pistol. "It's unloaded, now get the hell outta here. Oh yeah, there is one more thing . . ."

"What?"

"I'll see you Saturday."

*

Del handed the form to the telegrapher. "Send this off right away. If you get a response, bring it right over." The operator read the message and began to transmit it.

***To: Marshal Wesley Tompkins, Cheyenne**
2 cowboys killed by rustlers the night before last on the
Withers Ranch. Approx. 15-20 head taken, lost trail after
10 miles. All shod horses, one horse missing one shoe.

Deputy Marshal Delbert Beale, Laramie

"Raylan, this is likely to be the same gang that got the Timms' cattle two weeks ago."

"Both had a horse with a missing shoe," said Raylan. "I've been looking at every horse I see, but none with a missing shoe yet."

"Yeah, me too. If you do see one like that, don't confront him. Let me know, and maybe he'll lead us to the others."

"Marshal, what they did to those two cowboys was the worst thing I ever saw. There wasn't no need to strip 'em and shoot them so many times."

"It was ugly, that's for sure. Whoever did this is the same one that killed the trooper a while back. A man who would do something like this has a grudge against the whole world," said Del.

"You ever seen anything like this before?"

Del nodded. "More than once, though some of it was from the Comanches."

"You think this is from the Indians?"

"This ain't Indians."

*

94

Dolly stood on the porch watching two men put in the cabin's front door. The fireplace was finished, and the kitchen stove was in place. Del had a smaller heating stove put in their bedroom for the coldest winter nights. The workers had split and stacked plenty of firewood and finished the barn and corrals several days before.

Walking up behind her, Del wrapped his arms around her and kissed her on the neck. "I think we should celebrate tonight by letting me warm you up in our new cabin."

"Oh, Del, it's more than warm enough already," said Dolly, trying to keep a straight face. "Maybe later, when it gets colder outside, but we have a stove in the bedroom now, so that should keep me plenty warm."

"Miss Dolly, there is no substitute for a good man on a cold night."

"Well . . . I guess I could use a man to keep the firewood stocked."

"You have my word that I will always keep you warm by any method necessary. In fact, since the place is done, I think we should try out one of those methods tonight."

"I suppose we could, but I better not get cold."

*

Del pushed the chair back, put his boots on the desk, and pulled a packet of Buffalo Brand smoking tobacco out of the drawer, and rolled a cigarette. When Raylan came in, he slid the tobacco across the desk toward him.

"Thanks boss, I never tried this kind before."

95

"I found it on the trail where the two cowboys were killed. I think one of the rustlers dropped it. Since it's the first one like it that I've seen around here, it's something else to watch for, along with the missing horseshoe. I've gotta go meet someone, so hold down the fort until I get back."

"Will do, can I have another smoke?"

"Keep it, I prefer a good cigar."

Walking into the back of the livery, Del stepped into the dark stall and waited for his eyes to adjust. "Ike, you here?" asked Del, with his hand on his pistol.

"I'm here Marshal, next stall over."

"So, tell me what's new. What've you been hearing about this cattle business?"

"Nothing much different than last week. It looks like the gang you're interested in is still working this part of the country. The YK lost two good bulls a few days back. We tracked four rustlers several miles until we lost the trail."

"Were any of those horses you followed missing a shoe?"

"Yeah, how did you know that?"

"It's the same group that killed the two hands from the Withers Ranch. Ike, you gotta watch yourself out there. These are a bunch of murderers that don't care who they kill."

"That all Marshal? I got things to do."

"One thing, did you ever use Buffalo Brand smoking tobacco or know anyone that does?"

"Never heard of it. Why?"

"I want to know right away if you ever see anyone using it or if you see a horse with a missing right front shoe."

"That all?"

"Until next week."

Walking into the forge, Del waited a moment while the smith put a shoe back in the fire. "Andy, how's business?"

"Good Marshal, in fact, almost too good. I can't hardly get away from the place. What brings you in today?"

Pulling out a poster, he handed it to him. "I'm just out warning people to be on the lookout for this guy. He's running a gang of rustlers and horse thieves around here, and they've already murdered several people, including two good hands from the Withers ranch."

"I'll keep an eye open Marshal. Can I keep this poster?"

"Sure. I'm gonna hang a few more around town just in case someone has seen him. One of the gang rides a horse with a right front shoe missing, and the others are badly worn. I'd guess that all four of them might be needing some horse work. That's why I wanted you to know what was going on."

"I appreciate it Marshal. If I see anything that ain't right, I'll let you know right away."

"Thanks Andy. I got a couple of head that need full resets when you get time."

"Time is what I ain't got much of right now, but for you, I'll get 'em in. Just let me know when you need it done."

*

Del and Raylan rode slowly along the muddy trail, following the tracks of three Indians they had been following since first light. The day before, three good saddle horses had been stolen and a line shack of the YK ranch burned. The horses had escaped from the Indians and returned to the camp. Two cattle had been slaughtered nearby, and the track they picked up led east into the foothills.

Passing the remains of a small fire, they tied up the horses and followed the trail into a thin line of aspens, stopping to look through the trees at the trail ahead. In the distance, they saw the three Indians sitting alongside a beaver pond, talking loudly and laughing. Their horses fed on the damp grass near the pond.

Del studied the scene through his binoculars. "Raylan, that big bay has a brand on it. I can't make out exactly what it is, but it's damn sure a stolen horse."

"How do you want to handle it boss?"

"Only one way I know to do it, get your rifle."

The two men crawled to the edge of the trees and got into shooting position. At Del's signal, they fired, and two of the Indians slumped down where they sat. The third was on his feet running for the horses when he lurched forward and fell face first in the grass, taking a bullet from Raylan's second shot.

"Damn, that was one hell of a shot. Where did you learn to shoot like that?"

"Back home on the farm killin' jackrabbits. You ever see a jackrabbit plague?"

"Never saw one, but I heard of them before."

"We had a couple of bad ones where I come from in Kansas. They eat every single thing that grows, right down to the dirt. It got so bad that people were trapping them, clubbing them, and burning them out. It was a really ugly thing, and most people didn't want anything to do with it. A lot of them decided it would be easier just to pay me to shoot the ones on their property. Cartridges were expensive, so I got pretty good at it."

As Raylan gathered up the horses, Del looked over the Indian bodies. When one made a low gurgling sound, he shot him with his pistol, doing the same with the other two.

"They weren't dead?" said Raylan.

"It don't pay to take chances with these bastards. I learned that when I was killing Indians for the army."

"You were right about the brands, boss — all three of the ones they were riding are from the YK."

"I guess they have such good horses, the Indians thought they'd come back for more," said Del.

"What do you want to do with the bodies?"

"The wolves and the ravens gotta eat too, just take the guns and knives. Let's get going. It's a long ride home, so we'll stay at the YK tonight, and they can have their horses back."

*

"So, who the hell is that in the cell?" asked Del, walking into the jail.

99

"Meet Clarence Trumbell," said Raylan. "He got caught trying to steal two bottles of whisky at the saloon. Teddy caught him and brought him over yesterday."

"That's all he did, steal some whisky?"

"I guess he paid his fifteen cents for the food, and when they weren't looking, he stuffed the bottles in his coat and headed out the door. Before he got outside, the two bottles clinked together and gave him away."

"So Teddy got his whisky back?"

"He did, but I'm not sure what to do with Mister Trumbell now," said Raylan.

Del looked over the man in the cell. "So, Mister Trumbell, if there's one thing I really hate, it's a thief. To make matters even worse, you stole from my good friend Teddy. What do you have to say for yourself?"

"Sir, I have no money, no job, no home, and not even a good hat to my name. I spent my last fifteen cents on the bar food and one glass of beer. I simply needed something else to wash it down with. That is the plain truth, and all I have to say about it."

"Where you from, Mister Trumbell?"

"Most recently, Kansas City, by way of Cairo, Illinois, my home town."

"How did you get to Laramie?"

"I came in by coach two weeks ago. I have been camping down by the river since my money ran out."

"Mister Trumbell, what was your occupation when you had a job?"

"I was a school teacher sir. I taught in the city of Cairo until the end of the war. Reconstruction caused a huge boom but also destroyed a lot of folk's way of life. As I'm sure you know, Cairo is a border town, right at the confluence of the Mississippi and Ohio Rivers. Right after the war a lot of the good old Cairo families were uprooted by an unstoppable flood of niggers and unscrupulous men of all kinds. Many whites were forced to move out. I was one of that group."

"So, you thought you'd head west and find work?"

"Yessir, that's it exactly. However, I ran out of money by the time I got here."

"Are you a good teacher Mister Trumbell?"

"I have been told that by others . . ."

"Raylan, see to it that Mister Trumbell gets a meal. I will be back shortly."

*

When Del returned, he had Teddy, the bar owner, and a slim, pleasant looking, middle-aged woman with him. "Raylan, did he get his meal?"

"Yessir, Dolly fixed him a good one."

"Good. Mister Trumbell, this is Missus Margaret Walters, she's also Laramie's school teacher, and she will be moving away soon. She would like to talk to you about replacing her at our new school."

After a few minutes of conversation with Trumbell, she looked at Del and nodded. "I think he could work out Marshal. Let me know what you decide. I'll be at the schoolhouse."

"What do you think, Mister Trumbell," asked Del. "Can you handle the job?"

"Yessir, I can absolutely handle the job. I did it back home for almost nine years."

"Teddy, what do you think of the deal we talked about at the saloon, still good with it?"

"Sure, send him over whenever you're ready."

Del nodded. "Thanks. Mister Trumbell, I have a deal for you. If you agree to it, you will be released tomorrow morning. You agree to take the Laramie teacher's job for at least one full school year and clean Teddy's saloon, all the charges against you will be forgiven."

"Yessir, I will clean that saloon as good as you've ever seen it, and I promise I will be the best teacher anyone here has ever seen, and please, just call me Clarence."

"Clarence, I am Marshal Del Beale, and this is Raylan Davis, my deputy, good to meet you."

Stepping outside, Del and Raylan both lit up a smoke. "You still smoking that Buffalo Brand tobacco I gave you?"

"Yeah, I'm starting to like it. I might see if I can get some from Cheyenne next time I'm there. Del, do you think it's a good idea to let that guy be a teacher?"

"I don't know for sure, but I do know we got about three-dozen kids around here that won't have a teacher this year if we don't give him a try. People ain't exactly standing in a line waiting to get a teacher's job out here, particularly one that has such low pay."

"I suppose that's true, but he could just take off when you let him out."

"I'm betting he won't do that. He ain't really got nowhere to go from here."

*

Swinging the cell door open, he motioned for Trumbell to come out. "We'll get some coffee and talk about the deal you made. When we're done, you'll start cleaning Teddy's place. You will do everything he says without complaint. You're done when he says so and not before, are we clear?"

"Yessir Del, very clear."

"When he says you're done, I will take you over to the schoolhouse. There is a backroom with a bunk and a stove. You can sleep in the cell until that's ready. If you keep this place and the schoolhouse spotless and do whatever we need done, you can get two meals a day from the cafe."

"Thank you Del, I can't tell you just how much I appreciate this, you won't be disappointed, I can assure you of that."

"Something else you need to know," said Del. "This ain't like the part of the world where you came from. You gotta watch what you say to people. You call someone around here a nigger, and he

103

might just put a bullet in your head. I suggest you forget all of your troubles from Cairo and just go about minding your own business."

"Very good advice Del, thank you, I will take it to heart."

"One more thing, no whisky while you're staying here. And if I catch you in the schoolhouse with whisky on your breath I'll shoot you myself."

*

"Boss, you just missed Tom James from the /J ranch, that big spread up on Place Mesa," said Raylan.

"I haven't seen Tom for quite a while. It's rare for him to be in town. What did he want?"

"Someone got away with several head of horses two days ago. He was here for something else but wanted us to know someone was operating in his part of the world. I asked him if he had any idea who they were. He said he had no idea, but it looked like there were three of them, and one horse was missing a shoe."

"That sounds familiar. I'm going over to the telegraph office to let Cheyenne know about the three Indians and the YK horses we recovered. I'll fill them in on Tom's business too. They may decide to put together a posse that can stay out until they catch them."

Chapter 14

Anny was interviewing two Fort Laramie soldiers when they heard shouting near the front gate. Four wagons came to a stop next to the wall. The horses were completely lathered and frothing from the mouth. Several men and women climbed out, shouting and waving for help.

One man had a young child in his arms and another laid a woman on the grass and covered her with a blanket. "We need a doctor — please help!" said the man carrying the child.

By the time the fort doctor and several other soldiers got there, all the families from the wagons were gathered around. "What happened here?" said the doctor, kneeling over the young girl.

"She's been shot. The Indians attacked us about six days out of the fort. We were traveling with Pastor Jonathon Jeffers on our way to Oregon when we were attacked by the savages. The group had become lost and turned around several times," said the man, taking several large gulps of water. "At one point, we stopped for nearly three days until Pastor Jeffers finally convinced us to keep going. We were the last four wagons in the group and quite a ways behind the others because we'd been delayed by a broken wheel and axel. Pastor Jeffers kept on going, telling us to catch up when the repairs were finished."

"Sir, I'm very sorry, but your daughter is dead. The bullet passed through her heart; she was killed instantly," said the doctor. Kneeling, he pulled back the blanket covering the women. "Is this your wife sir?"

The man nodded. "She is my wife, Sara, and the girl is Irene, our only child. I am James Peterson; we are originally from Ohio."

"Are there any more injuries in your group?"

"No sir, the others right here are all okay," said Peterson, now sobbing uncontrollably.

"And what about the rest of the train, are there injured people with them?"

"I couldn't tell for sure; we were quite a distance away from the others, and they were completely surrounded by more Indians than could be counted. I would be surprised if there were any that lived through it."

As they talked, a Major named Carhart and several other troops came up and asked them how far out they were from the fort when the Indians attacked. "We've been on the trail for nearly a week since we left the fort, but we made painfully little progress, due to breakdowns, and I must say the arrogance of Pastor Jeffers. We were maybe twenty miles from the fort at most. He insisted we keep moving even when some were breaking down, or at times when we had lost the trail. That is why we weren't with the others when they were attacked."

"Then how did your wife and daughter get killed if you weren't with the others," asked Carhart.

106

"We'd just finished the repair when we realized what was happening. As we started to turn back, two of the savages saw us and gave chase. They fired several times, and we all returned fire, and they turned back. They were only two, and we had six rifles. I believe they preferred to join the carnage going on with the others than face our rifles. Sadly, two of their shots found Sara and Irene, they were in the last wagon," said Peterson, breaking down again.

Major Ian Carhart, a twenty-year veteran of the Western Indian Wars, motioned for the troopers to gather around. "Sargent, put a full detail together and head out immediately, see if there is anything to be done for the people, then get after the Indians before the trail goes away. Corporal, strip these horses and turn them loose down at the river. Maybe they can be saved. Then find Chaplin Rogers, tell him what's going on, and prepare two graves."

*

Anny watched as the last of the travelers entered the fort, "It's so sad Morgan, that little girl never hurt anyone . . ."

"You remember that preacher and what he said to us just before we left the fort?"

Anny nodded. "He said that he and God would get them to Oregon safely and that we should mind our own business."

"Looks like one of them didn't do their job so good," said Morgan.

"Do you believe there is a God?"

"I kind of like to think there is, but he's just got too many people down here to watch over at one time," said Morgan. "I think you gotta take care of yourself in this world, and he will take care of you after you are dead."

Anny nodded. "I think that's a very good way to look at it."

*

When the members of the wagon party were safely in the fort, Anny spent most of the day interviewing them, filling her tablets with notes of the attack and pencil drawings of their descriptions.

In the morning, they walked with James Peterson and the rest of the travelers to the cemetery for the burial service. Deciding to stay for another day, she was able to spend more time listening to the survivors' stories of their whole trip, starting in Ohio.

"Morgan, I'm having trouble reconciling the Indians that I have met and talked with here at the fort, to the stories that these travelers have been telling me."

"Missus Anny, the Indians are used to living their life any way they want. The white man has challenged them, not just for their land, but for their way of life. The Indians at the fort for the treaty meetings understand that their life is changing. They are at least willing to listen to what the government is offering in exchange for a safe route for the railroad. The ones that attacked the wagons, whatever tribe they are, do not care about any kind of agreement with the whites," said Morgan. "They hate the white man and all he represents. I don't think the government will ever understand that."

"What happens if the tribes here at the fort don't agree to the terms?"

"They will ride away and go back to their old life."

"And that could mean attacking more whites?"

"Yes Ma'am, that's possible. They have all done it before, and there is no reason to think that they will change."

"It's hard to believe that someone as friendly as Black Bear could do something like that," said Anny.

"When you write your stories about your time with the Indians, you should not let people think that they are all kind and gentle like Black Bear has been to you," said Morgan. "You need to tell them the reality of it too. You need to tell them what you have seen on this trip. This is dangerous country, and it is not for everyone."

"I understand what you're saying. I will work hard to be as accurate and detailed as possible," said Anny, closing up her tablet. "Let's plan on leaving in the morning. Mister Becker is anxious to get another story for the Leader."

*

CHEYENNE LEADER

Returned from my recent trip to Fort Laramie and the ongoing treaty negotiations with some sadness from recent events that occurred there. There are many more Indians at the fort than in my other trips. This is considered a good sign for ongoing talks with the government. However, as I was interviewing several soldiers about their life on the prairie, a great shout went up, and

I was directed to four wagons that had stopped at the front gate. The cries for help brought the fort doctor and many others to the scene. One of the members in the wagon had a wife and daughter killed by Indian bullets as a result of a vicious attack on their wagon party. The mother was Sara, and the daughter, a beautiful child of twelve, was called Irene. The father is James Peterson, and they were traveling to Oregon from Ohio. He lost his whole family in the attack.

The army Chaplin arranged for burial in the Fort Laramie cemetery, and many of the officers and men, as well as a few Indians, attended the service at the gravesite. We do not yet know the fate of the rest of the members of Pastor Jonathon Jeffers' party, as the army detail assigned to do the job has not yet returned. I will have a proper report on this when I return from my next trip.

The talks continue much as they were before the recent attack. Everyone involved in the negotiations understands that not all tribes want to participate in a treaty of any kind. A small amount of research will show that a treaty signed in this very fort in 1851 was immediately ignored by both the white men and the Indians. The Indians all know this, and so do the officials working for the government. It remains to be seen if this one will be viewed any differently, even if signed by all parties.

*

As Boyd watched a small group of S/4 cattle, he heard the shot and backtracked through the trees to see what it was. Riding into the clearing, he saw Ernesto bent over a deer, starting to dress it. "Good shooting, she'll make a good supper tonight."

"Sí, she is a nice fat one, but we might have to share her with a few others."

"Share her? With who?"

"With the indios watching us through the trees. I think they may have wanted her for themselves before I shot her."

Looking toward the tree line, Boyd spotted them sitting quietly on their horses, staring at the two cowboys. "Ernesto, I don't think we can eat this whole deer."

"No, Señor Boyd, I think that would be too much for just the two of us. Maybe the indios would like to have some fresh meat too?"

"I think one backstrap will be enough for us. I'm sure the rest will be put to good use."

Ernesto wrapped the meat in a cloth and put it in his bag. Boyd waved toward the Indians, pointed at the carcass and mounted up.

*

The fourth of the S/4 line shacks had been completed by the time the aspens started to show their color. Boyd and Ernesto laid in a supply of firewood and fired up the stove. Cutting up the meat from the young doe, Boyd dropped it in the skillet of hot grease. Adding a few spices from a small pouch he always carried in his bag, the cabin warmed up with the smell of a good supper. Tossing a pair of apples to Ernesto, he sat two on the table for himself and brought out the whisky. "Damn, it's getting pretty low. I need to remember to bring out another jug. It looks like we're in need of some beans too."

"Sí, both would be good. I will bring more the next trip," said Ernesto, cutting the apples into pieces. Fishing out the deer steaks, he put several on both plates. "Señor Boyd, this is very good steak. What is it you do to make it taste this way?"

"I just use a few things that my mother showed me. It's all mixed together in this leather pouch. I carry it with me all the time. I was a cook for buffalo hunters once, and on a long cattle drive from San Antonio. You learn to do a lot with very few supplies when you're out there," said Boyd. "Where do you come from, Ernesto?"

"My family is from Zacatecas, down in Mexico. They came to San Antonio after spending a year near Juarez. My wife Elena and my two children are there, and also my Madre and brother. That is where we sent the money. My brother Jesus works for a farmer in the area. What of your family, Señor?"

"I have no family left. I was from South Carolina, and my brother was the only family I had left before the war started. He was killed early in the war."

"I am sorry to hear that. Señor Boyd, I will make you a member of my family."

"Thank you Ernesto, I don't know what to say, but I'm not sure your mother and brother would want a red-haired, ex-Confederate soldier in their family."

"Señor Boyd, every man needs a family, it is settled — now you have one."

Boyd didn't know what to say. He'd never heard of such a thing before. He reached out his hand for Ernesto's, "Thank you my friend, that is a wonderful thing for you to do. I would be proud to be part of your family."

*

After a long day in the saddle, Boyd reached the ranch just after dark. Turning out his horse, he walked into the cabin and collapsed on the bed. It was past seven when he woke up, and he didn't realize that Flora was in bed with him. He woke her up when he got out of bed.

"Pew . . .! Boyd Stamps, you smell bad this morning, go get cleaned up," said Flora, "and maybe I'll make you something to eat."

"I'll get cleaned up, but you gotta give me a kiss first . . ."

"No way am I gonna kiss someone that smells like a buffalo — now go!"

"Okay, I'll get cleaned up, but you better make it worth my while . . ."

"Just get clean, and we'll see what happens when you get back."

When he got back to the cabin, Flora had already set two plates on the table with beef steak, potatoes, and tortillas and was waiting for him. "See what can happen when you do what I tell you?"

"Yes Ma'am, I see it now. What time did you get in bed? I don't remember anything after I hit the blankets."

"Not all that late. I was helping father with some things."

"Flora, this is very good, but why are we eating beef?"

"One of the hands found a steer with a broken leg, so everyone eats a little beef this week."

"A prairie dog hole?"

"Yes. He said he heard the steer bawling. When he got there, his leg was still stuck in the hole. You know, I do like buffalo better. You would make a girl very grateful if she had some to cook up."

"I will order some fresh buffalo hump just for you my dear. Since we're done with breakfast, and I'm freshly cleaned up and kinda cold, maybe we could cuddle together, just to get warmed up a little?"

"I suppose that would be okay, as long as you don't have anything else in mind. You don't have anything else in mind do you reb?"

"Oh, absolutely not, nothing at all. I just want to get warmed up a little, and don't call me reb."

"Well, okay, I guess it'll be all right then," said Flora, sitting down next to him.

"Speaking of smell, I detect something different about yours, you smell like some kind of a flower or something."

"Oh, yeah, I forgot to tell you. I tried some sweet cologne at the dry goods yesterday. Do you like it?"

"I guess it's okay . . . I'd have to get used to it though."

"Now, where were we? Something about getting warm?"

"There's one more thing," said Boyd. "This is really something that needs to be done naked . . ."

"Naked? Why does it have to be done naked? I don't understand."

"When you're out on the prairie, and it's snowing hard, and you can't get a fire started, this is how you keep warm, everyone knows that."

"But it's not snowing right now," said Flora.

"This is just practice for when it does."

"I guess it will be okay then."

Chapter 15

The small advertisement on the back page of the Leader read:

'Wyoming Women's Betterment Society'

**Meeting every Saturday morning at 10 amin the back
of the dry goods store. Open for discussions on all women's
issues. See Anny Timms for further information.**

"Anny, what's this in the Leader about a Women's Betterment Society?" asked Dean.

"That's what I was telling you about before. I want to write about things that concern women on everyday issues and on things that we can work on for the future. Have you forgotten already?"

"No, I remember we talked about it. I just didn't realize that you were having formal meetings."

"We've had lots of casual get-togethers with some of the ladies around here before, but now we have an official organization."

"That's right, I remember, you ladies think you'll get the vote, right?"

"That will be one of the topics, but not the only one. What about the new cattleman's association and the building you've been talking about? How's that coming along," said Anny, changing the subject.

"I'm still rounding up ranchers. There's a lot of interest, but trying to get them all in one place at one time is proving to be a chore."

"Maybe you should have Mister Becker print up some posters and send someone from ranch to ranch with them? You could also put an advertisement in the Leader, but I don't know how many ranchers will see it."

"Maybe you could be the secretary for our new association. You're good at all this sort of stuff."

"I'm sure you'd like that, but I already know what I'll be doing in the future. Unless I happen to get pregnant, which sadly, doesn't seem likely, I'll be writing about women and life in the American West."

"What about adoption? We talked about that before. If you really want a baby that bad, then go ahead and get that Indian baby at the fort."

Anny shook her head; the frustration obvious in her face. "Too late for that now. If we ever have a child, it will be ours. I've got work to do; you must have somewhere else to be?"

She watched Dean ride out of the barn and follow the trail into the trees. Sitting down on the bed, she broke down in tears, sobbing until she was too exhausted to cry anymore. It was something she hadn't done since childhood. After a while, she dried her eyes and went back to her desk. She knew he would never change, his drinking and hate for Indians seemed to get worse with time. He was a good man in most ways, and if this was the worst it would get, she could work around it.

*

The big excitement at the fort that morning was that word had been passed down that Red Cloud and Sitting Bull, chiefs of the Oglala Sioux, would be in camp soon. "Morgan, I can feel the excitement in the fort. Wouldn't it make a wonderful story if we could talk with them?"

"Yes Ma'am, it would. It is one of the things that the government is waiting for. If they don't sign the agreement, it is possible that the others will refuse too."

"If they don't all agree to a treaty, what would happen to the railroad?"

"I am sure the government would continue building it anyway, but the Indians will make them pay dearly for it."

"You really think they would continue to build it knowing the danger involved?"

"Yes Ma'am. Did you see all those new soldiers that have been arriving in the last few weeks? They are loaded with building materials and plenty of supplies to start building the forts needed to guard the tracks. The government never cared much about the Indians' rights before. I see no reason to think they would start now."

"It's been a few days. I think it's time to head back home," said Anny, sliding her books into the wagon. "Plan on coming back in about two weeks. Maybe the chiefs will be here by then."

Morgan nodded and began to hitch up the team. "We should be back before dark Ma'am. I have plenty of jerky and a few apples for the trip."

Climbing into the seat next to him, she grabbed an apple out of the bag. "It's a beautiful clear morning Morgan. If we're lucky, we might even see some buffalo or some pronghorns along the way."

After an hour on the road, they stopped alongside a small stream to have some lunch and fill their canteens. When they returned to the road, Morgan started the team into a long curve. When the road straightened out, they saw three men sitting on horses right in the middle, two of them wearing white hoods. Morgan stopped the wagon and picked up his Winchester, pointing it at the man in the center. "What is it that you want? Tell me now, or I start shooting."

"Mister," said the black man in the middle, not wearing a hood. "You really think you can get all three of us before we get you?"

"I guarantee I can get two of you for sure."

"That still leaves one of us left. What do you think will happen to your lady friend once he kills you?"

"One more time Mister," said Morgan, still holding the rifle on the man in the middle. "What is it that you want?"

"We're here to rob you. Just put down the rifle, give us your money and your valuables, and we'll be on our way. It's very simple, and nobody gets shot."

"Morgan, we really don't have much of value here," said Anny. "Maybe we should let them take what they want so nobody gets hurt?"

Morgan stared at the men for a moment, then lowered the rifle, and the two hooded figures rode up to the wagon. One man climbed inside and found a few coins in her bag that she carried for emergencies. The two men rode back to the front. "Shit boss, there ain't nothin' here that we want."

Before the leader could respond, Morgan pulled a pistol from his waistband and shot one hooded figure off his horse. Firing again, he hit the other hooded man in the hand as he started to turn around. The man in the middle fired one quick shot, then the two bandits spun around and raced off.

The team lurched forward and bolted down the road out of control. Realizing that Morgan wasn't on the seat next to her, Anny grabbed the reins set her feet against the wagon, pulling back with every bit of strength she had. When the wagon started up a steep hill, it began to slow, and she regained control of the horses.

Turning around, she drove back to the spot where the dead outlaw lay sprawled in the road with a trail of blood in the dust. Stopping the wagon, she saw Morgan sitting up in the grass next to the road. There was a large blood stain just above his left hip. "Are you okay? Lay back, let me take a look at it."

"I am sorry Ma'am, maybe I shouldn't have shot at them. I never woulda missed any of them if I was using my rifle. They were a bit far for the pistol. Those are the three horse thieves the Marshal has been looking for."

Pulling up his shirt, she looked at the bloody wound. "It looks like the bullet went straight through. Let me get something to bandage it with, and we'll get you to the doctor in Laramie."

"Missus Timms, I don't think I can drive the wagon right now. Maybe we should wait until someone comes along that can help."

"You need to get in the back of the wagon," said Anny as she wrapped him tightly around the waist with her extra shirt. "Take my hands and try to get on your feet."

He was able to get up with her help and made it to the back of the wagon. While she steadied him, he climbed in and laid down. Before they left, she caught the bandit's horse and tied it to the wagon. Pulling off the dead man's hood, it was someone she'd never seen before. Noting his thin blonde hair, ragged beard stubble and small, close set eyes might help identify him to the Marshal. He was the one that took her money out of the wagon, so she fished it out of his pocket, took his belt, holster, and pistol, and put it all in the hood. Dragging the bandit off the side of the road and onto the grass, she climbed into the wagon and grabbed the reins.

Back on the road, she looked at Morgan, "Are you doing okay back there?"

"Yes Ma'am, much better. I think the blood has stopped flowing."

"Good, we'll be in town soon enough. Morgan, how do you know that those three are the men the Marshal is looking for?"

"The man in the middle, the big black one with the beard, he is called Sylvie. I saw him on posters before, and he is riding a horse with a YK brand on it. They are wanted for killing two cowboys on that ranch. That's why I shot. I figured they were planning to do the same to us."

*

"He's a very lucky man Missus Timms," said the doctor. "The bullet glanced off the edge of the seat rail and went through his side from front to back. I cleaned it out and sewed him up. He's going to hurt for a while, but he's gonna heal up fine."

"Thank you doctor. Morgan, let's get you back to the ranch where you can rest up."

"Ma'am, I have to ask," said the doctor, washing up. "Did you drive the team all the way back from the attack?"

"Yes, I did. Someone had to do it. Why do you ask?"

"Not many women can handle a team of horses that well, particularly after they've been spooked like that."

"She saved my life," said Morgan. "If it was not for her taking charge, I would still be out there. I likely would have bled out by now."

Anny shook her head. "If he hadn't recognized them as wanted men, both of us might be dead right now. Doctor, have you got any pills for the pain?"

"Here's a tin of morphine pills. Take one when the pain is the worst. Good work to both of you. I'm glad you're okay."

*

Dean and Boyd helped Morgan into the bunkhouse. "Dean, that is one hell of a Missus you got there," said Morgan. "She stopped the wagon, patched me up, got me in the wagon, and drove us all the way to town to get me to the doctor."

"She is a good woman, that's for certain," said Dean. "Tell us what the hell happened out there."

After Morgan told them the story, he laid his head back. "The pills the doctor gave me are making me a little hazy. I think I need to sleep awhile." Closing his eyes, he was out instantly.

"Boyd, you need to get the Marshal," said Dean. "He may want to recover the outlaw that Morgan shot."

"I'll take care of it. Anny said the horse has a YK brand on it, and it's missing a shoe like we've been hearing about from the ranchers that lost horses and cattle recently. There may be some reward money in it for Morgan."

*

Anny Timms' adventure with Morgan Reese and the bandits had the whole town talking. Mister Becker, at the Leader, gave her plenty of space for the story.

*

Cheyenne Leader

This reporter had quite an exciting trip from Fort Laramie last Tuesday. Perhaps the term "exciting" may be too gentle of a word to describe it. First though, I need to report on the treaty business, my reason for being at Fort Laramie. After several days, the government officials and the Indians alike are excited to hear that Red Cloud and Sitting Bull, two powerful chiefs of the Oglala Sioux tribe are expected in camp soon. The government knows that their cooperation will be important in getting the others to sign the treaty. The fort is now stockpiling material and receiving more soldiers in anticipation of starting on the construction of new forts to protect and supply the railroad.

In my last report, I told of the attack of a party of fourteen wagons of devout missionaries from Ohio and how four wagons had made it back to the fort with two of their members killed by Indians. I attended a meeting with the captain of the detail of soldiers that made its way to the site. The news is as bad as everyone feared. All members of the Jeffers party were dead or missing. All men had been killed in a way that was worse than even the experienced soldiers had seen in the past. The pastor himself was mutilated beyond any words that I will repeat here. All the women were dead but for the very young ones and the girls, and they are missing. All wagons and possessions had been burned. The troopers had the sad job of burying the dead. The survivors from the original four wagons were able to provide a good list of the members of the party, and they are taking on the responsibility of notifying the families in Ohio. Another larger detail has been dispatched to track down the murderers and recover the hostages. I hope to have a report sometime in the future about the rescue of the missing party members.

The event that I referred to at the top of the story is about my friend and bodyguard, Morgan Reese, getting shot by a bandit on the road back to Cheyenne. In simple, straightforward words, he saved my life when we were accosted by three bandits. Two were white men that were wearing white cloth hoods, and the third, a stout negro man with a bald head and a full beard, sat on his horse in full defiance of any concealment. He seemed to be advertising to the whole world that he was afraid of nothing. After an attempt to rob us, they found little of value but for a few coins in my bag. Morgan quickly saw they were riding horses stolen from the YK ranch near Laramie. He also realized that they were likely to kill us because everyone knew who the negro man was. As he raised his pistol toward us, Morgan reacted by pulling his Colt pistol and shooting the two masked bandits, killing one and wounding the other. The negro man fired once as he and his partner, now bleeding, spun around and rode off. His bullet had glanced off the handrail of the seat and went through Morgan's side, just above his beltline. Our good doctor was able to patch him up, and he is now resting comfortably. He is a genuine hero, and this lady reporter will be forever in his debt.

*

When Mister Becker pressed for more information on her part in the holdup, she chose not to write about it. "I don't want it to appear that I did anything to prevent the crime. All I did was drive Morgan to the doctor. I am the reason we were on that road, and he is the reason I am alive today."

The whole town soon knew the full story, and it was all that was talked about for days. Anny's Saturday meetings of the *Wyoming Women's Betterment Society* filled up the back of the dry goods store with many standing in the doorway or against the walls to hear what she had to say.

Wearing her trail clothes to the meetings, she would set her big hat on the desk at the applause of the crowd. Walking up to a large blackboard at the front of the room, she rolled up her sleeves and wrote the word *suffrage* in large capital letters. When the crowd quieted down enough, she asked if there was anyone there that did not know what the word meant. Most knew the word, but not everyone had a good understanding of the meaning.

"The word suffrage means the right of women to vote and participate in all functions of your government. It is most often heard in relation to giving women the right to vote, but it can mean giving the same rights to any group, like the negros for example. Now that they have been freed from the bonds of slavery, they will no doubt be seeking their own path to complete equality by means of suffrage," said Anny. "The Wyoming Territory will be forming its own legislature soon, and I want every one of us to be included in it, exactly like the men are."

Whenever she spoke at the Saturday meetings, a few would get up and leave, but there were always more than enough to take their place. After a few weeks, the women had formed into groups to draft petitions for the soon to be new legislators. Anny had invited two women from the national suffrage movement to give a talk in Cheyenne, and they were very well attended. The Wyoming Women's Betterment Society soon became a strong voice in the territory's future.

*

Dean walked into the cabin and straight to Anny, putting his arms around her and kissing her on the cheek. "How was your meeting today?"

"I don't know. I wasn't there. Lea Pritchard is running it now."

"Really? What's going on? Did you give up on getting the women the vote?"

"Of course not, everything is fine, but I need to get back to the fort, they're getting close to finishing up the treaty, and I need to be there."

"When are you leaving?"

"First thing in the morning. If it looks like they are close to the end, I may stay a little longer. I wouldn't want to miss the big moment."

"Well, I for one will be happy when all this business is done and over," said Dean. Grabbing the whisky, he poured himself a full glass. "At least then, you can spend your time here at the ranch, and I don't have to worry about you being around all those murdering savages."

"There has never been any reason for me to worry about the Indians. They've never made me feel unsafe on these trips."

"Never felt unsafe? Morgan got shot on the last trip!"

"Not from the murdering savages, as you call them. The Indians have never given us a problem. I've told you that before."

"They oughta put a bounty on their heads, that would get rid of them fast enough," said Dean, reaching for the bottle.

Chapter 16

"I like this time of year," said Dolly, setting a plate of fresh biscuits on the table. "It's starting to cool off, the leaves are turning, and I even saw a small bunch of buffalo come through on the other side of the river."

"Too bad I wasn't here; I might have taken one. We could use the meat," said Del.

"As much as you've been gone lately, I don't know when you'd have time to eat it."

"I know, we've been down a deputy since Raylan's horse broke his arm, but he should be back in a couple of weeks. Wesley is sending us one new man this week and one more next month. There are so many cattle out there that it's like an open invitation to steal all you can. The chances of getting caught are pretty small."

"Does that mean you'll be spending more time around here? It would be nice to have you around. I miss you when you're gone for days at a time."

"That's what I'm hoping for. The way things were, someone had to be at the jail most of the time. It seems like there was always at least one thief or someone shooting at something, all of them waiting to see the judge. Now, when we catch rustlers or horse thieves, we put them on the train to Cheyenne, they have a bigger jail. I suppose Laramie will be needing a bigger jailhouse one of these days too."

Dolly hugged him for a moment, then kissed him. "I love you, and I just worry about you when you're gone."

"The new deputies will help a lot. When I do have to go away for a night or two, I'll set something up for you in town. That way, you won't have to be out here all alone."

"I don't really like spending too much time in town. What if I only stayed in town on nights you're gone, and I have to work at the cafe the next morning?"

Del nodded. "I think that sounds fine, but I'll still have a deputy check on you when I'm gone. You know, if you don't like town, you don't have to work at the cafe at all."

"No, I'd be bored. I like baking, so I'll stay there for now."

"Maybe I'll be late for work today," said Del, "I haven't finished up these biscuits yet. When I'm done, I'm sure we can find something else to do."

*

Del watched as the last of his horses were turned into the new pasture. The weather had started to cool down and the aspen, and oak were already showing their color. He had a covered porch built on the front of the cabin facing the river, and Dolly had turned the rebuilt cabin into a warm, comfortable home for the pair. A large sign across the entrance to the property said: *Maguire Ranch.* When the Clyde Harper homestead on the north side of their property came available, Del bought it and added another 160 acres to their ranch.

The Laramie Marshal's Office had grown to four deputies and had to keep to the peace in Albany County, more than 4,000 square miles of wild, wide open country. The railroad had moved far enough west to take much of its rough trade with it. Del felt bad about what the next towns down the line would be going through, but Laramie was slowly starting to settle into a more civilized routine, and that was good for everyone.

Rustlers and horse thieves were about half their work, and at least two deputies were out somewhere in the county at any given time.

Open range cattle outfits took their chances when they turned their cattle out. Often, by the time they realized some were missing, the thieves were long gone. The Marshals were called in several times a year, only to find the cattle weren't gone after all, they just couldn't find them.

"Raylan, who's our latest guest?" asked Del as he walked into the office.

"I don't really know. He ain't talking."

"Really? Where'd you find him?"

"I caught him hiding in Otto Peters' milking shed. I followed his trail from a homemade pen I found up in the hills with six head of YK steers in it. I figured he was out looking for more."

"How'd he end up in Otto's shed?"

"He had tied up his horse in the trees and went to the shed on foot. I followed him and waited by the door until he came out and grabbed him. I guess he must've had a deep craving for a drink of fresh milk."

"Did you talk to Otto?"

"Yeah, I had him look through the shed to see if anything was missing. He said it looked okay to him. However, he offered to shoot him for me, so I wouldn't have to bring him back to town."

"That was kind of him. What about the cows? Did you turn them back out?"

"Yessir, they're back on the range. His horse is at the livery, and his rifle and pistol are in the rack."

Del looked at the scruffy-looking rustler sitting on the bunk. Small, thin, and dirty, Del could smell him from the cell door. "What's your name Mister?"

The rustler never spoke or looked his way. "One more time, what's your name?"

When he didn't answer the second time, Del pulled out a sheet of paper from his desk and labeled it 'Unknown Rustler.' Filling out the form, he wrote: "Prisoner's name unknown, caught in possession of six head of steers carrying the YK brand. Caught by Deputy Raylan Davis on Otto Peters dairy operation." Signing it, he handed it to Raylan. Send Wesley a wire and tell him about it, then take him to Cheyenne on the next train. No need to keep him here any longer."

"Ike, you in here?" asked Del, standing in the empty stall.

"I'm here, just like I said I would be."

"You got some news for me," asked Del.

"Just remember our deal Marshal, if anybody finds out I'm here, I'll be done for on that ranch."

"I haven't forgotten, let's hear it."

"The story I've been hearin' is that this gang that's been workin' the area got a couple of its members shot up. One shot dead and one with a crippled up arm or something. I heard that the black guy in charge is recruiting a couple of new hands."

"You know who they might be?"

"No sir, but I heard that one of the YK range hands was talking shit about the cow boss and how he wanted a job doin' something else. Everyone knows he was hooked up with some rustlers down in Colorado a year or two back, and nobody's seen him for a few days."

"And what's this hand's name?"

"Everyone calls him Gate, but I ain't sure what his last name is."

"What's he look like?"

"Kinda medium tall, not fat, but stout and he has black kinda shiny lookin', slicked-back hair. Looks like a dandy if you ask me."

"Shiny black hair? What exactly do you mean by shiny?"

"Not really sure, but some of the guys say it's something he puts in his hair, so he looks good to the women."

"Anything else you can think of?"

Ike shook his head. "Can I go now?"

"Headed for the saloon?"

"It's Saturday ain't it?"

*

Anny slipped the holster and the Colt pistol she took from the dead bandit into her travel bag. Morgan had taught her to handle and shoot the pistol. She would never tell Dean she was a little nervous about the trip, but it did make her feel good to have it nearby. Kissing him goodbye, she climbed into the wagon, and Morgan snapped the reins and headed for Fort Laramie.

The aspens were already dropping their leaves, and the recent blast of cold air made her wrap a scarf around her neck and put on her gloves. The trip had been uneventful except for a lone badger watching them go by from a pile of rocks and a few pronghorns feeding along the far ridges.

It was obvious that the fort had more people than before. It looked more like a big city than an army post. A new encampment of lodges sat about a mile away from the fort, close to the main road. After setting up their wagon by the river, Anny put a fresh tablet and several pencils in her bag, and they headed for the fort.

One of the first people she encountered was the camp doctor. "Hello Missus Timms," he said, tipping his hat. "Back for another story?"

"Hello doctor, I'm always looking for a good story. What have I missed lately, anything I might want to write about?"

"The most excitement was when Red Cloud and Sitting Bull came in three days ago. You saw the new lodges when you came in?"

"We did. Does this mean that they will agree to sign the new treaty?"

"I don't think anyone really knows yet. General Sherman and the rest of the government people have been in a meeting with them for two days, but no word yet."

"Then I need to head over there, thank you for the information," said Anny.

"One more thing, I heard that Chief Black Bear is looking for the white woman with hair like fire. I believe that's you."

"I'm flattered that he would remember me. I will see him before we leave. Thank you again."

"Have a good day Ma'am, nice to see you again."

"It looks like you have made quite an impression on the chief," said Morgan.

"Do you have any idea what he may want?"

"No Ma'am, you never know with an Indian."

When they arrived at the headquarters office, a soldier opened the door for them and followed them inside. "Thank you Captain," said Anny.

"You're very welcome Ma'am. Are you Missus Timms?"

"Yes, I'm her."

"I just want to say that I liked your stories in the Cheyenne Leader very much. You are a very engaging writer."

"Why thank you for saying that Captain."

"Tucker, James Tucker. It's nice to meet you. I've always wanted to be a writer myself, but all I write these days are a never-ending river of official army reports. But one of these days I will finally get a little time for my own writing."

"Captain Tucker, If I can ever do anything to help, please let me know. I live on a ranch just outside of Cheyenne, so I'm easy to find."

When she looked around, she realized that they were in a small group of soldiers, along with the fort's officers. "I'm sorry, I didn't realized that I was interrupting your meeting. I just wanted to let you know that we're here."

"No problem Ma'am," said Captain Tucker. "We just returned from chasing down the Indians that attacked the Jeffers party. You may not want to hear this Ma'am. There are some very unpleasant details to it."

"They won't bother me Captain. If it's okay with you, I'd like to stay."

"Very well Ma'am. For the last two weeks, my detail has followed the trail of the Indians that attacked the Jeffers party. We followed them all the way up in the north end of the Laramie Mountains. When we caught up to them, it was late in the day, and we waited through a long cold night without a fire or shelter, then surrounded the camp just before sunup," said Tucker. "Then we watched until the braves came out of the lodges and started toward the horses. We were able to separate most of the braves from the lodges this way and engaged them on the spot. We killed eleven in the first rounds of fire, as they were not prepared to fight at that moment."

"Captain, what of the missing women and girls?" asked Anny.

"When we opened fire, the rest of the men in camp rushed from the lodges firing their rifles. My men killed thirteen more braves; two of them were young boys that were killed while they were shooting at us. As we cleared out each lodge, we found none of the expected female hostages, save for one fair-haired girl of about eleven or twelve years."

"You found no sign of the other missing women and girls?" asked Anny, writing down every word as fast as she could.

Captain Tucker hesitated for a moment. "Ma'am, we did find some evidence, but as I told you before we started, there are some very unpleasant details here."

"And I said it wouldn't bother me. Please continue."

"Yes Ma'am. I believe we were able to account for most, if not all the murdered members of the party. We have no bodies, but we found the proper number of fresh scalps to account for them. There were dozens of them hanging from the lodges. We also found a lot of possessions taken from the wagons."

"Captain, what has the young girl you rescued said about it?"

"She's yet to say anything," said Tucker. "She's with the doctor in the hospital right now."

"And what of the rest of the camp?"

"We confiscated or destroyed all of the firearms and recovered a few personal items like watches and rings as well as a few small, framed photographs. When we were ready to leave, we gathered the scalps and took them with us," said Tucker. "I did not want any Indian to have them, so when we were far away from the camp, we gave them a proper burial and said a few words over them. Our detail took two casualties, neither of them serious. There will be an official report ready in a few days."

"Thank you Captain Tucker," said Anny, closing her tablet. "Will you allow me to see the child before I leave?"

"I'll walk you over to the hospital and talk to the doctor. I'll leave it up to him."

Anny waited while Captain Tucker talked with the doctor. He motioned for her to come in. "Missus Timms, you can try and talk with her if you like, but if she seems to be getting upset, you'll have to stop. None of us have heard her speak yet, she just sits there quietly, looking straight ahead."

The girl was tall for her age and very slim, with intense blue eyes and thick blond hair that had been crudely cut off close to her scalp. She had rope burns and scrapes around her neck and wrists and a long cut down her right shoulder that had been stitched up by the doctor. Sitting down next to her, Anny touched her hand and got no response. Gently touching her hair, she looked at her beautiful face. "Sweetheart, is there anything we can do to help you?"

The girl turned her head and looked at her as though she just realized someone else was in the room. The girl reached her arms out, touching her hair. Anny gently pulled her close and hugged her, and she began to cry in great heaving sobs. They sat together for a long while and Anny began to cry for the second time since her childhood. When one wave of tears started to settle, another would follow. Anny rocked her back and forth, holding her tightly and caressing her hair until both of their tears started to slow. The doctor walked up and put out his arms. "Missus Timms, I can take her if you'd like."

"What will happen to her now?" asked Anny, with the girl still clinging to her.

"I think the army will arrange for her to be taken back East and try to find some family to take her."

"Back East? Absolutely not. I'm taking her home right now and giving her a warm safe place to heal. If there's a family found some time in the future, everyone knows where she'll be."

"Missus Timms, please, I can't let you take her . . ."

"It's already decided. You are not equipped to take care of her, and I am. She's coming with me, and I don't care what you, the army, or anyone else says about it." The child held tightly to her, "We're leaving now."

Walking toward the wagon with the girl in her arms, Captain Tucker and the doctor watched her go. "I think this is best for the girl," said the doctor.

"I agree," said Tucker. "I just hope the General sees it that way too."

"Morgan, did you notice all of the photographers here now? I think we should get a few photographs."

"Yes Ma'am, that would be a good thing for the folks in Cheyenne. Maybe some pictures of the Indian Chiefs would be interesting."

"I think I would really like a picture of me with Chief Black Bear to hang on my wall, and one with Laura in my arms."

Morgan nodded. "Laura? I think that is a very good name for her; it was my mother's. Maybe I could get in one with you too. I have never been in a picture before."

On a bitter morning in late November, the word spread through the camp like wildfire that the last of the chiefs in the Indian peace commission were ready to sign the treaty. In an oversized army tent surrounded by Indians and soldiers, the officials of the government and the leaders of each tribe sat with pens, inkwells, and papers spread on a buffalo hide on the ground.

Photographers took several shots of the historic moment as both sides made their marks on the documents. Anny had spoken to a photographer before the event, and she and Morgan were photographed with Black Bear and again with Laura in front of the historic signing tent. After the ceremony, the Indians returned to their camps and began to take down their lodges for the move. Watching them preparing to leave, Anny knew she would miss seeing the men race their ponies and gamble, and she loved the strong, beautiful Indian women as they cared for their children and their lodges.

"Morgan, where will they go from here?"

"To their winter camp Ma'am. Most tribes have a place where it is a little more sheltered and has good water and wood."

"It seems like a difficult life to me."

"Maybe it does to us, but to the Indians, it is the way it has always been."

*

The next morning the fort was nearly empty of Indians except for a few that worked for the army. Anny thanked everyone that had helped her with her interviews while Morgan hitched up the team.

"Morgan, this has been quite an adventure for me, but never did I think I would meet this beautiful child."

"Do you think Mister Timms will love her the way you do?"

"No, but I don't really care. He's got his cows, that's all he cares about."

"You will have your words and your pictures too Ma'am. I think when you write your books, you will find that others will like reading about all that you have done."

Anny pulled her cowboy hat down, tightened the string, and rewrapped her scarf against the cold air. She put Laura against her chest and wrapped an extra blanket around them. "I believe that we're about to see our first winter weather. The fire will feel good tonight."

By the time the wagon reached the ranch, several inches of snow covered everything. Walking into the house, she put her bag on the table and stripped off her winter clothes. Wrapping Laura with a dry blanket, she sat her in front of the fireplace.

"Anny, you had me worried," said Dean, staring out the window. "I thought you might get snowed in at the fort for a few days."

She gave him a hug and a kiss on the cheek. It was obvious he'd been into the whisky before they got home. "No, it's kind of boring up there, now that all the Indians have left."

"They actually got the Indians to agree to a treaty?"

"They signed everything yesterday. This morning they were already gone from the fort and headed for their winter camp."

"Well, that's good, maybe all them savages will freeze to death, and we won't have to worry about them anymore," said Dean, stumbling back against the table while he talked.

Anny took his arm and led him toward the bedroom. "Okay my handsome husband, that's enough whisky for one night. It's time for bed." She would wait until morning before she introduced him to Laura.

Chapter 17

Anny watched as the first bit of blue sky showed between the clouds. The storm had stopped an hour earlier and left a deep cover of snow. "Could have been a lot worse," said Dean, sitting down beside her.

"Sweetheart, come with me. I have someone I would like you to meet." They walked into the front room, and he saw the young girl wrapped in a blanket, sitting on his overstuffed chair.

"Who the hell is this?"

"This is Laura. She's the only survivor of the wagon party attack that I wrote about."

"So what's she doing here?"

"She needed a safe place to stay while the army tries to find some family back East."

"How long is that gonna take?"

"Dean, it will take as long as it takes," said Anny, "and we're going to love her like she's our own child, do you understand me?"

"Okay, fine, I know you've always wanted a child."

Glad that was over, she kissed him on the cheek and poured him a cup of coffee. "Do you think the cattle came through it okay?"

Dean stared out the window. "We may have lost a few weak ones, but I don't think it'll be too bad, they're tough animals."

"I think the cowboys are going to have some miserable days looking for them," said Anny.

"They're a pretty tough bunch themselves. I'm sure they'll be fine," said Dean. "What are you working on this morning?"

"This will be the last of my reports from the fort. I know I'll miss it."

"What are you going to write about now?"

"I have a whole list of interesting things to write about. I'm starting to put all of my work into one file. I plan on making it all part of a book someday."

*

Cheyenne Leader

Sadly, this will be my last report from the Fort Laramie Treaty negotiations. The Indian Peace Commission, comprised of the leaders of the Arapaho, Oglala, Brule, Miniconjou and Yanctonais tribes, and the United States Government's Indian Affairs Commission, have at last reached an agreement suitable to all parties. The tribes have left the fort and gone their separate ways. It remains to be seen if this will be a lasting peace, but the U.S. is moving ahead with plans to build a series of forts along the new railroad route to California.

This is also the last report on the Jeffers wagon party of the Oregon bound, Ohio immigrants that were attacked and murdered by a rogue band of Indians west of the fort, and it's also a sad one. The army sent a detail to track down the killers and caught up with them in the Laramie Mountains. When the camp was finally located, they were able to see many scalps hanging from the lodges. Waiting until first light, they engaged them and killed all of the adult males in the camp that had fired on them, with the detail suffering only two minor casualties. Five older males were not involved in the fight and surrendered. The scalps were removed and placed in a bag, and later buried along the trail with a proper service. A contingent of soldiers remained at the camp and will lead the rest of the band back to the fort for relocation to a reservation. One young girl about ten or twelve years of age was rescued and is currently recovering in my home until family members are located in Ohio.

I will continue to report for the Leader, as needed by the editor, and on other topics like the Wyoming Women's Betterment Society, of which I am proud to be a part of. I will cover any local stories that come up, and hope to do some stories on the Wyoming Territory's ranches and on politics as they develop.

*

Boyd sat a pot of beans on the table and dropped two steaks on the plates. "There's more steak, so eat up." Three cowboys sat around the table, devoured the steaks, and shoveled the beans in as fast as they could. Boyd kept the food coming as quickly as they could eat it. When they had finished up everything, he brought out a large can of peaches, a fresh jug of whisky, and four cups. "Leave me a bite of those peaches please," said Boyd as he loaded a few more sticks of wood in the stove.

They were all full and warm after two straight days on the range, checking on the cattle from the back of a horse. Boyd poured them a good shot of whisky and finally sat down. One more good drink, and they were all ready for the bedrolls. "Ernesto, did you find many dead cattle?"

"Sí, there were about thirty-five caught in the bottom of the lower breaks on Snake Creek. They couldn't get up the bank, and the snow had drifted completely over them. Also, it was about the same farther up the creek, about four miles or so. I saw perhaps several hundred that were okay and another small group of sixty or so about two miles south of here that had managed to find a little grass."

Reports from the other cowboys were nearly the same as Ernesto's. In the morning, they mounted up and started the search again. Boyd made his way to the other line shacks to find out what the rest of the cowboys had been seeing. The cowboys from the other shacks were out searching but had left notes for him with their counts.

*

Waking up to a cold cabin, Boyd fed the stove and put on some water for coffee. Looking around, he realized that Flora wasn't there and he didn't see her coat or hat. Warming a few biscuits and leftover gravy, he ate quickly and headed to the ranch house for the weekly S/4 association meeting.

145

Walking into the house, he stomped the snow off his boots and hung up his hat. Everyone was there but Flora. As they poured themselves a cup of coffee, Dean held up the whisky. "Anyone else? It's pretty cold out there," he said, pouring some in his coffee.

Nobody took him up on the offer. "Well then, let's get to it. Boyd, how did the cattle look? Did you find any dead ones?"

"Yes, quite a few."

"Quite a few? How the hell many is quite a few?" asked Clifford Platt.

"My estimate is about a five percent loss across the range, and it could be even higher."

"Oh that's just bullshit!" said Dean. "There ain't no way that many cattle could have died, the goddamn snow ain't more than a foot or two deep, how many hands you got out there checking on them?"

"All of them," said Boyd.

"How many is that again? I forget," said Dean.

"We got nine hired hands, myself and three more day workers I hired to help out. The dead animals are frozen solid, so I told the day workers to recover what good meat they could from the closest ones before it got too warm and give it to anyone that needed it."

Before the conversation got any farther, the door opened, and Flora walked in. Sitting down at her regular place next to Boyd, she took off her hat and boots. "Sorry I'm late. Did I miss anything?"

146

"No, nothing too important," said Dean, "Unless you consider thousands of dead S/4 cattle as something to talk about."

"Thousands of dead cattle . . .? Boyd, is that right?"

"Your boyfriend is the one that did the counting," said Dean. "Tell her, Boyd."

He told the group about all the dead animals they had found. "Most of the dead were in low spots and got drifted over, the live ones looked healthy, but they were having trouble reaching the grass."

"That's just more bullshit Boyd," said Dean. "There are millions of buffalo out there, and they don't have any trouble finding the grass when it snows!"

"That's enough," said Cliff Platt. "A cow ain't nothing like a buffalo. A buff will use his hooves and head and work until he gets to the grass. A cow will stand around with his ass end in the wind until he gets buried or freezes to death."

Wilf Rickard had listened to the discussion long enough. "Cliff is right. In the summer, things are good. During the bad winters, cattle can't always find enough feed. That's why we're working on a plan to grow additional feed and to fence in some of our pasture. That's for the horses too."

"Well, if you ask me, you're all worried about nothing," said Dean. "A good calf crop next spring will make you forget all about this."

"Next spring, I'll be starting to fence some of my ground too," said Rickard. "Then, in the fall, when it's time to gather, I'll start taking my cattle."

"Wilf, I hope you will reconsider. The grass and water out there are still free."

"Dean, I've already made up my mind on this. It's not gonna happen all at once, but it's gonna happen."

*

Flora and Boyd walked to his cabin after the meeting. "You've been pretty quiet today, something bothering you?" said Boyd.

"Yes, there is," said Flora, "but let's get inside first. It's cold out here."

They sat side by side on the bed. "I'm listening."

"Boyd, I'm going to have a baby."

"Really? I'm going to be a father? When?"

"I'm not exactly sure, spring sometime. How do you feel about that?"

"It's not anything I've ever thought about before, but yes, I think it would be wonderful to have a child."

"Well, I'm glad to hear that," said Flora. "Now, let's see what I can find for breakfast."

"Flora, I can smell the flowers on you again . . ."

"Yes, I do like the smell. It's kind of like lilacs, don't you think?"

Chapter 18

Raylan Davis slogged through the muddy street and into the jailhouse. Del sat with his feet up, smoking a cigar, and looking at the headline of the paper.

"What's going on this morning? I see we have a new customer."

"Ezekiel Jones, a farmer's son from south of town. He's just another drunk sleeping it off, except this one had a little disturbance with one of Teddy's girls last night."

"Which one?"

"Olive, he tried to cheat her out of her money, so she hit him over the head with a pitcher, knocked him colder than a block of ice," said Del. "The bartender carried him over here last night."

"So, he still owes her the money?"

Del shook his head. "She went through his pockets and found he had more than enough money to pay her. I suspect she likely got herself a little extra for the trouble. Teddy even made him pay for the broken pitcher."

"That Olive is a pretty one for sure, but she can be mean when she wants."

"Well, I can't attest to that, but it sounds like I know someone that can . . ."

"That's just what I heard around town," said Raylan.

"I'm sure. I'm going over to the cafe; you can turn him loose when he wakes up."

The recent snow had melted quickly, turning the dirt streets to brown muck. Every horse, wagon, and buggy in Laramie was covered in heavy layers of thick mud. Picking his way across the street and down the sidewalk, he followed the muddy trail into the cafe.

"Morning Marshal, looking for Dolly?" asked the waitress.

"Good morning June. Yes, please tell her I'm here."

Dolly came out with a steaming cup of coffee and a canning jar of sugar. "How's my favorite Marshal this morning? Did you get your drunken cowboy taken care of?"

Del took a sip of coffee and nodded. "Raylan's watching him now. He just had a little dispute with one of Teddy's girls. He'll be fine when he wakes up."

"You want a steak? We just got some fresh buffalo about an hour ago. I've been holding out a couple of potatoes for us too."

"That sounds real good. Can you get away for a few minutes and sit with me?"

"I'll put something on for both of us, and then I've got to put some pies in the oven, give me a few minutes."

As they finished up, Raylan walked up to the table and took his hat off. "Sorry to interrupt you Ma'am. Marshal, Ike King is over at the office, he wants to talk to you."

Dolly kissed him and gathered up the dishes. "I need to take the pies out anyway. What kind would you like for home?"

"Apple would be good. I'll see you tonight."

"Ike, what brings you out here in the middle of the week," asked Del.

"I'm just picking up some supplies. You remember that guy you asked about before, the black one on the poster?"

"Yeah, Sylvie Parker, what about him?"

"One of the new hands said he heard some saloon talk about him being around this part of the country. He also said its goin' round about how he took on a couple of new gang members."

"I thought we talked about that before. That ain't hardly new information," said Del.

"The new part is that he wants to get some extra men so he can pull off some kind of bigger job somewhere."

"Any of those people doin' all that talking have any idea about what the job is?"

"Only that it might have to do with the army and the supplies for the new forts."

Del lit his cigar again and leaned back in the chair. "Anything else?"

"No, but I thought you would want to know."

"Thanks, you can go back to work now," said Del.

"You ain't gonna tell anyone else I was here, are you Marshal?"

Del shook his head. "I never saw you."

"We haven't heard much about Sylvie for a while," said Raylan. "I was hoping maybe he was dead by now. What do you want to do about it?"

"Nothing right now, but I got a couple of thoughts on the subject when things dry up a bit."

*

The train ground to a stop in front of the Cheyenne station. Del stepped down and walked toward the two men leaning against the wall. "Wes, Boyd, it's good to see you," said Del, shaking their hands. "Wes, how about we go to that fancy restaurant of yours, what's it called, the Chophouse Bar? Riding the train always makes me hungry."

After the meal, Del handed each of them a cigar. "These were a gift from a rancher for helping him out with his rustler trouble. Wes, what do you think about this deal with Sylvie?" The waitress set each of them up with a whisky while they talked.

"Well, you two know Sylvie Parker better than I do. Tell me a little something about him."

"We met him down in Brownsville," said Del. "The army transferred me and Tom Lee Daggart from chasing Indians in New Mexico to the South Texas coast near the end of the war. Sylvie was an escaped slave that had signed up with the black Indiana unit of the Union Army. We met at the fight on Palmito Ranch, and I gotta say, he was a damn good soldier too."

"Boyd, what about you? You were a reb, right?"

He felt his face flush and shook his head. "Wesley, don't call me a reb. I was a conscript, and I didn't have a choice — you understand?"

"Boyd, I meant no disrespect. I wasn't trying to stir up any bad feelings," said Wesley, offering his hand to him.

Boyd shook his hand and nodded. "After the war, the four of us were all in need of a job, so we signed on with a buffalo hunting outfit up in the panhandle. A couple of months in, Sylvie took off in the middle of the night with two good horses and some other stuff, and that's the last we saw of him."

"Yeah, the next time we heard anything about him, it was for his stealing some Mexican horses," said Del. "He's one tough son-of-a-bitch, and he hates any kind of authority."

"Sounds to me like he's had a good long run," said Wes. "Maybe it's time for someone to look into the problem?"

"I think you may be right," said Del. "I might know a committee that could do it."

"That sounds like a good idea, here's to finding Sylvie," said Wes, holding his glass out for a toast.

"To finding Sylvie," said Boyd.

Del touched their glasses and made another toast, "Here's to killing the son-of-a-bitch . . ."

Downing one more round of drinks, they walked outside to finish their cigars. "You remember what it was like before the railroad came in," said Wesley.

"Yeah, there wasn't much here, but it was peaceful when we brought that first herd up," said Boyd. "Since then, every possible kind of outlaw and con-man in the country followed the rails into town."

"At least most of them moved on," said Del. "But every now and then, there's one that needs a little sorting out."

"Officially, I was never here, you know that, right," said Wes.

"Neither were we," said Boyd.

Chapter 19

The **Wyoming Women's Betterment Society** banner hung over the door. The group had grown enough that the local Methodists allowed them to use their church for their meetings. As many as fifty women attended most meetings and were participating in the work of the suffrage movement. Petitions had been written, signed, and circulated to the new group of politicians.

General Grant had just been elected president and would be leading the country now, and as Anny knew, this was the time to push the issue of women's suffrage into the headlines. Walking into the church wearing her trail clothes, what Dean called her cowgirl getup, she put her hat on the table. Walking over to the chalkboard, she began like always by rolling up her sleeves and writing the word 'suffrage' in large, all capital letters.

When the room was quiet, and all eyes were on her, she would begin her talk. At the end, she always closed with, "Ladies of the Wyoming Women's Betterment Society, thank you. Now remind me again, what is it we are working for . . .?"

In unison, they shouted, "Everything the men have!"

Anny looked at the crowd and said it again, "One more time, what is it we are working for . . .?"

Again, they all shouted, "Everything the men have!"

"Thank you all again for being here to fight for our rights. It will be one of the most important things you ever do."

Anny and the society women had accumulated several petitions full of women's signatures as well as a good number of men's. They began to work in earnest to talk to anyone and everyone that might have to do with the future of Wyoming.

"The territory has five times the number of men than it does women," she said when she spoke to groups. "Why should we allow them to tell us what we can and can't do? The new Wyoming Territory will end up just like every other territory and state, run by a bunch of crooked old white men who believe that if you aren't an Anglo-Saxon male, you couldn't manage to take care of your own business, and we all know that's a bunch of horse pucky!"

When she had the crowd at this point, she would pause for a few seconds, then say, "ladies, remind me again, what is it we are fighting for?"

The room would erupt in a resounding "everything the men have!," and the cheering would go on for several minutes.

"Blue skies Anny, just like I tried to tell them at the association meeting," said Dean, staring out the window. "The snows all melted, and the cattle are fine. By next spring, there'll be hundreds of new calves and plenty of grass for all of them."

She sat in front of the fireplace with Laura in her arms, rocking her gently back and forth. The girl had not spoken yet, but she was seldom out of Anny's sight except when she was speaking to the society meetings, and two of the members cared for her while she was talking.

"Anny, did you hear what I said?"

"I'm sorry, I didn't hear you sweetheart."

"Forget it."

She turned back to Laura and held her until she fell asleep. "Dean, will you come and take her, please. Put her on the bed. I think she'll sleep for a while."

Anny covered her and closed the door. "What were you saying a minute ago?"

"I just said that the association members were worried about nothing, the sun is out, and the snow is melting fast. The cattle can get all the grass they need."

"I'm sure they'll feel better about it now that the weather has improved. Have you noticed that Laura is getting more comfortable here? She is eating better and sleeping better now."

"I hardly even know she's here, she's always with you."

"Maybe you could start to show a little more interest in her. I think she's afraid of you."

Dean shrugged. "I'll try, but I don't know much about kids."

"Then we'll both learn together."

*

"You do know what a Christmas tree is, don't you?" said Flora.

"Yes, I do know what a Christmas tree is. We had them when I was a little kid," said Boyd.

"Then go find me a nice tree for the cabin, and I think Anny would like one for the main house too."

"You do know I have a ranch to run, don't you?"

"This ranch will be here when you get back, and it'll look a lot better with a couple of Christmas trees. And I hope you know I will be expecting a nicely wrapped present under the tree come Christmas morning, maybe something all shiny and pretty?"

"A tree and a present? Flora Dere, you are one demanding woman, is there anything else I need to do to make you happy?"

She kissed him on the cheek and headed for the door. "That's all for now. If I think of anything else, I'll let you know."

*

On the trail to the first line shack, Boyd spotted a small stand of spruce trees just before he got there and decided he would cut a pair of them on the way back. As he stared into the trees, he spotted a lone cow buffalo looking at him. Remembering Flora's comment on how much she liked fresh buffalo meat, he tied the horse off to a bush and grabbed his rifle. The buffalo never moved; one shot from the rifle, and she dropped in her tracks.

Walking over to the buffalo, he looked up to see Ernesto riding toward him. "Hola, Señor Boyd. You hunting meat for the ranch?"

"Yeah, buffalo meat and trees," said Boyd.

"Trees Señor?"

"Christmas trees Ernesto. I need two Christmas trees to make the women happy. I decided to cut them here, and then I saw the buffalo. If you could use the meat, I'll just take the hump."

"Sí, we can use it. I will go and get a couple of horses to pack it."

"I'll get started cutting her up, and we can pack the meat and drag the trees back to the ranch before dark."

With the meat tied on the extra horses, Boyd chose two trees and cut them down. Tying them behind his horse, the two cowboys started for the ranch.

"Señor Boyd, why do the Anglo's cut trees for Christmas?"

"Well, I don't really know. I think it's some old tradition from the bible or something. All I know for sure is that when I was a kid, everyone did it, so I guess we just did what the church people said."

The snow had been falling for nearly an hour when Flora saw them riding toward the barn dragging the trees behind them. Walking into the barn, she looked them over. "So you do know what a Christmas tree is . . ."

"Of course, I do. I brought you an early present too," said Boyd, handing her a canvas bag with the buffalo hump in it.

"You even remembered I was wanting some fresh buffalo meat. I'll take this inside and cut us off a couple of steaks right now."

"Don't forget about your part of the deal . . ."

"What deal would that be?"

"You said if I brought home some fresh buffalo, you would have something special for me after supper."

"I said that?"

"Yes Ma'am, you said those very words to me."

"Well, if that's what I said, then I guess I'll have to keep my word now, won't I?"

"That's the way I see it," said Boyd, turning his horse into the stall.

*

"Where did the tree come from," asked Dean.

"Boyd brought it over this morning," said Anny. "I think Laura will enjoy helping decorate it."

"I'll have Morgan set it up for you. I'm going into town for a while. I'm looking at a building lot in town for the new association."

"Dress warm, it's kind of miserable outside. You might stop and see if the dry goods store has any decorations for the tree."

Watching the buggy disappear down the lane, Anny sat down at the desk and went back to work while Laura played with a pencil and paper across the table. She was writing a story for the Leader about the suffrage movement and what the society was hoping to accomplish. She was also working on an idea for a small regular column about the cattle business. Her first pieces would be about the new business of shipping cattle by rail.

When Dean returned, he had a pile of mail and two quarts of whisky. When he handed the mail to her, she realized that he'd already been into the whisky. "Did you look at decorations for the tree?"

"Uh . . . no, I guess not. I just forgot is all."

Anny shook her head and turned to the mail. A thick package, wrapped in plain paper and string, had her name on it, and the name read: *Missus Anny "Cowgirl" Timms.* Inside were several photographs of her and Chief Black Bear, Morgan, and the signing of the treaty, as well as several other pictures from around Fort Laramie. With it was a note from the photographer telling her how much he enjoyed his visit with her and the photo of her and the chief. He said that if she published a book in the future, he would love to have a copy.

"Dean, do you want to see the photographs from the fort?"

Picking up one of the bottles of whisky, he headed for the door. "Some other time, I got a ranch to run,"

Anny sat down next to Laura and spread the photographs out in front of her. She looked at each one for a moment then moved to the next one. When she saw the picture with Anny holding her, she held it up excitedly, rocking back and forth in the chair and pointing to it. It was the first time that she had shown a smile or a reaction of any kind since she had been in the house.

Wrapping her arms around the little girl, Anny hugged her and began to cry. "It'll be okay sweetheart. I know that you're going to be fine. You'll get over this. I'll take good care of both of us, I promise."

Chapter 20

"Del, I think Laramie is starting to look like a real town," said Dolly, as they left the cafe. "The merchants have even started to hang a few Christmas decorations in their windows."

"Yeah, I heard Teddy is hiring several younger, prettier girls for the saloon."

"Oh, stop it, you know what I mean. They're building a sawmill across town and a butcher shop and a beautiful new church on the north side."

"Great, if there's one thing we really need here, it's more preachers. All they do is tell everyone that if they don't give him more money for God's work that they'll burn in hell for all eternity."

"That's just baloney, and you know it. They help a lot of people."

"All I know is that I put plenty of them bible thumpers in jail before, and more than one preacher too," said Del. "Some of the really devout ones came to my jail by way of Teddy's saloon."

"Let's talk about something else," said Dolly, "anything else but that."

"What about the cafe? I just heard today that it might be for sale, is that right?"

"Kate told me she was thinking about it. Yesterday she asked if I might be interested or know someone that was."

"Are you thinking about it," asked Del. "You're the best cook they've ever had."

"I might be interested, but if I did, I would need to hire a second cook and a new manager."

"You'd fire the manager? What's wrong with her?"

"Everyone knows she's a thief, but Kate won't fire her because they're related somewhere down the family line, second cousins, I think."

"Sounds like a lot of work to me."

Dolly nodded. "Del, I get bored on the days that I'm on the ranch, and you're at work. If I owned it, I would make it into a cafe and bakery. I'd run the business and do the baking, and someone else would do the day to day cooking. Having the extra money coming into the house wouldn't hurt either."

"As much as we're gone from the ranch has got me thinking about hiring an extra hand for the place," said Del. "We can keep our room in town and stay at the ranch whenever we can. We have enough horses and cattle that I don't want to leave the place alone for very long. Do you know how much she wants for the cafe?"

"I think about fifteen hundred, that's for the building and the business. The second floor is just used for storage. I think we could make it into our town place, that way we wouldn't have to rent a room."

"That sounds like a great idea. It may be a little high though, what if you offered her twelve hundred? Do you think she would take it?"

"Can we afford it?"

"I think we can work something out with the bank. Like you said, things are really growing here, and they like to see new business come to town."

"I'll talk with her today and see what she says. What about the new ranch hand?"

"I have someone in mind. I'll talk to him and see what he thinks," said Del. "There's one other thing I have to tell you about."

"What's that?"

"After the new year, Raylan will be acting Marshal, and I'm heading out with a couple of men to hunt down a gang of horse thieves and rustlers that are operating between here and Cheyenne. They're responsible for at least six murders, and someone has to bring this to an end."

"Why does it have to be you? There's plenty of other lawmen that could do it."

"It's my job Dolly. It's what I hired on to do. It's gone on way too long as it is, we can't take a chance they'll kill again."

"How long do you think you'll be gone?"

"I can't say. We don't know for sure where they're at, so I'll be gone until we find them."

*

"Ike, I'm surprised you made it into town," said Del, walking into the livery. "How's life on the ranch these days?"

"If you really want to know, it's just plain bullshit."

"What's going on? Does it have anything to do with horse thieves and murderers?"

"Naw, I ain't heard much about any of that lately. Everyone has been working their asses off trying to take care of the stock since the storms, and the owners don't give a shit about the hands. They cut our wages twice in the last couple of months. If we had anywhere else to go, we'd all quit that shithole today."

"Ike, what if I told you that I may be able to help you out with that?"

"I ain't gonna have to buy old man Yang's front window again, am I?"

Del shook his head. "That debt is officially paid. I'm asking if you want a job working for me on my place?"

"Your place? What would I be doin' there?"

"Horses, cows, feed, all the usual ranch work. It comes with a separate cabin and we can talk about the pay if you're interested."

"Hell yes, I'm interested . . ."

"Good, meet me at the ranch in the morning, and we'll work something out."

*

Del walked Ike around the property and the buildings. Showing him the new bunkhouse, he asked him what he thought.

"Are you planning for more hands in the future?"

"No, I built it just big enough to hold a couple of hands if I ever got that big, but I don't see that happening any time in the future. You can use it any way you want. It also comes with two meals a day at the cafe and the salary."

"Del, I definitely want the job. I can't thank you enough, and I promise, I'll work my ass off for you."

Del shook his hand, "Thanks, Ike."

As they walked toward the corral, a rifle bullet hit the barn tearing a chunk of wood off the corner. Before they could say anything, another one hit the barn just between them. Diving inside for cover, they both pulled their pistols and waited to see what was coming next.

"Did you see anything?" said Del.

"Nothing, it was all too quick. We're lucky we got inside."

"Let's get up in the hayloft. Maybe we can see something from up there." Before they could reach the ladder, another volley of shots tore off more chunks of barn wood and hit one of the stall doors.

"Them's pretty big holes Del. What the hell do you suppose he's shootin'?"

"A Spencer would be my guess."

"I don't remember seeing many of them around here, do you?"

Del nodded. "I know somebody that carries one, but I ain't seen him for a while. Let's get up that ladder."

Peering out between the cracks of the siding they couldn't see anyone in the trees. As they stared at the hillside, a large black man with a bald head and a full beard rode out of the cover and sat on his horse, looking down at the barn.

"Delbert Beale — I hear your lookin' for me . . . You the one that's been putting up these posters all over the county?" said Sylvie, waving one in the air. "Well, here I am! This is your chance old friend. Take your best shot!"

"Del, we'll never reach him with our pistols."

"Yeah, he knows that too, nothing we can do but wait and see what he's up to."

"So long old friend. I'll see you down the trail somewhere, and we can finish this." Sylvie threw down the crumpled poster and rode off.

"You know him Del?"

"I used to know him a long time ago."

Chapter 21

Del watched Boyd and Tom Lee step onto the platform as the engine smoke engulfed them. "Let's get inside. I'm freezing," said Tom Lee.

"Good to see you, it's been a while for sure," said Del, shaking his hand. "Sorry we drug you out of the sunshine this time of year."

"No problem. Case and I have been looking for some investments up here, maybe another livery business in Cheyenne or Laramie. That gives me a reason to be here and something to look forward to when I head home."

"I heard that you got a couple of little Texians running around the house now?"

"We have one boy, Jacob, and one girl, Maria. Sancha is going to have another one in the summer."

"Congratulations to you and Sancha," said Del. "Are Case and Thomas out hunting buffs now?"

"Yeah, they left in early November. You know what it's like. They'll probably be back as soon as the animals start shedding, maybe March or April."

"Better them than me," said Boyd. "I've seen more than enough of those big stinking things."

"I agree with that," said Del, "no buffalo hunts and no goddamn cattle drives. I'm happy with what I'm doing now. Let's get something to eat and talk about this. Tom Lee, you haven't met my girlfriend yet. Her name is Dolly, and she's the best cook this side of the Laramie mountains."

"Sounds good. We got somewhere to stay tonight?"

"We'll bunk at my place. Dolly is staying in town tonight, so we can have a drink, tell stories, and make a plan to kill this no-good son-of-a-bitch."

*

After a good supper and a little whisky, Del gave each one a cigar, and the three men talked about how they met, the buffalo hunting with Case and driving the longhorns from San Antonio to Cheyenne. Boyd reminded them of the battle of Tom Lee Creek and the arrowhead in his back. When the conversation finally got around to Sylvie Parker, Del asked them if they all agreed that Sylvie and his gang had to be stopped.

"Hell yes," said Boyd. "I've seen the damage he's done, and I knew two of the men he's killed."

"That son-of-a-bitch tried to kill me and my hired man just three weeks ago right here on my place," said Del.

"Sancha has been terrified of him for a couple of years, and I can't take a chance of him being around the children," said Tom Lee.

Del nodded. "In the morning, we'll take three saddle horses and one pack horse and head out."

"Any thoughts of where he might be?" asked Tom Lee.

"I hate starting out when the weather is miserable, but there are at least four of them, maybe more. The weather's gonna have them holed up somewhere. They'll be easier to find and less likely to escape than if it was summer. It's probably easier than hunting down Comanches in the desert, don't you think Tom Lee?"

"I don't care how hard it is, as long as it means stopping Sylvie."

*

Ike King had three horses saddled and waiting by the time the sun came up. "I'm just finishing up with the packhorse."

"You got everything we talked about," asked Del.

"Yessir."

"Remember what I said, your most important job here is to keep Dolly safe. We clear on that?"

"Absolutely clear, anything she needs. Where you guys headed?"

"Hunting," said Del. The three men mounted up, and Del took the lead rope for the packhorse and they headed out.

"Good luck," said Ike. When they disappeared across the sage flat, he walked into his cabin and checked his rifle and shotgun. Del had asked him to be sure they were loaded and to keep his pistol on his belt all the time.

*

After a long day's ride, they pitched their tent in a tight stand of spruce trees. Water trickled from an exposed rock face, filling a small pool. "I think this is good for tonight. We've got water and cover," said Del. "We better hold off on a fire tonight in case we're close to them." After dried meat and canned beans for supper, they crawled into their bedrolls and fell asleep quickly.

In the morning, they woke to find a light cover of fresh snow. Del filled them in on what he knew about the country around them. "There's a hundred old line shacks and prospector cabins scattered around these mountains. I'd say there's a dozen or so I know of that could hold several men for a while."

"Where do we start?" asked Tom Lee, stuffing a handful of jerky in his bag.

"There's one about three miles straight up the canyon just north of here. Last time I was up this way, it still had good pens and a decent roof, probably an old hunters cabin."

Quietly picking their way through the trees, the men climbed to the high points and used their binoculars to look for tracks in the snow. When they reached the cabin, there was no sign of horses or people. Backtracking through the trees, the snow covered them as they went. Riding into a smaller side canyon, they repeated their search of another shack, also empty.

After the day of searching, the only signs of life were a few deer, two elk, and plenty of rabbits. On the trail back to camp, Tom Lee spotted several grouse and killed three of them with rocks. "I think a small fire tonight might be okay. I'm hungry for fresh meat."

Reaching camp, they picketed the horses, and Boyd started a fire while Tom Lee cleaned their supper. "Which way tomorrow?" asked Boyd.

"Those were the closest ones that I know of, but it would have been damn lucky to find them so quick," said Del. "I'd like to take a ride on top of the mesa that runs off to the southeast. It's flat, and there's plenty of places that we can look down into the valleys for tracks. There is one good spot up there they could use as a hideout if the snow hasn't buried it already."

"How far is it?" asked Tom Lee.

"It's a long ride, but there are also several spots just over the backside of the divide. It used to have quite a few places strung out around there. They call it the Big Hill Camp. I think there was some mining going on there at one time."

"Well, you better eat up then," said Boyd, handing them each a stick with cooked grouse on it. "We'll need all our strength tomorrow."

They huddled close to the fire, quietly talking about the way they met in Brownsville. "Del, you remember when Sylvie pulled me out of the line of fire in my first night battle," said Tom Lee.

"Sure, you were standing there like a statue with balls whizzing all around you. How the hell both of you didn't get your head shot off is still amazing to me."

"It's hard to think that he's the same guy we're hunting for," said Tom Lee. "What do you suppose makes a man change like that?"

"I couldn't really say, but remember he was born and raised a slave, then he escaped and joined the army. He never liked being told what to do, I know that for sure," said Del. "He may have had a good heart deep down, but it just couldn't overcome all the bad stuff he suffered on the outside."

"Yeah, I suppose so. I remember all the scars he had on his back; it must have been terrible getting whipped all the time."

"I can tell you for sure that it was a terrible time for slaves," said Boyd. "My brother and me never had any slaves, but we were around them all the time. The only people that had a lot of slaves were the rich old white men that owned the land. The truth of it was, if you were poor and white like we were, they didn't really care much about you either."

"At least you didn't get whipped," said Tom Lee.

"Nope, nobody whipped us, but we were necessary for keeping their perfect society moving like they wanted it. Most of the slaves worked and lived on the farms, so someone had to do all the other work they didn't do."

*

Winding their way through the trees for several hours, they rode to the crest of the mesa and tied up. They looked down on what was a spread-out collection of tailings and crude, abandoned cabins. For more than an hour, they glassed the old camp without seeing any horses or tracks in the fresh snow.

"So much for the easy ones," said Del, mounting up.

"These have been the easy ones?" said Tom Lee.

172

"Yeah. Tomorrow I want to check some spots farther north. I got a hunch about a place down in a hole at the end of a canyon. I don't know if it has a real name, but I call it nasty canyon. I found it one time when I was elk hunting, it's a tough ride, but it has to be checked."

Tom Lee stood up and stretched a few times. "I ain't spent this much time in the saddle in a long time, and my skinny little butt hurts all the way up to my armpits."

"A few days in the saddle got you all wore out already," said Boyd.

"A few days in the saddle and a bunch more days getting to Cheyenne on a stagecoach, bouncing and jerking back and forth like I was riding a fresh bronc, has wore me out. Not to mention breathing in cigar smoke and fat man sweat, that didn't feel real good either."

"Don't worry, we'll get you back to town soon enough," said Boyd. "Then you can catch the next stage back."

"Yeah, I'm sure there won't be any of that going back," said Del. "Just soft seats and sweet-smelling pretty girls all the way home."

*

As the sky started to show some color, they broke the ice off the pool and filled their canteens then rode out of camp for the next canyon. For three days, they checked out every canyon, spring, and cabin they could find. Every night they came back to camp wet, tired, and hungry without seeing a sign of another human.

"Are we running out of places Del?" said Tom Lee as he chewed on the last of his jerky.

"We're getting close," said Del, "but I have one or two more canyons to check. They're kind of rough going, but we need to be sure."

After several hours in the saddle, they reached a sheer, dark-faced cliff, running for several miles. Large stands of aspen trees grew against the fractured openings in the rock. Riding along the face of the cliff, they cleared each stand of trees they came to. Near the end of the wall, there was a stand of trees much larger than the others with a steady trickle of spring water running out of it.

"I never would have found this place if the aspens and oak brush still had their leaves," said Del. "Let's tie up here, and I'll tell you what I know about it."

After a few mouthfuls of food and water, they were ready to go. "This opening goes into a narrow canyon, maybe three-quarters of a mile long. The whole thing ain't hardly ten or twelve feet wide for the whole length," said Del. "It's full of deadfalls, oak brush, and rocks, and it's muddy and dark as hell."

"Are you planning on taking the horses up it," asked Boyd.

"No, it'll be better to do it on foot. You could lead the horses through it, but it's just too much trouble. That's why I think this might be a good place for someone to hole up."

"What are we lookin' at on the other end," said Tom Lee.

"It opens up to a sage flat, ringed with rimrock. It's not much over a couple of acres. This spring starts on the opposite side of the flat and comes down through the canyon. When you get out of the canyon, on the left side, there's a big rock overhang that forms a deep cave and has been used as a shelter of some kind for years," said Del, taking a last swallow of water. "It's about as high as a man, and goes way back in. It's big enough to hold several men easy. At some point, the whole thing was walled in with logs and chinked with mud. I spent a night in there once when I was hunting."

"What're you thinking about doing when we get there?"

"We stop a little short, look it over, and decide then," said Del. "If they're up there, we'll see the horses and know how many we're dealing with. We all good with that?"

Boyd and Tom Lee nodded their heads in agreement.

"Check your guns, make sure they're all loaded, and you got extra cartridges," said Del. "If these guys are up there, they know there ain't no way out, so they'll be shooting for sure."

Del led the way, carefully stepping over rocks and logs and pointing out branches and other things to be avoided. Snowmelt dripped from the canyon walls, soaking them as they went. When the walls started to open up, he stopped.

All three heard the whinny of a horse at the same time. Edging ahead on his belly, Del looked between the branches and studied the scene with his binoculars. Backing off, he held up four fingers to the others. They nodded and moved several hundred yards back down the canyon.

"There's four horses, all of them just wandering around, " said Del. "I saw one man walk into the cave. It wasn't Sylvie, but I could hear a couple of different voices. There's a buck hanging in a tree and a little fire smoke. These are our boys, I'm sure of it."

Tom Lee pulled his pistol out and checked it again. "So, how do you want to do it?"

"There's no way to sneak up to the cave in daylight. It's probably a hundred yards from the last of the cover to the door."

"Then we gotta force them out of the cave," said Boyd.

"The horses," said Tom Lee. "They still need the horses; if they thought they were in trouble, they'd come running to see what was wrong."

"Maybe If we can make the horses nervous enough, they might come out," said Boyd. "What if I climbed above them enough to spook them with rocks?"

"I don't think all four will come out at one time no matter what we do. I thought we could smoke them out with a grass fire, but there ain't enough grass left for that. But, I got these," said Del, pulling out two sticks of dynamite.

"That oughta get them good and nervous," said Boyd.

"If we set one off, it'll get the horses moving and should bring at least one of them out the door."

"And if some are still inside, what then?"

"That's what the other stick is for. It'll take care of the logs in front," said Del. "Everyone ready?"

Moving slowly, the men reached the end of the canyon and laid flat in the brush, looking over the hideout. The horses were against the back of the cliff in the sun, and the men were nowhere to be seen. Del lit one stick and pitched it into the grass.

The horses lurched forward at the explosion and took off on a dead run before the last of the dirt hit the ground. Running in circles around the small space, they ran by the entrance of the cave just as two men rushed outside, knocking them to the ground. When they got to their feet, they both stumbled and fell again, each with a bullet in his chest.

As the dust settled and the horses calmed down, they watched the entrance to see what would happen next. After a few minutes, a familiar voice came from the cave. "Sargent Delbert Beale, is that you out there scaring all my horses?"

"You know it is . . ."

"Who else you got with you, Del? You surely ain't all alone, are you?"

"Just a couple of old friends, Boyd and Tom Lee."

"No shit? The four of us together again, how about that! Tom Lee, how's that pretty little wife of yours? I heard you got a couple of babies already. What's the plan, you trying to build your own army?"

"The plan is to kill you Sylvie."

"Kill me? Why would you want to go and do that?"

"It's just something that's gotta be done," said Tom Lee.

"Hey Boyd, you still cookin' beans for cowboys," asked Sylvie.

"No, I just work on a ranch."

"What I heard was that you run the Timms Ranch now and are carryin' on with some French dandy's pretty daughter, that so?"

"You heard right; everything is good with me."

"Okay Sylvie," said Del. "It's time to move on. You and your partner need to come out now, or we're gonna finish this with more dynamite."

"I ain't got no partner Del."

"We know someone else is in there with you."

They heard a single gunshot come from the cave. "It's just me now Del, no more partner. I'm coming out now, so don't go shootin' me." A pair of hands appeared at the door.

"I ain't gonna shoot you Sylvie. Come out slow and keep them hands out front."

Stepping through the opening, he stood up straight with his arms high and hands open. "Del, good to see you again."

"Boyd, grab the shackles and hook him up behind his back," said Del. "Tom Lee, check in the cave and make sure there ain't nobody alive in there, and be careful, no telling what kind of shit Sylvie might be trying to pull."

"I hear you and Miss Dolly are living together Del, that right?"

"Sylvie, you always did talk too much. Tom Lee, what did you find in the cave?"

"One dead outlaw with a fresh bullet hole in his head."

Standing in the sun, Sylvie's shiny bald head and dark skin made his beard, now mostly white, stand out. "I just don't get it," said Tom Lee. "You escaped from slavery and made it through the war. Why couldn't you just leave all that behind? What made you start killing?"

"It ain't nothin' I'd ever expect a white man to understand, 'specially a sorry ass reb like you. So, how's Sancha these days?"

"She's scared you'll come back again. That's why I put bars on the doors and windows."

"She sure growed up to be a fine lookin' woman," said Sylvie. "I was always hopin' to get a little taste of that someday . . ."

"You son-of-a-bitch," said Tom Lee, driving a punch deep into his gut. Sylvie doubled up then hit the ground face first, choking and spitting dirt.

"You always were a scrappy little shit. Take off these shackles, and we can see for sure who's the tough guy here."

"Nobody's taking off the shackles," said Del, stepping in between them. "Tom Lee, we ain't here to settle your personal vendetta, this is business. You and Boyd take him over by the trees. I'll be right there."

The skeletons of two dead cottonwoods reached across the spring. Standing him under a high branch, they waited as Del walked back, uncoiling a rope.

When Sylvie saw what was coming, he screamed at Del. "You sorry bastard, you ain't nothin' but another goddamn lyin' white man . . ."

"I didn't lie about nothing Sylvie."

"You son-of-a-bitch — you said you weren't gonna kill me!"

"No, I said I wasn't going to shoot you — I'm gonna hang you."

Throwing the rope over the branch, he made a noose while Tom Lee and Boyd held Sylvie up. Sliding the rope over his head, Del snugged it up against his ear and looked at him. "Anything you need to say before you die?"

Sylvie looked at him for a second, then shook his head. The three men jerked on the rope until his feet were off the ground, then tied it off.

After dragging the other three dead outlaws under the cottonwoods, they cut Sylvie down.

"This one has a messed up hand," said Boyd. "He's probably the one Morgan Reese shot on the way back from Fort Laramie."

"Yeah, and he's carrying a pouch of Buffalo Brand smoking tobacco like I found near the two murdered cowboys," said Del. He stuffed a wanted poster in Sylvie's shirt pocket. "Now we're done, let's head out. I'd like to get out of this canyon before it gets dark."

"Del, we should bury them," said Tom Lee.

"Murderers like them don't deserve a proper burying," said Boyd. "Tom Lee, it's over now, you gotta move on."

Looking at the bodies one last time, Tom Lee shook his head and walked off. "I guess that's best."

Rounding up the outlaw's horses, Boyd tied them together nose to tail and put a rope on the lead horse. Moving into the canyon, they worked through the deadfalls and rocks, reaching the aspen grove just as the sun set. Untying the outlaw's horses, he gave one a smack, and all four ran out of the trees and into freedom.

Chapter 22

Anny handed Laura a gift from under the Christmas tree. She looked at the gift, wrapped in red paper and tied with green ribbon, then looked at Anny.

"Just pull the ribbon sweetheart, like this."

When the ribbon came off, the paper loosened up, and the delicate face of a baby doll looked up at her. Her face lit up in an instant, and she pulled the doll to her shoulder, clearly delighted with it. She hugged the doll with one arm and Anny with the other and wouldn't let either of them go. Anny sat in front of the fireplace and watched her play with the doll until she fell asleep.

"Dean, there is a gift for you under the tree too."

Opening the package, he found a gold watch chain with a small gold coin hanging from it. "I noticed how worn yours was looking. I thought you might like a new one."

"What about the coin? I haven't seen one like this before."

"It's English. They have a custom that says if you carry a coin on your watch chain, you will never be able to be declared a vagrant because you can always show them you have money."

"I never heard anything like that before," said Dean, "but thank you for the gift. It's beautiful. I have one for you too."

Holding out a large box, she asked him to open it, so she didn't disturb Laura. He opened it and pulled out a new hat. "It came all the way from Philadelphia, and it's felt made from beaver hair. Your old one is looking pretty rough. I thought you might like this one to replace it."

"Oh, Dean, it's beautiful. Put it on me, I want to see if it fits."

Setting it on her head, he held up a mirror. "What do you think?"

"It fits perfect. Now I really do look like a cowgirl. I love it, thank you."

*

Flora laid in bed while Boyd made breakfast for them. When the cabin was warm, and the steak was frying, she threw off the covers and stood up. "Boyd, look, what do you see?"

He turned around to see her standing naked alongside the bed. "I see a beautiful woman looking at me?"

"Look again, what do you see going on here?"

"Well, I'm not sure what you want me to say?"

"My belly! Look how big my belly is, you did this to me. What have you got to say for yourself?"

"Uh . . . Merry Christmas?"

"Merry Christmas? Reb, there better be something under the tree to make up for this belly, or there's going to be trouble . . ."

"There might be something," said Boyd, "and don't call me reb."

Picking up a small gift from under the tree, he handed it to Flora, and she quickly tore off the wrapping. "It's called a cameo; an artist in Cheyenne carved the woman's face in it by hand."

"I know what a cameo is, just put it on me."

"The frame around it is real gold," said Boyd, closing the clasp.

Still naked, Flora looked at herself in the mirror. "It's beautiful. What can I possibly do to thank you reb?"

"You look like you might be a bit cold standing there with nothing to keep you warm but that little cameo. You can get under the covers with me, that would be a good start, and don't call me reb."

Wrapping herself in a blanket, she walked over to him. and kissed him on the cheek. "Boyd Stamps, you're a good man, for a reb. . ."

"Flora Dere, you'd be a perfect woman if you would just stop calling me that."

"I'll make a deal with you reb, I'll stop calling you that if you'll go into town tonight and have a couple of drinks with me."

"Flora, you know how I feel about that. I never was much of a drinker, and I don't think any good ever came from spending a lot of time in those places."

"Don't you ever want to get away from this place sometimes? I'm sure those cows won't notice you're gone for one night."

"Flora, I'm the ranch manager. This is my job. If I really want a drink, I can have one here any time. Why would I go all the way to town?"

"There's a lot of new people moving in around here. Maybe you'd like to meet some of them?"

"Maybe one of these days, but not right now."

"Boyd, you've been gone for almost two weeks, I get lonely."

"I'm sorry Flora, but you can stay with your father when I'm gone."

"Great, I'll just stay with the most boring man I know when my man is gone, no thanks."

"Flora . . ."

"Just shut up Boyd, I'm going back to bed."

*

The *Wyoming Women's Betterment Society* had been gaining members over the winter, and Anny's message of suffrage was one of the most talked about issues in the territory. She would take Laura with her to the meetings and rallies and introduce her as her daughter. It was much easier than trying to tell the real story over and over at every event. She liked the excitement of the rallies but was still unable to speak and shied away from any physical contact with the members. She did enjoy listening to Anny address the crowds, and then watch the response of the audience.

184

Nearly hidden behind the stacks of books and tablets, Anny finished writing her next article for the Leader titled, "Reaching for Statehood." Her last piece was titled, "Why a Women's Vote Is Important." The local men had a good laugh over it, sure that such a thing could never happen. Setting the tablet on top of the stacks of her books, she watched Laura playing with her baby doll. Sitting in the corner chair with a book in his lap, Dean was sound asleep. A nearly empty whisky bottle sat on the table next to him.

"Laura, sweetheart, let's get ready to go into town."

Wrapping her doll in a blanket, she went into the bedroom and came back wearing her coat. After dropping off the story at the Leader, they walked to the weekly meeting of the society. A long table had been set-up for the piles of posters, handouts, and the growing collection of petitions. Anny answered questions and filled them in on any new information. Potential delegates for the new territory were being contacted by members of the society in person and by mail.

The women of the society were relentless in their pursuit of suffrage legislation, and the day-to-day business of the society was now moving along without much help from Anny. She became a popular speaker and figurehead for the movement, always appearing in her trail clothes and big hat, and staying late to give interviews or talk to anyone that was interested. When she traveled out of town, Morgan was always by her side watching over her and Laura. By spring, she had been to all five counties in the territory and nearly every town that had at least a few women willing to listen.

Chapter 23

Pouring herself a second cup of tea, Anny and Laura watched as the spring storm piled snow against the barn. "Laura, have you seen daddy this morning?"

She shook her head.

"No? Neither have I. Maybe he went to town. If he did, he may stay there tonight until the snow goes away. Let's have some breakfast, and I'll read to you after, would you like that?"

She smiled and nodded.

The snow had let up by mid-day, and there was still no sign of Dean. She asked Morgan to go into town and see if he could find him, at least to make sure that he was okay. "Yes Ma'am, I'll saddle up right away."

Watching him disappear around the barn, she began to see a little sun through a break in the clouds. Several minutes later, she saw him walking back to the house. When the door opened, he walked straight to her and took his hat off. "Ma'am, I am very sorry, Dean is dead."

"Dead? What? How can that be? I thought he went to town?"

"No Ma'am, he's layin' against the barn, mostly covered in snow and all froze up. I saw his leg stickin' out when I walked by."

Anny sat down, unsure at the moment of what to do next. "Well, get Boyd and have him help you carry him into the barn for now. Then both of you come back to the house, and we'll decide what to do next."

"Yes Ma'am."

She took Laura into the bedroom and laid down, pulling the covers over their head. They lay for a while, and she began to cry softly. Watching her cry, Laura reached up and brushed the tears from Anny's face, then buried herself against her chest.

*

"I want to see him Boyd," said Anny.

"Missus Timms, he looks pretty bad right now. Maybe it would be better to let the undertaker clean him up some before you see him?"

"No, I want to see him and where he died so I can understand exactly what happened. Take me there, please."

Walking into the barn, she saw him lying across two bales of hay. His body was still frozen, twisted into grotesque contortions. "What do you think happened to him Boyd?"

"Missus Timms . . ."

"Please Boyd, call me Anny. We'll be working together now; we don't need to be formal."

"All right, Anny. I think he was looking for the privy and got lost in the storm."

"Here's what I think. He was looking for the privy in the storm but was so drunk he got lost, fell down, and died of exposure. Was there a bottle where you found him?"

Boyd nodded. "There was."

"What did you do with it?"

"I threw it in the privy."

"Good. That will be the last of the whisky in this house. I want to bury him up on the ridge, next to his father. I need you to get a couple of hands and prepare the grave. Morgan and I will go into town tomorrow and arrange for the undertaker and a stone."

"I'll take care of everything. Will the service be the day after tomorrow?"

"That will be fine. Thank you for all of your help. In a few days, we'll sit down and talk about the business and where to go from here. Are there any issues on the ranch we need to talk about before then?"

"No, everything is good right now."

*

The funeral was held at the gravesite, a place originally chosen by Dean for his father, Monroe. Now he will lay next to him on the land they both loved. It had a beautiful view of the ranch and the surrounding valley. Only the association members, the ranch hands, and Del and Dolly attended. Anny sent a telegram to Dean's brother David, in San Antonio, with the news. She put a short notice in the Leader without an explanation. If anyone asked, she told them he died in his sleep, most likely of a heart attack. She saw no reason to tell the whole world her business.

Sitting at the table in the ranch house, Anny poured Boyd a cup of coffee and a cup of tea for herself. "I need you to take over the day to day operation of the Timms Ranch," said Anny. "How do you feel about that?"

"Ma'am . . .?"

"Boyd, like I said before, we're past that, it's just Anny from now on."

Boyd nodded. "Anny, I will do whatever you need me to do, but I have to tell you that Dean and I didn't always see things the same way when it came to raising cattle on the open range."

"I know that you two had differences on the business, but I know little or nothing about cattle ranching. I want to put the operation in your hands, and I will support you in any decisions you make."

"Anny, if you're sure about this, I'll do it, but I'll need Ernesto to replace me. He's one of the best men I've ever worked with."

"Then we have to discuss wages and such things," said Anny.

"Let me talk to Ernesto about it, and I need to check on the branding crews while I'm out there. We can do it when I get back if that's good for you."

"Certainly, I'll be ready whenever you are."

"I should be back in three days, and we'll go over everything then."

She walked with him to the door. "Boyd, how is Flora doing?"

"Good, I guess, but I don't see her near as much as I'd like, though."

"When is the baby due?"

"She said sometime in the spring, maybe in April. I don't think she seems too excited about it though."

"I think she's just getting tired of being pregnant. I'm sure she'll feel better about it when she sees the baby."

"I sure hope so."

*

Ernesto and Boyd leaned against the fence at line camp one, watching the horses crop the new grass. In the distance, a few cattle could be seen feeding across a sidehill. "So, what do you think Ernesto, would you like to be cow boss for the Timms Ranch?"

"Sí, I would like that, it would mean more money for my family in San Antonio, and that would be good."

"The job is yours Ernesto."

"Muchos gracias Señor Boyd."

"How are the branding crews doing, any problems?"

"No Señor, they are doing good, but we spend most of our time looking for cattle. We set up the wagons and round up everything we can find, then move to another area and do it again. It takes all spring and part of the summer to find them and get them all branded. We're never sure how many we might have missed; they are spread all over the prairie."

"Yeah, they are. I'm hoping we can figure out a way to make that a little easier someday. Let's head back to the ranch. Missus Timms wants to talk about our new jobs."

*

"I'm glad you decided to stay with us Ernesto. Boyd says you are a great cowboy."

"Gracias Missus Timms, I will do a good job for you and the ranch."

"I know you will. There's one thing that I want to talk about as far as your new job goes. I plan on building another cabin for Boyd and Flora, so when their baby comes they can have some privacy. When it's finished, you can take the cabin that Boyd is living in now, will that be good for you?"

Sí Señora, I never believed that I would have a cabin to myself, muchos gracias."

"Boyd told me that you have family in San Antonio?"

"Sí, a wife, and a daughter and a son, although I have not seen them for a long while now. My Madre and brother also live there."

"Do you think you and your family could all live together in that cabin?"

He looked confused at the question. "Sí, I know we could, but they are not here."

"Here's what I would like to propose to you Ernesto. I would like to bring your family to the ranch to be with you. Would you be agreeable to that?"

191

Sitting quietly, he looked at her for a moment and nodded his head. Still quiet, his eyes filled with tears. "I do not know what to say Señora," said Ernesto, wiping his eyes. "I do not know how I could ever repay you . . ."

"You don't need to say or do anything. This is something I would like to do. I have decided to change the way the ranch is run," said Anny. "With help from you and Boyd, I want to make it more efficient and profitable. Boyd will be the manager of the ranch, and you will be the cow boss. You and your family would live here, on the ranch property with Laura and me and Boyd and Flora, and their baby, that is if you would like to."

"Sí, Sí, I would like that very much. I know my Madre and brother would choose to stay where they are, but when could we get my family here?"

"Boyd and I have a friend in San Antonio that will help us get that done. It may take a couple of months before they get here though. I will let you know when I get more information."

Standing up, he nervously held his hat in his hands, unsure of what to say next.

Anny put her arms around him and gave him a hug. "Welcome to our family Ernesto."

When he had left the house, Boyd asked if there was anything else she wanted to talk about today. "Just one thing. I was going through Dean's papers and found this. It's a deed of some kind, what do you think?"

Boyd read through the document. "It looks like a piece of property that was quitclaimed to Dean, maybe to cover a debt or something. I think it's a building lot in town."

Anny looked over the deed. "He may have got this property as a possible site to use as a new building for the association. Do you know anything about that?"

"Dean was trying to convince the members to build a place for the association and to try and bring other ranchers into it."

"What did the group think about it?"

"They were cautious, but willing to listen. I believe Dean was thinking about what the new politicians were going to do about open range ranching. I think he was looking to form a group for a more powerful voice against them."

"That sounds like him. He liked politicians even less than he liked Indians. Next time in town, I'd like to see the lot. Maybe I will have a use for it one day."

Chapter 24

Del watched as Ike King did his best to hold onto a small sorrel bronc. After he had the first jumps out of him, the horse spun around and tore off down the fence rail, trying to scrub him off. When that didn't work, it raced across the pen and stopped short, pitching Ike over the rail, landing him hard on his backside.

Del was still laughing when he stood up and brushed himself off. "Ike, that was one ride you're not likely to forget."

"That's the third time I've been on that nasty son-of-a-bitch, and the third time he threw me off. I gotta say though, running me down the rail was a new move for him. But I'm gonna break him, or he's gonna break me, that much I'm sure of."

"Ike, I appreciate you watching over things while I was gone. The place looks real good," said Del. "You're welcome to that horse or one of the others we have here if you'd like one."

"Thanks, boss. I definitely would like to have this one. Now all I gotta do is figure out how to ride him, and he might make a good saddle horse."

"I think the two of you will become good friends one of these days."

"I guess we'll see about that," said Ike. "So, how was the hunting trip?"

"Long and tiring."

"Did you have any luck?"

"It was a lot of work, but we did well."

"Good, glad to hear that," said Ike. "I'm gonna head to town for supper. I'll see you in the morning."

*

"So, what's happening at the cafe," said Del. "Is Kate ready to sell yet?"

"I think she's getting close; her health isn't all that good, and she's in there from open to close every day," said Dolly.

"Did you make her an offer?"

"I told her I could pay twelve hundred for everything. She asked for a couple of weeks to think about it. I'm still waiting for an answer."

Del wrapped his arms around her and gave her a good hug. "I'm so glad to be back, I missed you."

"I missed you too," said Dolly, "it's been pretty quiet around here, I hope you don't have to take a lot of those long trips anymore."

"I think I'm gonna leave those things to the young guys from now on. I'm getting too old to sleep on the cold hard ground."

"You just stick around here Marshal. I'll see to it that you have a soft place to sleep."

"I've been waiting to hear that for the last couple of weeks, and to hear you say that you've cooked up something special for this old man."

"How about biscuits and gravy and a big buffalo steak? Will that be special enough?"

"That will do just fine. So, how was Ike while I was gone, any problems?"

"None at all. He's been taking good care of the place and checking with me every day. I like him."

"Has he been wearing his pistol every day?"

Dolly nodded. "He did. How did the trip go? Everything end well?"

"It was good," said Del. "Saw a lot of pretty country and came across a nest of rattlesnakes in one place — I never liked snakes."

*

"I just came from the bank. It's done, Del, the River Cafe is officially ours!" said Dolly.

"Congratulations sweetheart," said Del, giving her a hug. "What's next?"

"I'm changing the name to the River Cafe and Bakery. I'm having a new sign made right now. Then I'll be closed a few days for cleaning and a few changes and reopen on Monday morning."

"What about the new cook and manager?"

"Already taken care of, they'll both be there tomorrow, helping with the cleaning and getting ready to open."

"So how did the old manager take getting fired?"

"Not real well. Kate had paid her the last of her wages, but I guess she figured the job was hers forever. She screamed at me for a minute, and then she cried some, then she called me a bunch of names, took a pie and left."

"She took a pie?"

"Yeah, she said they were made when Kate still owned the place, so she was taking one."

"Probably a cheap price to get rid of a thief," said Del.

"That's what I thought too," said Dolly. "Speaking of food, I have a couple of elk backstraps that were left at the cafe. I'll cook them up for supper."

"If there's two things that I really love, it's the owner of the River Cafe and Bakery and elk steaks."

She kissed him and walked into the kitchen. "Thank you my love. We have more than enough steak for Ike. You want to invite him in?"

"Not a chance. I want you all to myself tonight."

"Well, you got me, but I'll cook it all up, and you can give the extra to him."

"Sounds good. Tomorrow I want to take a look at the new building and see what it will take to make the upstairs into a place for us to stay when we're in town."

*

"Raylan, take a look at this telegram from Wes," said Del. "You ever hear anything about this guy before?"

Looking at the telegram, he walked over to the wanted posters on the wall. "It kinda sounds like it could be this guy boss," said

Raylan, pointing to a poster on the bottom row. "Split Nose Bob, wanted for stealing horses up north in the Bighorns."

"Yeah, that's the guy Wes is talking about. I know he used to work the border country between here and Colorado. I heard he got in a fight with his partner over a girl and got his nose sliced in the process. The poster says he's well known as a horse thief. Wes said he's moved up to murder now. I guess a rancher and his son confronted him, and he shot them both. He wants us to find him and his gang."

"That's a long ride boss, I'll go," said Raylan. "I can take Henry Becker with me. It's time the new guy got some saddle time."

"That's fine, but plan on being gone a while. You're gonna be heading up into the hole-in-the-wall country, and you might run into more outlaws than you're looking for."

"We'll be careful. Besides, I've always wanted to see that part of the territory."

"Then plan on leaving in the morning."

Chapter 25

Boyd reached around Flora, caressing her belly. "I think it will be soon. What do you think?"

"How would I know? I never had a baby before, and I ain't about to have another one, that's for damn sure."

"Not even one more? Just for me?"

"Not for you, not for anybody — ever."

"Flora, I smell whisky on your breath. Where were you drinking at?"

"I was in town for father. I just stopped in for one drink. It's nothing, Boyd."

"Flora, I know that you are in town a lot when I'm gone. I smell the cigars and the whisky, and the flower perfume."

"You're gone a lot, and I get lonely . . ."

"I'm sorry Flora. It's all part of my job. I worry about you when I'm gone, but now that the baby's close, I think you should stay at the cabin."

"Well, great," said Flora. "I'll stay here if you will. I'll be bored out of my mind, but I'll stay."

"Flora, I can stay at the ranch until the baby comes. Then I can hire someone to care for you and the baby until you're ready to go back to work for your father. If you don't want to go back to work, that's fine too. Anny is planning on building a new cabin for us so we can live here on the ranch."

"Anny? What happened to Missus Timms? Sounds like you two are getting pretty close."

"Oh stop it, I only have one woman, and that's you, and you know it. With Dean gone, she asked me to manage the whole ranch. I report to her now, she asked me to call her Anny. She said if we were to work together every day, we should call each other by our given names."

"After the baby comes, I will be going back to work for father. He's getting old, and it's hard for him to get around."

"Any way you want to do it is fine with me, but you will live with me and the baby here, right?"

"I don't want to talk about this anymore, I'm going to bed."

Boyd walked over to the bed and pulled back the blanket. "I'm tired too."

"I'm sleeping alone, Boyd. I'm too big and too uncomfortable with you in the bed too."

Boyd helped her into bed and covered her up. "Then I'll see you in the morning."

*

Boyd had written down the names of Ernesto's family and where they lived and sent a telegram to Tom Lee explaining that they wanted to move the family from San Antonio to Cheyenne by the best means possible, and the Timms Ranch would pay for everything. Boyd got a return telegram from Tom Lee that said they found the family and that the move was underway. He would keep them informed as to when they left.

*

The work of the Betterment Society had been gaining the attention of the potential territorial delegates, and the women continued to lobby every one of them. Anny was often called on to give her suffrage presentation to various towns and groups. Always dressed in her trail clothes, her reputation proceeded her wherever she went. When the regular business was concluded, she would be surrounded by people wanting to hear about her time at the fort and her friendship with the Indians. In time, Laura began to love the trips and the attention she got from the other women.

The framed photo of her with Chief Black Bear was one of Anny's most prized possessions. Next to it was a photo of her and Morgan, with Laura clinging tight to her side. After enlarging her office and adding new bookshelves, she began writing stories for the Leader on all kinds of subjects. Everything from town issues to military issues and the cattle business, turned up in the pages of the paper.

She was also working on two different books at the same time. The first was stories about her travels in the West. She had decided to call it, *"Mountains, Indians & Buffalos, A Lady's Life in the American West."* The second was, *"An Issue of Equality, Western Women and the Fight for Suffrage."*

She kept a list of subjects she would like to write books about, and an even longer list of issues she wanted to report on that grew longer every week. Several of her reports on the treaty signing had been forwarded to eastern papers by the publisher, and a sketch of her done by a local artist was sent along with the reports. Her name and the picture of her in her cowgirl clothes were becoming well known in the East.

"Laura, would you like to go to town for a while? I need a few things for my office."

Running into the bedroom, she came back with her coat and a huge smile. She loved to ride in the buggy. Part way to town, Anny told Morgan to pull over. In the distance, she watched a small group of Indians as they rode across a sage flat and disappeared into the trees. Laura pulled herself close to Anny and turned her head.

"I miss seeing them Morgan. Someday I would like to learn to take pictures myself. I would never run out of wonderful things to photograph." Reaching town, they stopped at the dry goods, and she bought a few tablets and other supplies for the office. Walking to the counter they stopped, and Anny had the clerk take down a display of large candy lollypops. After Laura picked the one she wanted, they left the store and walked to the address that was on the deed she had found.

The address was a large corner lot just off the main street by one block. "What a great location for a business of some kind. What do you think Morgan?"

"Yes Ma'am, you could easily build any kind of business you want on a lot this big."

"Or — even a large meeting hall if that was your interest."

Morgan looked at the empty lot for a minute. "Yes, I could easily see a fine meeting hall sitting right here Ma'am. Maybe with a big sign in front that said: *"The Wyoming Women's Betterment Society"*."

"Why Morgan, that's a very good idea. I think I may have to look into that."

*

Tom Lee knew the stage trip from San Antonio would be difficult and dangerous for Ernesto's family, and he sent Arturo, an old friend and trail companion with them. Able to speak English and Spanish, he was absolutely loyal and fearless in any situation. He would see to it that they got to Cheyenne safely, and Boyd would hire him on at the ranch for as long as he wanted to stay.

The new cabin had been started and would be complete in a few weeks. "What do you think Boyd," said Anny, "will Flora like it?"

Boyd shrugged. "To be honest, I'm not sure if she would. I'm not really sure just what she likes right now."

"I imagine she's just tired of being pregnant. It can't be very comfortable for her. I think she'll get back to normal after the baby comes."

"I hope that's it."

"How's Ernesto doing? Is he excited about the family coming?"

"That's all he talks about; this is a really good thing you're doing for his family. His mother lives with his brother and chooses to stay there. But Ernesto can hardly wait to see his wife and children again."

"You know, I really like to think about it as our family," said Anny. "I never had children of my own with my first husband, or with Dean, and I have no living family that I know of. I consider Laura my family now, and hopefully, you and Flora as well as Ernesto and his wife and children."

"It's been the same for me all these years. I only remember my older brother. He took me in and raised me when my folks died," said Boyd. "When he was killed in the war, I had nobody left."

"All I ever wanted in life was a family of my own," said Anny. "I would be honored if you would consider being part of it."

"I can't think of anything I would like more than to be part of your family, thank you."

*

The excitement of seeing his family again was nearly unbearable for Ernesto. For the last week, he had made the trip from line camp one to the ranch every day to see if they had arrived yet. For the last week, Boyd would meet the stage in town every day. He knew Arturo from the buffalo hunt, and when he saw him get off the stage with the family, he walked over and shook his hand and embraced him. "Good to see you old friend. I hope the long trip wasn't too hard on everyone."

"It was hard on the family, but their excitement at seeing Ernesto made up for the rough ride." A slim, pretty woman with a young boy and girl, waited with Arturo. Each carried one cloth bag over their shoulder. When the introductions were made, everyone climbed into the buggy.

"Was there any trouble on the road?" asked Boyd.

"Nothing too bad, just a little problem with the weather and the rivers. Some of the way stations were kinda rough, and the food poor. But it is a long trip, one I would not like to make again any time soon."

*

Boyd drove under the Timms Ranch sign and pulled up to the barn. Helping the family down, Arturo asked if Ernesto was here.

"No, he's at the line camp right now, but this is about the time he comes to the ranch every day to check and see if they have arrived. I think he'll like the surprise he gets this time."

Arturo translated for Ernesto's wife, and she broke into a huge smile.

Anny greeted them and invited them into the house for refreshments. Inside, she sat a tray with lemonade and cinnamon bread on the table. A pitcher of spring water sat next to it. "Arturo, can you introduce me to our guests?"

"Sí, this is Elena, Ernesto's wife, and this pretty young lady is Sara, and this handsome young man is Martin." Each one nodded and smiled as he introduced them.

"Do they speak English?" asked Anny.

"Martin does pretty good. I think after a few weeks here, he will pick it up quickly. The others speak very little."

"Welcome to the Timms Ranch. I am very happy to meet everyone."

Ernesto stepped through the doorway and everyone turned to see who it was. In an instant, it was chaos, Elena ran into his arms, sobbing and kissing him. At first, the children hesitated, then Ernesto dropped to the floor with his arms wide open — "Por favor, ven a ver a tu padre. . .!" The children ran straight to him, bowling him over — all four were crying and laughing at the same time.

After he composed himself enough, and everyone stopped crying, he stood up with his family still clinging to him. "Muchos Gracias, Missus Timms, there is no way that I could ever thank you for what you have done for us."

Wiping away her own tears, she put her arms out, and they all embraced. "Ernesto, I'm so happy it worked out for everyone. Would you like to go to your cabin now?"

"Sí, we would like that very much."

"Boyd is in his new cabin now, and yours is ready for you and the family," said Anny. "Morgan, would you walk them to the cabin please?"

Boyd and Anny sat at the table watching out the window. "Anny, that was quite a reunion. I almost cried myself just watching it."

"Boyd Stamps, who are you kidding? I saw your eyes, there was a tear or two in there."

"I think you're mistaken; cowboys don't cry . . ."

"Another myth of the cowboy shattered forever," said Anny.

Chapter 26

The Timms Ranch was changing quickly since Ernesto's family arrived. The sound of children playing was something Anny never thought she would hear. Laura watched the children play in front of the cabin. Anny explained to her what was happening and asked if she would like to play with the children. She pulled her baby doll close, looked down, and shook her head.

"It's okay sweetheart, it's something new, and it may take a while. I just want you to know that they're very nice, and they would never hurt you. Whenever you would like to visit with them or play with them, they would like that, do you understand?"

She nodded and turned back to the window to watch them.

While they were watching the kids, Boyd came out of the cabin, running toward the house. Anny met him at the door. "Is something wrong?"

"I think the baby is coming — I need help."

"Get Ernesto and have him send Elena over to the cabin. I'll meet her there."

Running to Ernesto's cabin, he told him the baby was coming and asked if Elena could help.

"Sí, no problema, she has done this many times before. She will be right there."

After nearly an hour, Anny stepped out of the cabin and waved for Boyd. "Come and meet your new cowboy."

Flora looked at the baby then at Boyd. "Here's your son, now you have someone to help you run the ranch."

"He is our son Flora, not just mine."

Ignoring his comment, she handed him to Boyd. "I wish you could have shared in the pain of delivering our son. Do you have a name for him?"

"No, not yet, what do you think it should be?"

"I have no thoughts on it. He's your son, you name him."

"Okay, then I will name him Alexander Boyd Stamps, and I'll call him Alex."

"Fine," said Flora. "Now that it's done, can I get a little sleep?"

Boyd sat on the bed with the baby rocking him back and forth. Ernesto told him that Elena would stay with the baby while he and Flora rested.

Boyd's world was now baby Alex and Flora. He built a new bed for him and helped Flora with anything she needed. Ernesto took care of the ranch business in the first week. When Flora declared she was ready to go back to work, Elena offered to care for the baby while Boyd went to check on the ranch.

After three days of riding the range, he returned to the cabin to find it empty. He walked to Ernesto's cabin and knocked. "Ernesto, this is Boyd. Do you know where Flora and the baby are?"

The door opened, and Anny stepped out, followed by Elena with baby Alex in her arms. "Boyd, I'm so sorry, but Flora is gone," said Anny.

"Gone? What do you mean, gone? Is she dead?"

"Right after you left to check on the cattle, she brought the baby to Elena, then saddled a horse and left the ranch, and she hasn't come back."

"She never said where she was going?"

"I wasn't here when she left, and Elena doesn't speak English."

"Then I have to go to town and find her."

"Boyd, I don't think she's coming back, she left this with the baby," said Anny, handing him a cameo necklace with a gold frame. "It was in the baby blanket."

Turning red in the face, he ran for the barn and saddled the first horse he came to and headed for Cheyenne. Reaching the Chophouse Bar, he went straight to the bartender. "Have you seen my girlfriend in the last few days?"

"Who the hell is your girlfriend?" asked the surprised bartender.

"Flora Dere, my girlfriend is Flora Dere, do you know her?"

The bartender nodded. "Sure, everybody around here knows Flora, but I haven't seen her for a couple of days. I heard that her and Charlie Cooper left for Chicago."

"Who the hell is Charlie Cooper?"

"He's a railroad detective. Cheyenne is on his route; he is in town for a couple of days every few weeks. So Flora was your girlfriend? She told everyone she was Charlie's girlfriend, and they were going to have a baby and move to Chicago after it came."

Boyd's head was spinning, and he felt sick. Walking outside, he sat down on the step, took several deep breaths, and tried to reconcile the mother of his son with the woman he just learned about. Saddling up, he rode to her father's house and pounded on the door. When Basquiat opened it, he asked him if he knew where Flora had gone.

Leaning heavily on his cane, the old man shook his head. "I'm sorry Boyd, I haven't seen her for at least a month, I'm a little worried myself. If you find her, will you let me know where she is please?" Boyd rode back to the ranch, in no real hurry to get there.

Elena continued to take care of the baby while he spent the next three days alone in the cabin. On the third morning, Anny knocked on his door. "Boyd, you need to eat, I have some food for you. Open the door please."

The door opened, and Boyd stood looking at her. "You're a mess, move out of way, please, so I can put this food down."

"Anny, thank you, but I'm not hungry."

"That's horse pucky, and we both know it, now move out of my way," said Anny, pushing her way past him.

"I'm fine, really. I'll be making a trip to the line shacks tomorrow."

"Boyd Stamps, you listen carefully. Here's how it's going to be. You are the father of a new son, you are my ranch manager, and you are my friend. You smell bad and you look bad, now sit down and eat this food before it gets cold."

"Anny, I'm sorry, I don't feel too good. I miss Flora."

"Well that's just too bad, you have responsibilities, so eat up."

"You just don't understand . . ."

"That's just more horse pucky, and I don't want to hear it. I lost my family when I was very young. My first husband was shot in the war and suffered horribly from his wound before he finally killed himself. My second husband got drunk and wandered off in a blizzard, and froze to death and neither of them left me with any children. You have a beautiful son and by God and be dammed, you will start caring for him right now. Now finish eating, head down to the creek, and get yourself cleaned up."

Boyd said nothing else as he finished the meal. Picking up a towel and a bar of soap, he headed out the door. When he got back, Anny had cleaned up part of the mess in the cabin and left a pile of clothes near the door.

"These need to be washed. You do know how to wash clothes don't you?"

"Anny . . ."

"Boyd, I expect my manager to be managing my ranch tomorrow morning, and I expect him to look like a manager too, you understand?"

Boyd nodded. "I'll be on the job tomorrow."

"Now that Ernesto has taken your job, you won't need to be gone as often. You won't need to be gone several days at a time; he can do it. You said he could handle it, right?"

"He can do it. He's a really good man."

"Good. I talked to Ernesto and Elena yesterday. She will take care of the baby during the day, and when you have to be gone from the ranch. In the evenings, while you are here, you will take care of him. She will teach you everything you need to know, and I expect that you will compensate her properly."

"Anny, I wish I knew what to say besides thank you."

"There's nothing else needed."

*

Laura was proving to be an exceptionally bright young girl. Still unable to speak, she understood everything that she saw and heard without a problem. Anny worked with her every chance she had, teaching her to read and write. There was no evidence that she remembered anything from her life with her family, but she picked up on the lessons very quickly. Once she understood the alphabet, she was able to connect the letters with a picture of the object, and it began to come back to her much faster.

Each time something became clear to her, she would light up and look to Anny for confirmation. She was given books on many different subjects like animals and stars and a large copy of an illustrated dictionary. She loved the books about history and ones with stories of explorers. Everyone who knew her brought her a new book for her collection. Picking out words she didn't understand, she would write them out, and Anny would explain what the words meant.

As her reading and writing improved, a local Cheyenne school teacher came in several days a week to tutor her. "You know Anny, I think she still retains most of the basic learning from before the tragedy. She learns much faster than my other students of her age," said the teacher. "When I started Laura on math, she understood the concept of adding, subtracting, and multiplying quickly. Division was a little slower, but from the moment she understood it, she seemed to love working out every problem she was given."

As the weather warmed up, she ventured outside, at first with Anny at her side, to watch Ernesto's children play in the grass. She still wasn't ready to play with them, but she enjoyed watching. One morning as Anny was working, Laura came to her desk and pointed outside toward the kids.

"What is it sweetheart? Do you want to go outside and play with the other children?"

She nodded, and took Anny by the hand, leading her outside. Walking up to kids playing, she stopped and watched them for a minute, then looked up at Anny. Letting go of her hand, she handed her the baby doll and walked over to the kids. In minutes they were all running around like they had been playmates forever. This time Anny couldn't wait to get to the bedroom. She started to cry as she watched them play.

*

Boyd hung up his hat and sat down across the table from Anny.

"How's baby Alex doing today," asked Anny.

"Well, he's loud, he never stops kicking, and sometimes he's really smelly, but he sure is beautiful," said Boyd. "His bed is right alongside mine, and I don't get all that much sleep. Sometimes I wake up because he needs something, and sometimes I wake up worrying about him, even when he's sleeping. Sometimes I just like to watch him sleep."

"It sounds like you've got a good start on being a father."

"I sure hope so."

"Okay, let's talk about the ranch and your ideas for the future. I gather you don't like the open range system as much as Dean did?"

Boyd nodded and pulled out his notebook. "The basic idea of free grass and water sounds good. The government allows you to run your cattle on the land for free. A lot of ranchers like to use the example of the buffalo. If millions of buffalo can survive out there, then so can the cattle. They both eat grass, and it's free. But buffalo and cattle are very different animals. Buffalo are tough and can find forage in any weather, or they'll migrate to somewhere else. Cattle don't do that. They will turn their back in a blizzard and freeze to death where they stand or get buried by drifting snow."

"So, how would you change things?"

"Our cattle are spread out across a hundred miles of prairie along with the rest of the association's cattle and anyone else who wants to turn theirs out. It's first come first served. Even if we keep doing business like we are now and continue to have mild winters, we still have a lot of cowboys out there on horseback, branding calves, caring for sick cows, and gathering them when the time is right. We feed them, pay them, and provide them with horses, and that's a lot of expense for the ranch. We need to make sure that the cattle have feed and water available at all times. We have to protect them from the times when the winters aren't so mild."

"Is that possible when they're scattered all over the territory," said Anny.

"It's not, and that's the problem. I believe we will need to start growing our own feed, build pens, and fence our ground into pastures. Then, over the next couple of years, we should reduce the herd size to something more manageable. And we have to sell all the horses we don't need for our own use."

"How many cattle do you think we have right now?"

"I have it in my book as about sixty-five hundred without the new calves. I think that Dean's book would show it much higher, but I think this is a reasonable number. We lost quite a few to the early storms and rustlers, and some loss to theft of unbranded calves and a few more to the Indians."

"Boyd, I trust your judgment on this. The Timms Ranch is in good financial shape right now thanks to Dean's frugal management. But I agree that things will change with more people moving in and an unknown bunch of politicians about to start running things. So it's time to go ahead and get started on it."

"One more thing, I think we should look into buying more ground in the future," said Boyd. "As we start to raise more feed, we'll need more pasture ground."

"I'll start looking into it as soon as I get to town," said Anny.

Chapter 27

The new sign above the window said: ***River Cafe & Bakery.*** Del sat across from Dolly while he finished his breakfast. "The place is packed; you might run out of food the way it's going today."

"It's still hard to find certain things like potatoes," said Dolly, "but the new butcher shop is working out well. They have plenty of everything. They even smoke a few hams when they get a fresh load of dressed hogs."

"Then maybe I'll retire and stay home. I'll just sit around all day eating ham and pie, and smoking cigars . . ."

"Don't quit that job yet, I could never make that many pies," said Dolly, "I have to go to work now, so skedaddle, we need the table."

"Yes Ma'am, I'm going to work now. How about a cherry pie tonight?"

"Just go!"

*

Walking into the office, Del sat down and put his feet on his regular spot on the desk. Lighting up a fresh cigar, he picked up the pile of mail and sorted through it. Two new wanted posters for his wall, a bill from the livery, and another one from the dry goods store were the only things of any importance. Looking up at the sound of the door, he saw Raylan walk in.

"Glad to see you're back. Where's Henry?"

"He's at the doctor's place. He took a bullet from old Split Nose, nothing too bad though."

"How bad, exactly?"

"It just grazed his cheekbone and clipped his ear. He'll have a good story to tell about the scar for sure."

"Tell me all about it."

Raylan took off his hat and sat down, wiping his face with his bandanna. "It was a long dry dusty ride for sure. The wind was worse than usual for most of the trip. After a few days of looking, I found a couple of really remote ranches and talked to the owners and a few of their hands."

"Let me guess, nobody knew a damn thing?"

"Most of them said that, but after we left one ranch, a cowboy by the name of Able Gustafsson caught up to us and had some things to say. It turns out that the rancher and his son that were killed were his kin, and he wanted to shoot ol' Bob himself, but he was a bit timid about going after him alone. He said there were three of them."

"Go on, this sounds interesting."

"He wanted to come along, so I told him he was a temporary deputy, but he had to do exactly what I said. Turns out, he was a good hand and a good shot."

"So they're all dead?"

Raylan nodded. "They're all in the ground. Able's information was good, and we caught up with them after a long days ride. From a spot up on some rimrock, we saw a makeshift pen with maybe fifteen horses in it. Two men were sitting by the fire, and Bob was off somewhere else, probably answering the call. We were too far away to be real accurate, so we closed the gap some and got a good shooting position. When I called out to them, Bob came running out of the weeds, and the other two opened fire right away. Henry killed one of them with the first shot, and that's when Bob clipped his ear. I killed the second one and shot at Bob several times."

"You killed Bob?" said Del.

"I wasn't even close. Bob was on a dead run toward the horses, and Able made a spectacular shot and hit him in the ear. If you ever need another deputy, he'd be a good one."

"You know there was a five-hundred-dollar reward on him?"

"Yeah, I thought I would put him in for it. It was his people they killed. I gave him the saddles and anything else he wanted, 'cept the guns, I brought them back."

"Good idea. What about the horses?"

"Able thanked us and said he would get them back where they belonged. Most of them had family brands on them."

The door opened again, and Henry walked in with a wad of white gauze taped to the side of his head. "Well, Henry, it looks like you got a good story to tell everyone when you get old," said Del.

"Yessir, I do, but I'm good with just the one story. I ain't wantin' to see any more bullets that close to my head again. Bob fired that bullet from his pistol while he was running. Most men would never have gotten this close."

"You boys did a hell of a job up there. Why don't you go over and get some grub, then rest up, and I'll see you tomorrow."

*

With the ranch in good hands, Anny Timms was able to spend more time with Laura and her work for the society. No place had ever recognized women's suffrage before, and Anny and the society were determined to become the first. After receiving an invitation from a women's group in Laramie, she agreed to come to give her talk and see if she could enlist more women in the cause. She hadn't been there recently and looked forward to the train ride.

After the train got up to speed, she enjoyed seeing Laura watch out the window as the prairie rushed by. The fresh spring grass blanketed the countryside as far as she could see. After a few miles, several pronghorns raced alongside the train, and she tugged at Anny's sleeve to be sure she saw them too.

When they reached the Laramie mountains, they saw several Indians sitting on horses watching the train go by. Laura turned and put her head on Anny's shoulder. Sometimes the sudden sight of Indians still made her nervous, and they rode the rest of the way in silence. Stepping off the train, Morgan followed them with their bag. Several women met them at the train including Dolly, and their host, Lenetta Haynes, wife of the local mortician, G. Ronald Haynes.

After proper introductions, they walked to the cafe for refreshments. "You bought the cafe, how wonderful," said Anny, "It's always great to see a woman go into her own business."

"Well, Del was a real help," said Dolly. "He introduced me to the banker, and they helped with the money."

"Everyone needs a little help getting started. I'm glad it worked out for you."

"Thank you. Would anyone like a fresh piece of pie and coffee," asked Dolly.

"Laura, would you like a piece of pie," said Anny.

She nodded and pointed at the case. When Dolly pointed at the first pie, she shook her head. The next one drew a big smile. "Do you like cherry?"

Laura smiled and nodded again. "I'm not sure she ever had it before," said Anny, "but I guess she'll find out."

Laura took the fork and picked out a cherry, touching it to her tongue. Smiling, she put it in her mouth and ate it. Wrinkling her nose, she broke into a huge smile and finished the pie.

"It looks like you have a new customer," said Anny.

"We have rooms for you and Morgan at the Laramie House, we can walk over there whenever you're ready," said Lenetta.

"How many women are you expecting tonight?"

"It's hard to say. The room will hold at least a hundred. A lot of them say they will come, but there is a lot of resistance from their men. Some will stay home just to avoid the conflict."

"It can be hard to overcome all the old prejudices in the men of this country. That's what the society is all about," said Anny. "How does your husband feel about the issue?"

"Ronald is just like all the other men around here; he thinks women should stay home and take care of the house and the kids. Missus Timms, thank you for coming. We're looking forward to hearing you talk."

*

The room was buzzing about hearing Anny Timms speak. She was very popular and starting to become famous throughout the Wyoming Territory as well as in the Colorado and Utah territories on the subject of women's rights. Even those who weren't interested in the issue had followed her newspaper articles on the treaty and the Indian tribes and wanted to meet her.

Above a large blackboard was the banner reading: *The Wyoming Women's Betterment Society.* When Lenetta Haynes walked out in front of the board, the room quieted down. "Ladies, I would like to introduce you to Missus Anny Timms."

Walking over to Missus Haynes, she shook her hand and thanked her for the invitation. When the applause subsided, she took off her big hat and put it on the table. Rolling up the sleeves of her western shirt, she walked over to the board and picked up the chalk. Like always, in big letters, she wrote the word suffrage in all capitals. "How many of you know exactly what that word means?"

A lot of hands went up, but just as many didn't know the word. "That's more hands than I see in a lot of places," said Anny. "I think our cause is getting stronger. Women's suffrage means, literally, to give women the right to vote. But, not only do we want the right to vote, we want more than that! We want the right to serve in political jobs, and we want to be able to serve on juries. In short — we want everything the men have!"

When the applause died down, she went back to the blackboard and wrote:

THERE IS NO COUNTRY IN THE ENTIRE WORLD THAT HAS GIVEN WOMEN THESE RIGHTS!
THE WYOMING TERRITORY WILL BE THE FIRST PLACE IN THE WORLD TO DO IT!

After another wave of applause, she resumed her speech and held the audience for another half hour, then opened it up to questions.

Seven women stood up and quietly left the room. "Thank you for coming ladies," said Anny.

Before she could continue, two men walked in and physically pulled women from their chairs. Morgan had been standing at the back of the room near the door. Stepping forward, he grabbed the men and separated them from the women, he looked at Anny.

"Gentlemen, if these ladies want to leave, they can do it without your help. Ladies, it is up to you."

Both stood up and walked out. Morgan blocked the door as the men tried to follow them.

"Lady, just who the goddamn hell do you think you are?" shouted one of the men. "Ain't no woman of mine gonna listen to any more of this horseshit. Ain't no way any woman is ever gonna vote on anything."

"Well, sir," said Anny, "men like you are exactly the reason we are doing this. You should just go on home and get ready for it because you can't stop it now."

"What's next lady? You gonna let all the beaners and pigtails vote too?"

Anny nodded at Morgan, and he grabbed the man by the arm and walked him out the front door, the second man followed on his own.

"Ladies, I'm sorry that you had to see such an ugly thing like that happen," said Anny, "but I've seen it before, and I'm sure all of us will see it again before we get this done."

For the next hour, she answered all their questions and told a few interesting stories about meeting Chief Black Bear and watching the tribes race their ponies. A long table held the petitions ready to sign and stacks of flyers for handouts. They included a list of names of possible candidates for the new territorial delegates from their area.

Walking back to the hotel, Del joined them. "Missus Timms, it's nice to see you again," he said, tipping his hat.

"And it's good to see you too, Del, but please, we know each other well enough, no need to be so formal. Please, just call me Anny."

Del nodded. "How was the meeting tonight? Was there a good turnout?"

"It was nearly full. Most everyone seemed to enjoy it."

"Everyone but that nasty old man Jenkins and his son," said Dolly. "They tried to drag their wives out of the meeting like a couple of animals."

"So I heard," said Del. "Raylan was outside the door when it happened. I think he might have explained to them, rather firmly, how they needed to calm down a little before they went home."

"Thank you Del," said Anny. "Unfortunately, I think it may not be possible to change the minds of men like these. I hope their women are okay."

"I asked Raylan to stop by their places and check on the two ladies in the morning, just to make sure they were okay."

"Thank you for that Del."

*

Dolly and Lenetta walked to the cafe for breakfast. After the meal, Laura tapped on Anny's arm and held up a small tablet with 'cherry pie' written on it. "You want a piece of cherry pie for breakfast? I thought pie was just for supper?"

Dolly looked at the note. "You know what? I think there might be a piece of my special breakfast pie left. Would you like it Laura?"

She nodded her head and wrote, 'yes, please.' "Would anyone else like a piece of my special breakfast pie?"

"Maybe I will try one myself," said Anny. "Morgan, how about you?"

"Yes Ma'am, I would like very much to have a piece."

"Then it's pie for everyone," said Dolly.

*

On the ride home, Laura wrapped herself in the blanket as soon as they sat down. After a few miles, she pulled it from her face and began to watch out the window. Several groups of pronghorns watched as they went by, and two hawks floated over the grass looking for a meal. She tugged on Anny's sleeve and showed her the tablet. She had written 'birds' and the word 'hawks' followed by a question mark.

"Sweetheart, that's exactly right. Those are hawks," said Anny, giving her a hug.

At the station, Boyd waited for them with the buggy. "So, how is baby Alex doing," asked Anny.

"He is good, a little louder maybe, but he seems to be happy. He likes it when I sit with him in the rocker in front of the fireplace. It puts him to sleep quickly. Then I can hold him in my arms as long as I want. It's my favorite part of the day."

"I'm glad to hear that. He's a beautiful child."

"Thank you, how was your trip?"

"It went very well, thank you. I think we have quite a few new members in Laramie willing to fight for the cause. Anything going on at the ranch that I need to be aware of?"

"No problems, we're marking out the new pastures and pens and finding the property lines. While you were gone, I saw Basquiat Dere in the dry goods store. He told me that he would like to talk to you about selling his property."

"Really, he wants to get out of the business?"

"He said he wants to go back to France. He misses Flora and needed her to run things for him. He doesn't look too good, and he says he has no reason to do it anymore."

"Doesn't his property border ours?"

"Yes, all along the northeast side. We would have even more water access than before."

"Please tell him we would like to talk to him as soon as possible. We can come to his place if he would like."

"I'll do that right away."

"In the morning, we can talk about how to enlarge the ranch if we buy the property."

Chapter 28

"Del, what are they building down by the railroad tracks? I see a lot of lumber piled up by the rails," said Dolly.

"New cattle pens, and loading ramps and more barracks for the coolies and the men loading the cars. They're getting ready for when they start shipping cattle."

"Why do you call them coolies?"

"Beats me. That's just what most people call them. I think it just means a Chinese laborer. They're a pain in my butt most of the time. They get crazy on opium and lose most of their money gambling and get in fights. I quit locking most of them up. Their track boss handles all of that small stuff. The new cattle facility means more business for Laramie and more people moving here, and, a lot more pies to bake and steaks to cook."

"You remember what it was like when you came to town just a few years ago," said Dolly. "It's hard to believe it's grown this fast."

"I remember," said Del. "I see they're building the town's first permanent bank right now. When the bankers put down roots, it's a good sign things are going to grow."

Dolly kissed him goodbye and headed for the door. "I have to get going. Today's baking day, will I see you for lunch?"

"I have to see about a couple of missing horses out at the /J Ranch. It may be supper before I get back."

"Then there'll be fresh pie in your future for sure. See you tonight."

Del and Henry rode up to the barn and tied off to the fence. Tom James came out leading a horse and greeted them. "Hello Tom," said Del. "This is my deputy, Henry. I understand you lost a couple more horses?"

"Three to be exact. These weren't just ranch horses; these were three well-bred studs that I just bought. I wanted to start improving my herd. Hell, I ain't even had them a week."

"When did they get them?"

"Night before last. I had them in the barn in separate stalls. The next morning they were gone."

"They were branded right?"

"Sure, /J on the left hip."

"Were they shod?"

James nodded. "Fresh set on every one of them. Just finished them the day before."

"What do they look like?"

"Two sorrels, one is solid color, one has a black mane and tail and one light dun with black feet. I had two hands tracking them, but the trail ran out after a couple of miles."

"Let me check around, and I'll let you know what I find. No sense in spending days in the saddle if your guys said the trail ran out."

"Thanks Del, those studs cost me six hundred apiece. I hope you can find them."

"So Marshal, what's next," asked Henry as he saddled up. "Are we going to go looking for them?"

"No, I think I might know where they're at."

"You do? Where are they?"

"We'll go looking for them tomorrow. I'll explain then. Just don't say anything about this to anyone."

"I won't tell nobody about it."

*

The next morning Del and Henry headed into the foothills. After several hours, they tied up in a stand of broken timber and walked to a jumble of boulders where they could get a look below. They saw a small, rundown camp at the end of the canyon. As they watched, a man walked out of the barn leading the three missing horses into a separate pen. "Shit boss, how did you know they would be here?"

"I'll tell you about it later. Let's go and have a little talk with these guys first. Make sure your badge and pistol can be seen when we go in, pay close attention, and be ready for anything."

Riding into the ranch, several hands came out of the barn to see who was here. One man clearly stood out from the others. Well over six feet and three hundred pounds with a stringy gray beard, and a long trail of tobacco juice down his shirt, he walked straight to the two lawmen.

"Moss, it's been a while," said Del, with his hand on his pistol.

"Not near long enough Marshal. What do you want?"

"You know damn well what I want, I need those three studs you stole from Tom James, and I need to take you to jail."

"Like I told you the last time I saw you Del, I ain't going to no jail."

"Like I told you the last time I saw you, if I caught you in my county again, I was gonna kill you," said Del, cocking his pistol and pointing it at the man's head.

"There's four of us here Del, at least one of them will kill you before it's over. Are you willing to try it?"

"I don't care nothing about them, only you. I'm willing to bet that I can put a .45 slug through your head before anyone gets me. So the question is, are you willing to try it?"

Running his greasy fingers through his beard, he stared at Del. "One of them is my boy. I don't want him hurt," said Moss, motioning for him to come over. "This is Matt, you leave him go free, and I'll come in quiet."

Del never took his eyes off of him. "Henry, if there's trouble, you kill him first."

"I'm on him Marshal," said Henry, his pistol already pointed at the boy.

"Moss, if you have him return the horses to Tom James, I'll let him go. If he doesn't do it and get out of Albany County, you know damn well I'll find him — then I'll kill him."

"What about the others?"

"When the horses are back with Tom, they all go free. But if I see any of them in Albany County again, including your boy, I'll kill them on the spot."

Ordering his son to return the horses, he told him to saddle up a horse for his ride to town. Handing his pistol to Del, he said he was ready. "So, you're takin' me back to Laramie so you can hang me?"

"Nope, I'm gonna take you back to Laramie and put you on the train to Cheyenne. They handle all that legal stuff these days."

"So then they're gonna hang me in Cheyenne?"

"Yep."

*

Henry locked the cell door and removed the shackles from the old man's wrists. "Okay, Del, you said you were gonna tell me how you knew where to find them. I'm listening."

"Yeah, I'm listening too," said Moss. "How the hell did you know where we were?"

"I got spies everywhere," said Del. "When you work with all the ranchers in the county, they tell you things. One of their cowboys told me about seeing four men riding into a stand of quakie trees, just a few miles from where we found you. One of them matched your description, Moss, since we'd met before, it was obvious who it was. It's kinda hard to keep outta sight when you're that fat."

"Screw you," said Moss.

"Well, how did you know it was him that stole Tom's horses?"

"Well, old Moss kinda thinks he's an expert on horse flesh, ain't that right old man?"

"I forgot more about good horses than most men could learn in a lifetime," said Moss, laying back on the bunk. "When do I get something to eat?"

"Moss likes to steal good horses, especially ones like Tom's studs, they bring more money."

"So, how'd you know where they were at?"

"My hired man said that when he was riding for a local ranch, he cut several sets of tracks leading off into the dark timber below that ridge where we spotted them. He saw them a couple of times while he was working cattle in that area. He figured it might have been rustlers, but he never saw them taking any cattle. When he came to work for me, he filled me in on what he saw. Two days later, I heard that Moss was back in my county again."

"So, why did you let the others go?"

"If I took Moss in alone, I figured we'd have to try and take all of them right there. When he told his boy to take the horses back, I knew he wouldn't go against his father. Besides, I didn't want anyone hurt in a shootout."

"Both of you would be dead if you had started shooting," said Moss.

"Yeah, yeah, but you're the one in the cell now, ain't you? Tomorrow you can take him for a train ride. I'll wire Wesley and tell him you're coming."

*

The engine ground to a stop in front of the Laramie station, and Del and Henry walked out with their prisoner in shackles. Climbing into an empty car, they walked him to a seat near the middle. "So long Moss, have a good trip," said Del.

"I'll see you in hell Marshal."

"You just might be right about that Moss," said Del, as he walked out of the train car.

Just before the train pulled away, two more deputies entered the car with their rifles and took a seat near the prisoner. "All this just for one old horse thief . . ." said Moss, looking at the deputies.

"For you, your boy, and the other two horse thieves," said Henry, "just in case they decide to show their faces between here and Cheyenne."

The deputies opened the windows and stuck their rifles out, settling in for the ride. The trip was uneventful until a few miles from Cheyenne, when three riders appeared on the horizon, just out of rifle range. As the train passed, they spurred their horses and headed toward town, disappearing over the ridge. Moss watched them ride off without speaking.

When the train pulled into Cheyenne, Marshal Wesley Tompkins and one deputy were waiting on the landing for their prisoner. When the exchange was made, everyone walked to the territorial jail. After the deputy locked him in one of the six cells, Moss laid back on the bunk.

"Why so quiet Moss, were you expecting someone to meet you here," said Tompkins.

"Screw you Marshal, and all the rest of you."

"You'll be happy to know that tomorrow is a court day, so you won't have to wait long for your trial," said Wesley. "If everything goes well, you could be hung by the end of the week."

Before he could answer, the front door swung open, and several deputies walked in with three prisoners in shackles. Tompkins unlocked three cell doors and put each of them in a different one. "Did they give you much trouble when you caught them?"

The lead deputy laughed out loud at the question. "No, they were riding along the road like you figured, looking kinda fat, dumb, and happy. When we rode up on them with our guns out, they were so startled they just gave up. Not the smartest horse thieves we've ever seen."

"Recognize these guys Moss?"

Shaking his head, he sat up in his bunk. "What the goddamn hell were you thinking? Jesus Christ almighty, you could have been long gone by now, instead, you're all gonna get hung right alongside me."

"Father, I took the horses back like you said to do, but I wanted to get you out of here," said Matt, "I'm sorry."

"Oh, just shut up."

"Shit Moss," said Wesley, " we ain't never hung four at a time before. I better get to work on a bigger gallows. Henry, we got four horse thieves in our cells without firing a shot, and they even brought back the stolen horses!"

Damn, it's been a good week for the law. Tell Dell good job and thanks for the telegram. He figured we would see them somewhere along the way, and he was right. When's your train back to Laramie?

"About two hours," said Henry, snapping his watch closed.

"Then let's go over to the Chophouse and have a big steak and a couple of drinks while you wait. It's on the government."

Chapter 29

Boyd and Anny sat at the table across from Basquiat Dere at his home in Cheyenne. The man looked sad and tired. His time in America had worn him down to a bent over shadow of his former self.

"Do you like this house Anny?" asked Dere. "I built it for Flora, hoping she would get married and settle down here and carry on the Dere name in America. Now it's just a great big house full of nothing but one broken down old Frenchman."

"It is a truly wonderful house," said Anny. "I'm sorry your dream didn't work out."

"Well, it's just the way it is. So, you are interested in buying the ranch, is that right?"

Anny nodded. "I am interested if it's something I can afford to do. Have you settled on the price you want for it?"

"Yes, but let me tell you what I have and what I would like to do." said Dere. "I have the original homestead of one-hundred-sixty acres, plus another hundred-sixty acres on the east side of it. There's a good ranch house, barn, bunkhouse, and various outbuildings. I have the cattle and the horse business that will go with the sale. Here are the most recent head counts," he said, handing her a folder.

"Boyd understands these things better than me. If he says it's good, then I'm fine with it."

"One more thing," said Dere. "I know that you weren't aware of it, but I have decided I want the house to go with the sale too."

"You're right. I never thought about the house. I guess that will depend on the price," said Anny.

He handed her another folder. "This is the price for everything. I have also talked with the bank and had them prepare several different proposals in the event that you would like to procure a loan."

Opening the folder, Anny spent a few minutes looking over the information. "Mister Dere, would you give me until this time tomorrow to study this and get back to you with my answer?"

"Certainly, I will see you tomorrow then. One more thing, I would truly love to see my grandson once before I leave. Boyd, would you consider bringing him here for a visit when you come?"

"Mister Dere, I'm so sorry, I never even thought about it. I'll bring him tomorrow, and you can spend as much time with him as you like."

"Thank you." The old man rose from his chair, leaning heavily on his cane, and walked them to the door. "Until tomorrow then."

*

Anny watched Laura playing with Ernesto's children while Elena rocked baby Alex on the porch. "Boyd, this is a beautiful family, don't you agree?"

"It is for sure Anny."

"Okay, let's talk about this offer from Basquiat. Do you think the Timms Ranch will benefit by adding that property?"

"You know how I feel about open range ranching. It will eventually die as more people move in and the Indians get moved onto the reservations. I think that the answer to successful ranching in the future will be owning your own ground and feeding your stock from what you grow," said Boyd. "So yes, I think it will not only benefit the ranch but will put us ahead of the rest of them in the future."

"What do you think about the price?"

"I think that it's about right or maybe a bit high. It's a lot of money, but I wouldn't know much about the value of his house."

*

Basquiat sat on the overstuffed chair with baby Alex on his lap. Tears ran down his eyes as he gently rocked him back and forth. The baby closed his eyes and fell asleep in his arms. "I'm sad that this has to end today, I would like to see him grow up."

"If it would help, we can send you photos as he grows," said Anny.

"Yes, that would be nice, thank you. There is something else that I would like to do for him if it is okay with you."

"What is it?" asked Boyd.

"I would like to leave some money for him, perhaps for a college back east or whatever he might need in the future."

"That would be wonderful," said Boyd, "thank you. If you want to set up an account at the bank for Alex, just let us know how to handle it, and we will see to it that you will get regular reports with the photographs."

Dere nodded and handed Alex back to Boyd. "Anny, is our business complete?" asked Dere.

"I think that's everything. The bank has approved the loan, and we take possession on the first of the month.

"Then I'll see about booking passage to France right away."

*

Boyd was acquainted with several of the cowboys from the Dere ranch, and with the old-timer that managed it, a famously grumpy old man by the name of Philip Singleton, and called Flip by everyone that knew him. He'd been managing cattle outfits for twenty-years and had the reputation of being tough and outspoken but fair to deal with. He'd been managing the whole Dere Ranch since before Flora left.

The two men spent several days riding the property and looking over the cattle and horses. "As I understand it, you want off the open range, that right?" asked Flip.

Boyd nodded. "I want to have the whole operation off of the range within the next two or three years."

"You're gonna give up all that free grass and water? Why would you want to go and do a thing like that?"

"For one thing, these two ranches are close to the railroad, and that's our future. The less time we spend out on the range, the less expenses we have, and that means more money in our pocket. For another thing, a really bad winter could cripple the business as we know it right now."

"Well, I think you're full of crap Boyd, but you're the boss, and whatever you say goes. What do you want me to do first?"

"Ranch business as usual, let me know if there are any problems. When you get time, let's find all of the property lines and set some corner posts, so we have somewhere to start."

"I'll get on it."

*

The summer was the busiest that Anny had ever experienced. Even when she was covering the treaty at Fort Laramie, she wasn't gone this much. Laura, her, and Morgan traveled all over the territory, talking about suffrage to anyone that would listen. She had met with most of the potential delegates and got to know many of them personally.

At her town meetings, she still got a lot of questions about the treaty and her meeting with the Indian chiefs and was becoming something of a local expert on the subject. Her book, *Mountains, Indians & Buffalos*, *A Lady's Life in the American West*, had just published, and the first boxes of books had arrived by train several days ago.

"Morgan, I think we will bring a few books with us to the next meeting, in case there may be someone interested in them after the talk."

"Missus Anny, I think you will need more than a few books," said Morgan. "Everyone is talking about it in town, and you were already well known around the territory."

"I doubt there's all that much interest, but if you really think so, go ahead and put some more on. We're taking the train to Rawlins, so it won't be a problem."

*

The brown summer prairie whizzed by, and Laura seemed almost mesmerized by it as she stared out the window. This trip, they didn't see any Indians or pronghorns to break up the open country. Reaching Rawlins, the hostess, a short, plump woman with white hair and dark eyes, took them to the hotel. "I'm Mary Hayden, my husband John is the mayor of Rawlins. It will be several hours before the event; you can rest here if you like. We have a cafe, and they know to charge everything to me."

"Thank you Mary. Do you mind if I ask you how your husband feels about the suffrage issue?"

"Unfortunately, he doesn't even want to talk about it. Like all the men around Rawlins, he thinks it's the dumbest thing he's ever heard of. He says that women already have more rights than they'll ever need."

"Well, that's too bad for them, because we're about to change that."

"I hope so Ma'am. Can I ask you one question before I go?"

"Certainly, and please call me Anny,"

"I recently heard that you wrote a book about your experiences with the Indians. Where could I get a copy? I love to read."

"I have some with me now. I'll sign one to you if you'd like." Laura opened the box and handed one to Anny. After inscribing it, she gave it to Mary. "I hope you enjoy it."

"I know I will, and thank you for all your support Missus Timms. All the women of the territory appreciate what you are doing. We will see you at six this evening. The hall is directly across the street."

*

Anny watched from her window as the women began to enter the hall. Dressed in her usual trail clothes, she pulled on her boots and walked toward the door. Laura picked up her hat and followed her down the stairs. Meeting Morgan and Missus Hayden in the lobby, they escorted Anny into the hall and to the front of the room. When she was introduced to the ladies of Rawlins, the applause could be heard across the street in the lobby of the hotel.

After her talk and the question and answer time, she began to get questions about the book. She told people that she had brought some books with her, but they were in her room. If they would like a book, she would be happy to meet them in the hotel lobby.

As she walked across to the hotel, a group of interested followers fell into line behind her. By the time the crowd was gone, she had given away all thirty copies she had brought. She also had a list of names that would like a copy sent to them. "Missus Anny, I think you could have brought another box and still not had enough," said Morgan.

"I admit I am pleasantly surprised. I would never have thought this would happen or even could happen. I guess I'll have to order some more when I get back."

"You are famous Ma'am; everyone wants to meet the lady who talks with Indian Chiefs."

As they waited on the platform for the train, Morgan noticed a tall bearded man wearing a leather work apron that had been standing back against the station door. Walking with a cane in his hand, he approached them, yelling at the top of his voice. "Just who the hell do you think you are, filling my wife with all your foolish crap?" said the man, suddenly raising his cane above his head.

In an instant, Morgan had taken the cane away from him and jerked his arm behind his back, causing him to scream even louder. "You no-good son-of-a-bitch, you let me go right now!"

Morgan twisted his arm a little more. "If you stop talking, I will let you go. Do you understand me?"

"Yeah goddamn it, I understand just fine, now let me go."

Loosening his grip, the man calmed down. "Now, sir, you will tell us your name, and you will apologize to the ladies, then you can tell us what is on your mind."

"Okay-okay, just let me go."

Morgan let his arm go but kept a good grip on his apron. "My name is Amos Best. I'm a wheelwright. Every time you and your dimwitted daughter come to town, my wife ain't no good for nothing for weeks. All she talks about is women getting the vote. That's just crap, and everyone knows it."

"Mister Best, your wife deserves every right you do," said Anny. "And my daughter Laura, is not dimwitted. She can read and write better than most adults. She hears perfectly, but she just can't speak, a condition that I very much wish you were afflicted with right now. Why don't you just go back to work and leave us be? We have a train to catch."

"Tell him to leave go of my arm, and I'll go away and hope to never see you again."

Anny nodded at Morgan, "It's okay — you can let him go."

"As soon as he apologizes to you and Laura, he can go," said Morgan.

"Alright, I apologize, now let me go."

Morgan turned him loose, and he walked away, shouting about how women would never get the vote and to never come back to Rawlins again.

"Thank you Morgan," said Anny. "It looks like he forgot to take his cane with him."

"I don't think he needed it to help him walk. He needed it to help him find a little extra courage. Now I have a new cane, just in case I need a little extra courage someday."

"I don't foresee a time you'd ever need any extra courage," said Anny.

*

Cheyenne was excited about the territorial assembly meeting to be held in October. The town was the designated capital of the territory, and a lot of people, many of them potential delegates for the new government, would be in town.

Nobody knew this better than Anny and the women of the society. They lobbied everyone they could find about the issue. Since all the delegates would be men, Anny herself spent a lot of time with their wives, daughters, and girlfriends. She explained to them that once the assembly was chosen, they would immediately start making laws for the territory. If they were ever to get equal rights, now was the time they needed to convince their men that they want to be included in the new laws. By the time the meeting was over, twenty-two delegates across all five counties had been appointed, with one member chosen as the first representative to the U.S. Congress.

"I believe we have done well so far," said Anny at the next local meeting. "But now is not the time to relax. Those of you that have access to one of the new delegates need to keep the issue in front of them."

On the tenth of October, the women of the society and every other woman in the new Wyoming Territory got their wish when Territorial Governor John Campbell signed the world's first women's suffrage bill into law.

*

"Congratulations Anny," said Boyd. "All your hard work paid off."

"All the hard work of several thousand good women paid off. I was just one voice."

"Well, congratulations to all several thousand of you then."

"Thank you Boyd," said Anny. Embracing him with a long hug, she suddenly pulled back. "Oh Boyd, I'm sorry, I didn't mean to be so forward. Please forgive me."

"Nothing to forgive Anny. I liked it. It's been a long time since I was touched by anyone but Alex."

"Thank you. I'm glad you are okay with it, I liked it too."

Not quite sure what just happened, Boyd sat down at the table and pulled out his notebook. "We have found all the property lines and set corner posts for when we start building the fence. I have found a buyer for the seventy extra horses we have; they will bring in some good cash for the ranch."

"What about the horses from the Dere Ranch?"

"They have a good remuda, but not a lot of extras."

"Have you thought about what feed we'll grow when the fields are fenced?"

"I found two long-time farmers that are willing to teach us about growing our own feed. When the time comes to lay out the fields, we may want to hire one of them full-time." Both of them sat quietly, looking across the table at each other. "Uh, well, I need to see about the horses," said Boyd.

"And I need to work on my article for the Leader," said Anny.

Chapter 30

Del leaned against the rail of the pen and lit up a fresh cigar as he watched Ike work a new horse. "How many have you broke now?"

Dropping a rope over his neck, he led him to the fence. "This is number fourteen, and he's been a real pain in my ass so far."

"It looks like he may have some mustang in him. He's kind of small and stocky for a ranch horse."

"I think he's all mustang, he's knot-headed as all hell, and he kicks and bites. He definitely don't like the idea of a halter or the feel of something on his back."

"I'm headed for town. I got a new deputy looking for a young, well broke saddle horse. He should be coming by this afternoon. Show him what you got."

"We got several he can pick from."

"He's a tall stout black man. His name is Davis Benson. If he finds one he likes, let him take it with him.

"He must be the first black deputy in the county . . ." said Ike.

"I think he's the first one in the territory, but they're about to hire another one in Cheyenne."

"I worked with plenty of black cowboys, they're some good hands, but I've never met one with a badge before."

"There ain't too many that come looking for the job," said Del, "but the way things are growing, that'll likely change.

*

Walking into the cafe, he sat down, and the waitress set up his coffee and took a small jar of sugar down from a shelf. "Gotta take good care of the Marshal, he knows the boss," said the waitress.

"Speaking of the boss, where is she right now?"

"Let me get her."

Before he could say anything else, Henry came in the door and gestured to him. "Marshal, better come quick. There's a problem at the rail station."

Del was out the door before Dolly had a chance to talk to him. A group of workers stood around the bodies of two Chinese track workers lying face down in the ditch between the tracks. Both had their pigtails cut off close to their head.

247

"Goddamn, we ain't got enough trouble with rustlers and horse thieves, now we got dead Chinamen turning up all over the place. Del asked if anyone spoke English as he looked at the body.

"I do. I am their supervisor," said one older man. "I am Wei Zhou."

"What's this all about," asked Del. "They found another Chinese man on the edge of town last week; his pigtail was missing too."

"I think it is about opium Marshal, and who they are buying it from."

"What about the missing pigtails?"

"It is meant as an insult and a threat to those that challenge the opium dealer," said Zhou. "Marshal, I need to attend to the burial of these men and will have to take care of their business. I have to send their pay and possessions to their families."

"Henry, get the undertaker and have him pick them up," said Del. "Mister Wei, will you come with me to the office so we can identify them?"

He nodded and gave instructions to his men to help the undertaker with the bodies, then walked to the office with him.

"Marshal, I will take care of the notifications," said Zhou. "Did you want to talk to me about something else?"

Del nodded. "I didn't want to talk about it in front of the other men, but what can you tell me about who did this?"

"Thank you for that. There are just two places here that are large enough to sell the necessary amount of opium to cause this kind of trouble. One is Zhang Lee, he sells out of the back of the apartment in his dry goods store, and Sam Han, he has a place in the back of his worker apartments."

"Opium isn't illegal," said Del, "what else can you tell me about them?"

"Sam Han is the largest dealer. When he finds his customers have been buying from someone else, he often sends them a message with violence. I have heard that when their customers are under the influence, his workers come into the room and rob them of whatever they have. Most Chinese workers carry their money with them all the time because they have no safe place to keep it. The opium trade will not go away as long as there are so many Chinese track workers here, but these are two very bad men, and all of the workers would like to see them gone."

"They sound like someone the town of Laramie could do without. Thank you for your help Mister Zhou, we will look into who is doing this killing, and I will get back with you very soon."

"Thank you Marshal," said Zhou, as he walked out the door.

"Raylan, do you know much about these places?" asked Del.

"I know a little about them, but I've heard a lot of talk about how bad they are. It's not just the opium, but they both have prostitutes working the dens, and they're the ones robbing the track workers for them. The girls say that they have been forced into prostitution, and any girl that causes trouble is killed. Everyone is too scared to talk about it."

"See what you can find out about these opium dens and the two men Mister Zhou was talking about. There isn't anything to arrest them for unless the victims are willing to come forward and go to court, and I don't see that happening."

"Do they have the same problems in Cheyenne?"

"They do, and I'm sure every railroad town along the way does too."

"Maybe they need to be convinced to change their ways," said Raylan.

Del nodded. "Maybe so. Maybe a private conversation with Mister Zhou would be good. You could explain to him there's nothing that can be done legally the way things are now. Maybe the two of you can work something out."

"I'm sure we can come up with something."

"By the way, I will be in Cheyenne next week for a couple of meetings on the new territorial laws. I need you to watch over things while I'm gone."

"I'll take care of business boss, no problem."

Walking into the cafe, Del sat down, and the waitress came back to the counter. "Finally ready for that coffee?"

"Yes Ma'am, and some biscuits and gravy and a steak please, well done."

"Hello, Marshal," said Dolly, sliding into the chair next to him. "Emergency I assume? You left in a hurry."

"Yeah, two dead Chinese track workers, there was one killed last week too."

"What do you think is going on, some kind of feud?"

"Maybe. I gave it to Raylan to look into. He's good at these type of things."

"This town is growing too fast," said Dolly. "I heard it's well over a thousand people now. There must be at least a hundred or more Chinese workers that live here and work for the railroad that aren't counted, plus the ones that come and go with the trains, and it could be one of them."

"It could be. I'm sure that Raylan will do a good job sorting it out, enjoy your breakfast. I'll see you tonight," said Dolly.

Chapter 31

The headline in the special edition of the Cheyenne Leader was one that Anny had waited a long time to write:

December 10, 1869

Wyoming Women Win the Vote . . .!
Governor Campbell Signs First Women's
Suffrage Bill in History!

The Wyoming Women's Betterment Society held an open house and a party for all the women that had worked so long and hard for the cause. The former Dere house had the large society banner hung over its door, and the big front room had tables lined up with pies and cakes and punch for all the members and visitors.

Anny was asked to give a speech, and if she wouldn't mind, would she wear her trail clothes one more time and bring some of her books for the crowd. Wearing her best long-sleeve shirt, one with beautiful red and blue embroidery across the breast, she looked the part of a cowgirl. She wore a pair of leather riding cuffs decorated with silver conchos, a gift from the people of Rawlins for the events she had arranged for them, and a bright new bandanna. Her silver buckle was a gift from Dean as was the hat she always wore.

Many of the women of Cheyenne came by during the day, as well as a lot of local men. In the afternoon, Governor Campbell came by himself to congratulate the women for what they had accomplished and brought a photographer with him to commemorate the event. Lining up with the members, he positioned Anny and Laura in front of him, and they took several shots. The governor promised Anny a photo for the house and one for her personal use.

On the way back to the ranch, she could see clouds starting to roll in from the west, and the temperature began to drop. Covering herself and Laura, the first snow of the season began to fall. By the time they reached the ranch, everything was several inches deep in snow. Morgan pulled the buggy into the barn and helped them climb down.

"I always loved the first snowfall of the year," said Anny, "it makes everything look so fresh and clean."

Laura wrote something in her notebook and showed it to her. The note said, "I love it too."

"Well Morgan, we both love the first snowfall. What about you?"

"When I was a small boy, I liked the snow, it was fun to play in, but it's not so much fun now, just more work."

"Then, for today, we shall all pretend we are small children and love to play in the snow."

"Yes Ma'am, if that's what you would like."

"Very good, it's settled then, today we are all small children that love the snow."

"Yes Ma'am."

*

Boyd shook off the snow and walked into the ranch house for their weekly meeting. Sitting at the table, Anny came in and sat across from him. "Good morning cowboy. How is baby Alex this morning?"

"He's been kind of noisy. Elena says he may be getting his first teeth."

"Soon he'll be walking, and you'll have a lot of fun then."

"That sounds a little scary to me," said Boyd.

"So, what's going on with the ranch that we need to talk about today?" said Anny.

"Before we talk about that, I wanted to give you this," said Boyd, handing her a package. "I just got it from Tom Lee yesterday. It's more of the day to day journal that he kept on the cattle drive up from Texas. I think it's a few of the notes he made along the way. He thought you might be interested in using it in one of your books someday."

Opening to the first page, she read a few of the entries. "Boyd, this is amazing. I can definitely use this in my next book on the West. I'll send him a telegram and thank him when I get to town."

Laura came into the kitchen and sat down next to Anny. She had grown a lot since she came to the ranch. Her blonde hair had grown back long and thick, framing a beautiful, fair-skinned face with bright blue eyes. She could read and write as well as anyone that Anny had ever met, but she really stood out when it came to math. She loved everything about numbers and working out the problems.

She carried a tablet and pencils wherever she went, using it to communicate and to make her drawings. Animals were her great love, and the ranch house was full of her pictures. Everything from cows and horses to deer and elk caught her eye. Her bird drawings were often compared to well-known artists of the day. A picture of a fresh mule deer fawn in the grass was Anny's favorite, and it hung over the fireplace.

"Boyd, I've decided to make Laura the official bookkeeper of the Timms Ranch. She's much better at math than I am, and she likes working on numbers."

"That's wonderful," said Boyd. "I couldn't think of anyone I would rather work with than you Laura."

She wrote, "Thank you," on her pad, stood up, and gave him a hug. It was the first time that he'd ever seen her hug anyone but Anny.

"Thank you for that Laura," said Boyd.

She nodded and smiled broadly at him, then hugged Anny. As she walked back to her bedroom, Boyd looked surprised. "I've never seen her hug anyone but you."

"I'm more surprised than you are," said Anny. "I wondered if it would ever happen."

"After that, it's kinda hard to think of ranch business," said Boyd.

"I do have something else I would like to talk about."

"What is it?"

"About the other day, when we hugged . . ."

"Anny, I'm so sorry about that. I should not have . . ."

"Stop, please, it's okay Boyd. I've had time to think about it for a while now, and there's something I would like to say."

"What is it?"

"Anyone who knows me very well, knows that I'm a very outspoken woman who is willing to say what's needed to get what I think is important. That's how Dean and I came to be a couple, so I have a proposal for you. Please hear me out before you say anything. If you're not interested in what I have to say, then I give you my word, nothing will ever change between us and our relationship as it is right now."

Boyd nodded. "I'm listening."

"I believe that the Timms Ranch could become one of the biggest and best cattle operations in this part of the territory. Cheyenne is the perfect place to become an important center for cattle production. In fact, it already is. I - uh - we've spoken about how the shipping and our proximity to the rails is perfect for us."

"I agree Anny, but is that what you wanted to talk about?"

"No, it's not, just bear with me, please. I'm a bit nervous. I have this big ranch house, and I love Laura and the fact that she lives here with me. But the fact is, I'm lonely."

Boyd sat silently for a minute, hoping he understood what she was trying to say. "I know what it's like to be lonely Anny. I've been that way since Flora left."

"Then here is my proposal. You and baby Alex move in here with Laura and me. Elena will take care of the children, and I can help her and work on my writing while you and Ernesto take care of the ranch business."

"You want me to live here in the house with you?"

"Boyd, that's exactly what I'm proposing. I'm hoping that perhaps we are compatible as a couple. There, I've said it. I'm also hoping that you might feel the same way, but as I said, either way, nothing will change our relationship as it is right now."

256

Boyd nodded, his mind going over what he just heard. "I think that I'd like to sleep on this for a night. Would that be okay with you?"

"Of course, would you consider having breakfast with me in the morning, and we can talk more about it?"

"I'll be here. Thank you."

*

Boyd woke up to the sound of Alex crying. He picked him up and rocked him for a while. "What do you think, little cowboy? Should we go to live with Anny?" Hearing a knock on the door, Boyd got up and opened it. Elena walked in with an arm full of fresh laundry. Boyd took the laundry and handed Alex to her. "Thank you Elena. I have to go see the boss, she's waiting on me," said Boyd, setting the laundry on the bed. Walking outside, he was still wondering what he should do. Stepping through the ranch house door, he could smell breakfast cooking. "Good morning," said Boyd. "Something smells good in here."

"I'm teaching Laura how to make biscuits. She's becoming quite a good cook," said Anny.

"She can do math and cook? Next thing you know, she'll be running the ranch all by herself, and I'll be out of a job."

Laura walked over to him and wrote a note on her tablet. "Not out of a job. I don't want to work with the cows — they stink!"

Anny and Boyd had a good laugh at the comment, and Laura got a huge smile at the idea of making them laugh. Then she hugged both of them and went back to her biscuits. After breakfast, Laura sat down and went to work on a new drawing.

"Anny, before you say anything, let me say that I have given a lot of thought to your proposal. My answer is yes, but we will need to discuss a few things before Alex and I move in."

"Boyd, that is wonderful. I couldn't be happier right now. What is it you would like to talk about."

"First, I want to tell you that I have very little experience with women. Flora is the only woman I have ever been with, and even then, she was the one who educated me about such things. I may be a very poor husband in that respect."

"Boyd, I have only been with two men in my life. My first husband was in the Union Army and died by his own hand after receiving terrible wounds in the war, and my second was Dean, who was less interested in me than he was his cows and his whisky. I believe that we will be able to determine what is right for us as a couple. What else is on your mind?"

"Well, like you said, your first husband was in the Union Army. You know I was a Confederate soldier. There are still a lot of ugly feelings on both sides. The two of us living together may cause a lot of gossip, and it could affect our business."

"I've never cared one whit what other people thought about such things. If talking about us makes those people happy, then let them talk," said Anny. "As for our business, I plan on our ranch being big enough that they won't be able to affect us."

"Anny, how does Laura feel about this?"

"Laura, sweetheart, come here please," said Anny. "Boyd and I have decided that he and baby Alex will move in with us, but first, we want to know how you feel about that?"

She thought about it for a minute then wrote her answer on the tablet. She wrote, "Yes, please!" in large letters and smiled, hugging both of them. She quickly wrote another note and showed it to them. It said, "Boyd, can I call you Father?"

Boyd looked at Anny, "If it is okay with your mother, I'd be really proud to be your father."

Anny's eyes were already wet when Laura pulled the three of them close together. Her next note caused her tears to flow uncontrollably. It said, "Now we are a real family . . ."

Chapter 32

Del stepped off of the train just as it rolled to a stop. Cheyenne was noticeably colder than Laramie, and the wind much worse. He pulled up his collar and pushed his hat down a little tighter. Wesley Tompkins and another man he didn't know greeted him. "Del, this is my newest deputy, Eli Wood. He's only been with us a few weeks."

Del stuck out his hand. "Good to meet you Eli, I'm Delbert Beale, from Laramie."

The new deputy was very young, about the same height as Del, and very fair-skinned. Short hair and a thick, droopy mustache hung nearly to his chin. "The meetings with the new territorial attorney will probably be long and boring," said Wesley. "There's one this afternoon and one tomorrow morning. He's going to talk about the new laws that affect us. You should probably have stayed home; I could have filled you in on anything important."

"That's okay. Once in a while, a man just needs to get out of town for a couple of days. Sometimes when you get back home, you get a new perspective on things; you know what I mean?"

"Yeah, I think so. Let's get you a room and a drink while we wait for the politicians to talk."

"Eli, where do you come from?" asked Del.

"A small town west of Chicago called Lane. It was just me and my father. He was a blacksmith, and I worked for him. He got sick one day and died about a month later. They said it was diphtheria. I came out West looking for adventure, and when the train stopped here, I got off," said Eli. "When I first got here, I worked on a ranch. I was in town one day and walked into the Marshal's Office and happened to meet Wesley. I asked if he might need a deputy, and he agreed to give me a chance, so here I am."

"You didn't like the ranch work?"

"The work was fine, but I didn't like smelling like cowshit all day, so I thought I'd try something else. I figured as a deputy, I could be a lot cleaner and a lot warmer in the winter."

"Can't say as I blame you there," said Del. "I put in my time pushing cattle and killing buffalo, and I like this deputy job a whole lot better."

After two days of long, dull legal conferences, Del watched as the train to Laramie rolled into the station and took on water. "It was good to see you Del," said Wesley, "hope you have that new perspective on things when you get back home."

"So do I," said Del, stepping up into the car, "see you on the next trip."

*

Walking into the office, Del was greeted by Raylan and a man snoring in the cell. "Who's our new customer?"

"Just a cowboy that got drunk and fell over in the road. Nobody knew who he was, so I let him sleep it off here. He should be sober by now."

"Then kick him out. We ain't a hotel for drunken cowhands."

"I heard that," said the man in the cell. Standing up on shaky legs, he walked to the door and grabbed a bar to balance himself. "My name is Niles Dixon, from Sussex County, England. I most certainly am not a cowboy, but I am here hoping to meet some owners of large cattle ranches to discuss possible investments with them."

"How did you get here Mister Dixon?" asked Del.

"I arrived here yesterday by train. I started my search for ranch owners in the establishment you call a saloon."

"Did you find what you were looking for?"

"No, sir, I did not. I found nothing more than a thundering headache, a need for food, and the loss of my hat. Do you think you can put me on the road to a large cattle ranch?"

"What do you think Raylan, are there any large cattle ranches around here?"

"We might know of a few."

"Okay then, can you let me out of your jail please," said Dixon.

"It's not locked."

Walking up to the desk, he offered his hand to Raylan. "Thank you sir. I do appreciate your watching out for me last night. I likely would have froze to death if you hadn't taken me in." Offering his hand to Del, he thanked him too. "Your constable is a very good man, sir."

"Yes he is. Mister Dixon, just across the street and a few doors down, is the River Cafe and Bakery. If you're hungry, that's the best place in town to get a meal. We'll both be over there in a bit, and we can help you find a ranch owner to visit with."

"Thank you sir. I shall see you then."

When the door closed, Raylan pulled up a chair next to the desk. "How were the meetings boss? Anything interesting we should know about?"

"Just a couple of boring, longwinded politicians is all. So, what's been happening since I left, other than the Englishman?"

"Well, there are a few interesting things that you missed," said Raylan.

"Like what?"

"The night after you left, the two Chinamen that ran the opium dens disappeared. Nobody has seen them since."

"Really? Just disappeared in the middle of the night?"

"It looks that way. The next day Wei Zhou came in with the four girls that had been working the dens for Lee and Dau."

"Where are the girls now?"

"Wei decided to hire one of them as a cook and housekeeper, and Teddy hired two of them for the saloon."

"What about the fourth one?"

"Well," said Raylan, "she's with me right now."

"She's with you? Why is she with you?"

"I'm sorry boss, I know it sounds strange, but I like her, and I didn't want her to go to work for Teddy."

"How does she feel about it? Does she even speak English?"

"She speaks decent English and fluent Spanish, and Chinese of course. She said she was kidnapped from somewhere around El Paso, Texas, and has been sold to several men over the last three or four years. She and a friend were both about thirteen when they were taken. After a few months, her friend tried to escape and was shot dead right in front of her."

"So, she's a Mexican from El Paso?"

"No, she's Chinese and very grateful to be away from the dens."

"Is she pretty?"

He turned red at the question and nodded. "Very pretty boss."

"Well, good luck with that. What's her name?

263

"She is called Yu Yan. It looks like she was part of an operation that kidnapped young girls and moved them up and down the tracks from town to town. Every time another town was added, they were moved there and worked at the next opium dens."

"I hope it works out for you," said Del. "What about the dens, are they shut down?"

"They are right now, but Mister Zhou says it will just be a matter of time before a few more show up."

"I guess we'll deal with them when it happens. Let's go see the Englishman and have some food."

"That sounds good. Where are you going to point him?"

"I thought I'd take him out to the /J. I need to talk with Tom anyway. If he don't have any interest, I'll send him to Cheyenne. Maybe Boyd will know someone who's looking for an investor."

*

Niles Dixon sat on his horse between Del and rancher Tom James, looking at the cattle scattered around the prairie. "Mister James, how do you know how many cows you really have out there?"

"Well, it's more of an experienced guess Mister Dixon. When the time comes for branding and gathering, we have a formula for how many cows and bulls it takes to produce the number of calves that we brand," said James. "We've been doing it this way for years and find it to be very accurate."

"So, how many head do you have out there now?" asked Dixon, making a few notes in his book.

"It's hard to tell at the moment," said James. "It's branding season, and the cowboys are out on the range doing it right now. They should be done in a couple of weeks, and we can get you that number."

"What about last year, Mister James. Can I get those numbers?"

"I have them back at the ranch, whenever you're ready to go."

"What about loss? Do predators kill many? I've also heard that Indians and rustlers get their share, is that correct?"

"There will always be some loss. Wolves are probably the worst enemy. We kill them every chance we get. Rustlers get a few now and then, but that problem is not as bad as it was before the territorial government finally hired good lawmen like Del. As for the Indians, they don't get very many. The army is starting to get them moved onto the reservations as we speak."

Dixon made a few more notes in his book, then put it in his bag. "I'm ready to go back to the ranch and look at those numbers now."

*

"Whisky Mister Dixon?" asked James, setting a glass on the table.

"No, thank you. I do like a good glass of spirits now and then, but I don't drink while I'm doing business. Now, about those cattle numbers from last year?"

"Sure, let me get them."

Dixon studied the numbers on the sheet for a minute then copied them into his book. "You are saying that you have over seven-thousand cattle under your brand on the open range?"

James nodded. "That's the count after last year's gather."

"That's the count by your own formula?"

"Yessir, it is."

"Mister James, I believe that I have seen all I need for now," said Dixon. "As I said earlier, I represent a group of twelve wealthy investors, all from the south of England, who would like to invest in the cattle operations in this part of the country. I plan on looking at several different ranches and then making recommendations to them as to where their investments could realize the best return. Thank you for your time."

"Well I hope you liked what you saw today," said James. "We have several ideas about improving the business and could use a knowledgeable investor to help us get there."

*

On the way back to Laramie, Del and Niles Dixon talked about the cattle business and what it was like to live in this part of the country. "What do you think of Tom's operation Mister Dixon? He's a highly respected rancher around here, known to be a fair and honest man."

"Marshal, I think I will need that whisky when I get back. There is no way that Mister James knows if he has seven thousand cattle or seven hundred, not by any formula I know of."

Sitting at a table in the cafe, Del and Niles continued their talk about the ranching business and life in the territory. Dolly came over and sat down with them. "Del, introduce me to your friend. I don't believe we've ever met."

"Dolly, this is Niles Dixon, from England. Niles, this is my wife, Dolly. Niles is here looking at some possible investment opportunities in the cattle ranching business."

"Mister Dixon, welcome to the Wyoming Territory. It's always nice to meet someone from a more refined part of the world," said Dolly.

Removing his hat, he smiled at the comment. "I'm not convinced that we are much more refined in England Missus Beale, but thank you. Del said this was your cafe. Are you the one in charge of the fine meal I just had?"

"I confess it was me. Thank you for the compliment. Can I get you some more coffee? There's also fresh pie if you would like."

"I am quite filled up, but I plan on eating here tomorrow, so I will have plenty of time to sample more than one of those delicious looking pies," said Dixon.

"Del, I'll see you at home. Nice to meet you Mister Dixon."

"Marshal, can you point me to the best place for a night's rest please."

"Laramie's not all that big. There are only two good hotels at the moment. Let's take a walk over to the Laramie House, I think you will like that one. Are you going over to Teddy's saloon for that whisky before you turn in?"

"I think I will get checked in, then go over for a short nip. How about you Marshal?"

"No, I'm headed home. Be careful they don't get all your money."

Del stepped into the cabin and saw Dolly working in the kitchen. Walking up slowly behind her, he kissed her on the neck. Good afternoon my beautiful lady. How are you?"

"Don't you mean your beautiful wife . . ." said Dolly, not looking up at him. "I never heard you say that before."

"Well, if you like the sound of it, we can march right over to the judge and make it happen," said Del, kissing her again.

"I do like the sound of it, but we've talked about this before. I just can't do it."

"Dolly, we've been together for quite a while now. Can you at least tell me why you can't marry me?"

Stopping what she was doing, she pushed him away. "Okay Del, you deserve that much. The truth is, I'm already married . . ."

"You're already married? To who?"

"A man named Sam Chadwick. I married him when I lived in St. Louis a long time ago."

"And . . .?"

"Del, I'm sorry I never said anything before. Marrying him was a terrible mistake. He turned out to be a violent drunk. I witnessed him shoot a man off a horse, and the man died. He said he was going to kill me too, but they caught him, and he was sentenced to prison for twelve years," said Dolly. "The last thing he said before they took him out of the courtroom was to scream at me that when he got out, he would find me where ever I was and kill me."

"How long ago was that?"

"Eleven years. Del, I never did anything about divorcing him. I just ran."

Dolly started to cry, and he put his arms around her. "Let me send a wire to the officials at the Missouri prison and see if I can find out what his status is, and don't worry about anything, nobody is ever going to hurt you."

"I'm sorry, I should have said something before. I love you."

"I love you too Dolly. But when I get this straightened out, you know you'll have to marry me."

She put her head on his shoulder and sobbed, "Yes, yes, yes, yes . . ."

*

Two weeks later, Del walked into the office and found a telegram on his desk; it was from the Missouri Department of Prisons.

Dear Marshal Beale; as per your request for information on convict #183857, Sam Chadwick, our records show that he died from wounds received in a prison fight on July 17, 1866. Sincerely, Warden Benjamin T. Walker.

Dolly was already home when he got there. Walking up quietly behind her, he grabbed her without warning, spun her around, and kissed her full on the mouth. She kissed him back and pulled away slightly. "I must say I do love the attention, but why so romantic today if I might ask?"

Del handed her a card that he bought at the dry goods with red and blue prairie flowers painted on it. He had written, "I love you Missus Beale," and signed it Delbert. Inside the card was the folded up telegram from the prison.

As she read the telegram, her face lit up, and she pulled him back and began to kiss him again and again. "I didn't know Del, I'm sorry, I should have checked on this before . . ."

"It's okay, it's all over. We can get married now. That's all that matters." Dolly kissed him once more, then took his hand and led him to the bedroom. "Why Ma'am, whatever are you doing? We aren't married yet," said Del.

"Just shut up and get those clothes off cowboy, we'll get married when I'm done with you . . ."

Chapter 33

"It's good to meet you Mister Dixon," said Wesley. "Del says you want to meet with some of the ranchers around the Cheyenne area? Something about investing in the cattle business?"

"Yessir, I represent a group of twelve men in England that would like to invest in the cattle industry of the American West."

"Mister Dixon, this is my deputy, Colman Brown. He's familiar with some of the ranchers around here. Why don't you take him out to see Boyd at the Timms Ranch? He knows the business as good as anyone around here."

Brown nodded. "Mister Dixon, do you have a horse?"

"No sir, I assume I can get one at the local livery?"

"Follow me. We'll get you properly mounted."

"How far is this ranch Mister Brown?"

"About ten miles, why do you ask?"

"Just wondering how many miles my old English backside has left in it. It's still sore from visiting the ranches in the Laramie area."

"We'll take it slow Mister Dixon."

*

Anny and Boyd invited Dixon in for tea, a gesture that Dixon appreciated. "Thank you from an old Englishman Missis Timms. I haven't seen much attention given to the tea leaf out here in the West, mostly strong coffee and whisky."

Anny nodded. "I agree with that, particularly the whisky. I don't really drink either one, but I do keep my pantry well-stocked with several kinds of tea. So, tell us something about you and your investors. How did you come to be interested in our cattle industry?"

"This country loves its beef, and to us, it's just that simple. You have the cattle, and you have this magnificent prairie with hundreds of thousands of acres of free grass and water to fatten them up. Now that the railroad runs right through it, we would like to be part of helping the business grow even larger. The more beef that reaches the meat packers, the more money we all make."

"That sounds interesting Mister Dixon," said Anny. "Boyd is my partner, and he's the one that knows everything about the cattle and the market. He would be the one to discuss any new ideas with."

"Mister Dixon, there are others in our cattle pool," said Boyd. "We would need to have a meeting with them so they can hear what you have to say."

"That would be fine. Let me know the time and place, and I'll be there. Missus Timms, there is one more thing if I may. I wonder if I might get a copy of your book? I love reading about the American West, and I have heard good things about your work."

"Certainly Mister Dixon. I'm flattered that you even know of it," said Anny. "Let me get you a copy."

*

On the ride back to town, Dixon asked Brown if he would mind a few questions. "No, of course not, what's on your mind?"

"I have read so much about the American Civil War, and you are the first black man I have met since I got here. I wondered if you were a slave that was freed after the war?"

"No sir, I was born free, way up in New York state, but my folks had escaped from a South Carolina rice plantation nearly ten years before the war."

"Did you fight on the side of the union?"

272

"No, I was too young, but two of my brothers did. One was killed the first day at the Battle of Gettysburg, and the other one came home safely."

"I'm sorry to hear that. It must have been terrible right after the war. How do you go back to regular life after all the bloodshed?"

"You don't. You can stop the killing but you're never gonna stop the hating, and it's always gonna be that way."

"Is it better living out here in the West than back where all the fighting happened?"

"That's what I hoped for when I came out here, and I guess it is better, but it may be just because there's less people. Many of them came out here for the same reason I did, but the railroad is changing that pretty fast. There are new people from the east arriving every day."

When they reached town, Brown followed him back to the livery. "Thank you for your help Mister Brown. I really enjoyed our conversation."

"So did I Mister Dixon, please call me Colman."

Dixon nodded, "And I am Niles, thank you. I hope we have time to visit again before I leave."

*

Ernesto and the cowboys of the Timms Ranch had been gathering cattle and preparing to ship them for several weeks. Today they were moving the first herd from the ranch to the railroad for shipping. In a great swirl of dust, bawling cattle, and barking dogs, several hundred head were moved through town and into the pens next to the tracks. The drag man pushed the last few in and swung the gate closed.

Boyd rode up to Ernesto and stopped to watch the cattle mill around in their new surroundings. It was the first herd the Timms Ranch had committed to the railroad. "This is the new way Ernesto, no more long drives to sell our beef. Now we just move them from the ranch to the rails. It looks like old Monroe Timms picked a good spot for his ranch."

"Sí, a very good place to be sure," said Ernesto. "Branding and cutting the calves and gathering all these cattle out on the prairie does take a long time and a lot of work."

"Yes, it does, and that's why we're gonna change the system," said Boyd. "It's already eighteen-seventy, hardly five years since the war ended and not even three years since the railroad got here. I think in two more years, we should be completely off the open range."

Boyd rolled a cigarette as they watched two men, one from the railroad and one from the ranch, count each animal as they were loaded into the cars. As the cattle moved up the ramp and disappeared into the darkness, the railroad cowboys poked their sticks through the openings in the car to keep them moving to the back. When they were all loaded, one of the men doing the counting for the railroad handed Boyd a sheet of paper to sign. "Our counts matched Boyd, three-hundred and twenty head, just sign here, and we'll be rolling out."

They both signed a copy for the railroad and one for the ranch. Looking at the bill of sale, he nodded, "This is good Ernesto, very good," said Boyd. "Let's head back and get the next bunch ready. They'll have more cars here tomorrow."

Chapter 34

"Mister Dixon, it's good to see you again," said Anny. "Before we get started, I would like you to meet my daughter Laura. She's unable to speak, but in all of her other senses, she is quite exceptional. She's a partner in the ranch and will be participating in our meetings."

Dixon took off his hat and nodded to her. "It is my pleasure to meet you Laura."

She wrote a note and turned the tablet toward him. "Thank you, Mister Dixon, it is a pleasure to meet you too."

"Mister Dixon, this is Clifford Platt and Wilf Rickard, the other members of the S/4 Cattlemen's pool that was formed a few years ago when we first staked claims on our ranches," said Boyd. "If you would explain to them about your group's interests in the cattle operations around here, we would appreciate it."

They listened quietly as he outlined his proposal, then he asked if he could elaborate on anything or answer any questions.

"I may have a couple," said Platt. "Are you looking to be part of the day to day ranch operation?"

"No, we're only looking to be silent partners for an agreed upon percentage of the cattle operation," said Dixon. "That is if the cattle business is valued at five-hundred thousand dollars, and we provide one-hundred thousand dollars of capital investment, then we would share in the profits to the same percentage."

"And if there was no profit in one year, what would you have to say then," said Platt.

"All the members of our group are experienced businessmen and investors. We understand that there is no guarantee of success on any venture," said Dixon. "We also know that there will be many more good years than bad ones, your businesses over the last few years have already shown that."

"Mister Dixon," said Rickard, "we do our business much differently out here than they do in England. I think if we were to see a bad year, the investors might get nervous and want to change how things are done."

"I can give you my word that won't happen. We all intend to continue living in England. I don't see how we could run your operation from there. I'll be your one contact and travel back and forth as needed."

"Mister Dixon, if we were to decide to get into business with you, we would expect to be able to use the investment money any way we choose," said Boyd.

"That is correct. There are no stipulations on what you use it for, only that it goes into the cattle operation."

"What about the land and the buildings?" asked Platt. "I wouldn't be able to do something like this if I thought I was at risk of losing them to an outside investor."

"We are only interested in cattle. You can use the money any way you want to increase production. In the unlikely event that the cattle business failed, we would have no use for your property," said Dixon. "Can I answer any more questions for you?"

"Mister Dixon, I appreciate you taking the time to explain your proposal to everyone," said Anny. "We would like to think about it, and I'm sure we will have more questions. Would you be able to come back here Wednesday at the same time?"

"Certainly Missus Timms. I will be here then, and I will likely have more questions of my own. I look forward to seeing you on Wednesday."

"Wilf, Clifford, will that be good for both of you?"

Both men nodded. "Then let me walk you out. I will have a fresh pot of tea ready for you when you return."

As Anny sat back down, Laura slid her tablet in front of her. "Mother, I really like the way he talks. It sounds quite funny."

Anny read the message to everyone, and they all had a good laugh. "You're right sweetheart, it does sound quite funny."

*

Since the passage of the suffrage act, Anny had been receiving mail and telegrams from all over the country asking for her to

277

speak to women's groups. Utah and Colorado told her that they would be ready at her convenience, whenever she was available.

Her book was selling well in the East, and her publisher was already asking about a second one. He told her that the parts about the Indians were the most popular, and stories about her and Morgan's trips through the mountains were next.

Laura had become the secretary and bookkeeper for the ranch and for Anny's business. Sorting through all the correspondence for Anny, she made notes on each request and filed them according to the topic, and the date received. She quickly picked up on the ranch's financial business.

Anny had started to lay out her next book with all the stories she had gathered on her trips and the journal that was kept by Tom Lee. Laura had been reading the notes written by Del, Tom Lee, and Boyd about their time as buffalo hunters and trail cowboys.

She told her mother that it was very exciting to read about the buffalo, and could they go see them one day. She wanted to draw them for her collection. Boyd told her that they would take a ride soon and see if they could find some.

*

The S/4 pool members sat around the table talking about the offer that the Englishman had given them. "Now that you've thought about it a while, what does everyone think about it?" asked Boyd.

"I don't think it sounds all that bad," said Clifford Platt. "If that man wants to give me a bunch of money to do what I'm already doing, I think I might go along with him."

"Wilf, what about you?"

"Well, a couple of years ago, I would have jumped at it. But you all know my wife died last year, and the truth is, I'm just tired of the whole thing," said Rickard. "I have decided to sell everything and move to Missouri to live with my brothers. I wanted to hear what this Englishman said first, but nothing he said helps me at all. So does anyone want to buy a ranch and a herd of cattle?"

"Wilf, I'm sorry to hear that. I'll be losing a good friend," said Platt. "Boyd, we haven't heard from you yet."

"Well, by now, you all know how I feel about the cattle business. We've all done very well running our cattle this way. But with all the new people moving in, there will be more ranches and more homesteaders competing with the cattle for the same land. It will eventually kill the business as we know it," said Boyd. "I think we'd be smart to buy land now and fence the operation in."

"I think that's crazy talk," said Platt. "The free grass and water on the open range is what makes this business work. How can you feed all them cattle if you fence them in."

"Cliff, we're going to have to grow our own feed. That way, we won't have to depend on the government or the weather or anything else."

"Well, I ain't no goddamn farmer, and I never will be. I'm gonna see what that Englishman will do for me."

"Wilf, are you going to sell your operation right away?" asked Anny.

"As soon as I can get it done, there ain't no need to wait any longer."

"Then the Timms Ranch would be interested in making you an offer."

"Missus Timms, I would like to sit down with you and see what we can work out."

*

Anny poured Boyd and Wilf a cup of coffee and a cup of tea for herself. "Wilf, we really hate to see you leave the area."

"Thank you. I know there's a lot I will miss about this place, but since we never had any children, it's just too lonely living on the ranch. Both my brothers have big families, and I'm looking forward to spending time with them."

"I understand how you must feel. I don't like being alone either. Have you given any thought to how much you want for the place?"

"All I know for sure is that I want to sell everything in one deal."

"How many head do you have on the range right now?" asked Boyd.

"I'd say between three-thousand and thirty-four hundred, and we've already shipped this year."

"As I understand it, your land borders the old Dere Ranch," said Anny, "the one we bought?"

"Yes, it has a long common border. It would give the Timms ranch two more sections of land."

"What do you think Boyd, will that work for our purposes?"

Boyd nodded. "That would give us almost four-thousand acres of ground with good water on all of it. It would let us start growing feed in the spring."

"Wilf, let's all meet at the bank tomorrow morning and see what can be worked out," said Anny.

"Anny, Boyd, I will see you there tomorrow," said Rickard. "Thank you for everything."

*

Anny rocked baby Alex while Elena made breakfast for all of them. "Where are you headed today Boyd?"

"Ernesto and me are riding out to Wilf's place to see if there is anything we can do to help him out with his move. We need to look over the property while we're there and see if anything needs to be done right away. Wilf's manager is an old trail drive hand from Texas named Steve Butler. I'll have him continue to run that operation for now. The ranch house is not too big, but it's real nice. If he works out, I think we should set him up in the house."

"That's fine with me, does he have a family?"

"He's married, but I think their son and daughter left home years ago," said Boyd.

"Then it should work out good for them. I had planned on one or two more trips for the society this year, but it's already starting to get cold, so I think I'll put them off until spring. Boyd, have you seen any buffalo recently?"

"No, but I can ask around. Are you looking for meat?"

"No, I'd like to find one for Laura. She wants to draw one for her collection."

"I'm sure there's plenty around. I'll see if we can find her one."

Chapter 35

"Raylan, how is your new girlfriend working out? What's her name, Yu Yan?" asked Del.

"Yes. She's doing well, considering the rough life she's been living. She doesn't want to leave the rooms though. She's still afraid someone will kidnap her again."

"I can't blame her for that," said Del. "Why don't you take her to the cafe and introduce her to Dolly. She might be able to give her some work in the kitchen. I'll talk to her about it tonight."

"Thanks, I'll see what she thinks about it."

"Have you heard anything from Mister Zhou lately?"

"No, but like he said before, opium is part of their culture. With the trains coming and going every day, you'll never stop it."

"I just got this telegram from Wes; it says there were two Chinese bodies found outside of Cheyenne face down in a ditch with their pigtails cut off. There was another one the week before.

Whoever is doing this is likely the same one that was supplying the opium to our guys," said Del. "Wes thinks they might be trying to set up a new business here."

"I'll keep my eyes open," said Raylan.

"He also says that there were two attacks on new settlers west of Rawlins. Nobody was killed, but they were burned out of their homestead."

"Indians?"

"Could be, but the report said they think they may have been white men acting like Indians. They're not sure yet, but the horses were shod."

"I think this may be something we're going to see more of. People are filing for homesteads on open land that other people have already been using, like the cattlemen. I'm glad this one ain't in our county."

Del walked into the cafe and took a table in the corner. Dolly brought the coffee and sugar and sat down next to him. "Good morning, sir," said Dolly. "Your breakfast is being cooked as we speak."

Del nodded and poured the sugar in his coffee. "How is your morning going?"

"Quite well thank you. I just got engaged to a wonderful man, and I am very excited about it. Perhaps you know him, he's the local Marshal for Albany County?"

"I've heard of him before," said Del, "but I don't think we've ever met."

"Then I'll have to introduce you sometime. He is quite the handsome devil."

The cook interrupted them, setting his breakfast on the table. "Good morning Marshal. Anything else I can get you?"

Del shook his head. "I'm good, thank you."

"Enjoy your meal. I'll see you later," said Dolly, kissing him on the cheek.

"Dolly, there's one thing I wanted to ask you about this morning. You know that Raylan took in one of the Chinese girls from Sam Han's opium operation?"

"I'm sure everyone in town knows about it, why?"

"He says she's terrified to leave their rooms for fear she will be killed or kidnapped again. Is there any chance that you may have something she could do in the kitchen? Even something part-time would help. Just so she won't have to deal with a lot of strangers, and it might help her get over some of her fear of outsiders."

"I could maybe use her for some of the basic chores, preparing the food for the cook, and general cleanup of the place after we close, that kind of thing. It wouldn't pay much, and there's not a lot of hours."

"I'll talk to Raylan, but I think it could work out. You're a good woman, Miss Dolly, if you weren't already spoken for, I'd marry you myself . . ."

"You would be a very lucky man if that happened, but sadly, I'm already promised to the Marshal, you have a good day now."

*

Dolly and Del walked into the office of Judge Chapman and asked his clerk if they could talk to him. "Delbert, what do you want to see him about?"

"I want to see him about getting married . . ."

"Married?" said Chapman, walking out of the back room as he spoke. "It's damn well time you made an honest woman out of her Del."

"I threatened to lock her in a cell until she agreed to marry me. She finally gave in and said yes."

"Well, let's get this done before she changes her mind. Dolly, I don't know what you see in this man, but if it's what you really want . . ."

"I'm good Judge," said Dolly, still holding Del's hand. "If I change my mind, I'll let you know."

After the judge pronounced them married, they walked out of the office and toward the cafe. When they reached the door, Henry shouted at him from across the street. "Marshal, there's been a shooting at Teddy's place, Raylan's holding the guy right now."

"Well shit, some things ain't never gonna change," said Del. Kissing his new bride, he held the cafe door open for her. "I'll see you at home tonight."

Chapter 36

"So the Englishman is going into business with Cliff Platt?" said Anny.

"I just saw Cliff in town," said Boyd. "He said there was no way he could turn down the offer. It seems like Mister Dixon is in an all-fired hurry to get into the cattle business. I wonder if he and his investors really understand what could happen in a bad year."

"I guess he'll find out, just like the rest of us."

"That's true enough. If we have a couple of good years in a row, I think that we'll see a bunch more investors looking to get their share."

Laura smiled and wrote a note. "I liked him; I hope I can hear more of the funny talk."

Anny laughed and hugged her. "I liked hearing him talk too sweetheart."

"Things around here have been moving fast," said Boyd. "But I think it's nothing like what we're going to see in the next few years. The gates have been opened, and everyone in the country that wants land will be in a race to get here and get their hundred-sixty acres. If Cliff and Niles have a good season, there will be more investors looking for ranches to buy into."

"I can't say as I blame them Boyd. There was a time we were both looking for a better life."

"That's true, but I can't understand people like Cliff, they think things will never change."

Laura held her tablet in front of them and smiled. "Don't worry, I will not change."

"Really?" said Boyd. "You just wait until you see a cute boy that wants to be your boyfriend. We'll see if you change or not."

Laura flushed and shook her head. She quickly wrote out her answer, "No boyfriend for me. I will stay here on the ranch!"

Acknowledgements

Here I am again, deep in the debt of my intrepid readers who helped me take a bunch of words poured loosely into a manuscript and make a book out of it. They all see things that I don't, and each of them are my friends and are invaluable as test readers. Like always, if I have forgotten anyone, or spelled your name wrong, (Lenetta!) I apologize again and I will keep trying to get it right—thank you, thank you, thank you.

Nancy Entwistle, my bride of more than 53 years, I could not have accomplished anything in my life without you. Thank you for all your work on my writing, putting up with my endlessly wandering mind, and for keeping me on the straight and narrow.

Gary & Lenetta Haynes, two of my oldest friends in Colorado and a great tag team of readers. One gives it to me straight from a woman's perspective and one from a man's. I simply could not ask for better input.

Wesley Marshal, a friend since grade school, a scientist, great reader and friend for all his help.

Phil Singleton, friend since high school who probably taught me a thing or two he shouldn't have.

Bob Baker, good friend for 45 years that reads all my books and magazine work, and tells everyone he knows how great I am. The check is in the mail . . .

Bruce Flourquist, an online friend that has been a great supporter of my writing. We've yet to have dinner together, but when we do, the hot dog is on me.

Steve Butler, my fishing buddy and friend from the South. The virus may have kept us out of a good trip this year, but next year for sure!

Tim O'Byrne, editor of Working Ranch Magazine, long-time friend and cowboy advisor.

Liane Laroque, editor of my heart and all the words that I send her. My work is like a big word jumble, and she manages to get all of the words in the right place. I don't know how, but it comes back to me right! Keep on keeping me straight!

The photo on the cover is from the "Burying the Tomahawk" ceremony at Garryowen, Montana, on the 50th anniversary of the Battle of the Little Bighorn, June 26, 1926.

(719) 287-8063

blackmulepress.com